TRACK RECORDS

The very young Paul Gambaccini staggered his parents when he sat down and played his grand uncle's piano. What his family did not realise was that he was pounding out an atonal row. At his second lesson his teacher was horrified to hear he had spent the entire first week of study playing as if F natural were middle C. Paul has since found out where the keys are. Some of the other things he has learned about music are in this book.

Track Records

PAUL GAMBACCINI

ELM TREE BOOKS
London

This book is dedicated to Teddy Warrick

First published in Great Britain 1985
by Elm Tree Books/Hamish Hamilton Ltd
Garden House 57–59 Long Acre London WC2E 9JZ

Copyright © 1985 by Paul Gambaccini

British Library Cataloguing in Publication Data
Gambaccini, Paul
    Track records.
    1. Rock musicians—Biography
    I. Title
    784.5′4′00922   ML394
    ISBN 0–241–11447–0

Photoset, printed and bound in Great Britain by
Redwood Burn Limited, Trowbridge, Wiltshire

CONTENTS

Introduction   vii
Acknowledgements   xi
John Lennon   1
Elton John   7
Curtis Mayfield   15
Fleetwood Mac   23
Neil Young   31
Aretha Franklin   37
The Doors   45
Bob Marley   53
The Who   61
Jimi Hendrix   69
Bryan Ferry and Roxy Music   77
Marvin Gaye   85
Jerry Lee Lewis   93
Paul McCartney   101
Michael Jackson   111
Joe Jackson   119
Bobby Darin   127
The Kinks   135
James Brown   145
Elvis Costello   153
Frankie Valli and The Four Seasons   163
Queen   171

INTRODUCTION

THIS IS the easy part. After weeks of sweating over scripts, burying myself within reams of research and recordsworth of repertoire, I can pause for breath, look outside to see what the weather's doing, and find out what time it is. How pleasant to rejoin the land of the living on a sunny afternoon!

So much for the easy part. Now for the hard work – explaining what these essays are, how and why they were written, and how they have been edited for book form.

The pieces in this publication originally appeared in two series of programmes on Radio 1. They were the successors to a sequence of twenty-five originally broadcast in 1981. The series was conceived by producer Teddy Warrick, one of BBC radio's genuinely great men, with whom I had collaborated on *The Elton John Story* and *The Bee Gees Story* at the height of their popularity in the 1970s. The series involved dozens of interviews with not only the title characters but those people who had been involved in their careers. The eventual shows required scores of tape edits and a weaving together of script, interview, records and, in Elton's case, unreleased demos.

I was thrilled to have worked on the series, which were heard by millions around the world, and it seemed for a brief time that this might be a format in which I would want to do further work. Only a few major artists had been so treated, and plenty of worthy candidates remained. But when radio stations and syndication services on both sides of the Atlantic realised the commercial potential of this type of production they overdid it.

The benefit to local radio stations from bought-in biographies was considerable. At a fraction of what it would cost them to do it themselves, they obtained programmes made with facilities they did not have, featuring celebrities they could not reach. Their fee was not sufficient to pay for the production but multiplied many times over it provided the profit to encourage the making of more. Record companies recognised they could obtain coast-to-coast coverage of an act in return for merely a single interview and encouraged artists to co-operate. *Bill-*

board, the music industry bible, began running a full column of forth-coming artist specials.

The late seventies and early eighties were awash with broadcast biogs of both the deserving and unworthy. I realised the element of tribute and sense of event that had gone into our two projects had long been lost when an American chain presented an hour-long life story of a fashionable female artist with only three hits to her name. This over-kill put paid to my interest in any more *Story* series. The last artist Teddy and I considered treating in this manner was Rod Stewart, who preposterously suggested we interview him in Australia even though at the time he was living in a flat across the street from Broadcasting House. To turn a journey of a few feet into one of thousands of miles seemed so lunatic we gave up on Rod then and there.

In the spring of 1981 Teddy suggested a series of thirteen profiles of my favourite artists. These would be subjective studies of careers without words from the performers themselves. I was immediately taken with the challenge. If it failed the enterprise could be considered the ultimate in self-indulgence – a 'Why I like Elvis Presley in 3000 words or less'. There was also a danger of it seeming a case study in underachievement, voluntarily declining to seek statements from the stars themselves. But it also marked a turnaround of trends from the 'no-expense-spared' production number to the 'no-expense-at-all' approach. I liked the idea that, rather than hearing many voices, the listener would hear just one. The essence of radio is one-to-one communication. Here was a chance to speak person-to-person about the artists who meant the most to me. Could I manage to convey my enthusiasms and do so without compromising the objective element of the show, the biographical and musical elements?

There was another dare to accept. I had to give each subject, whether they had more than enough hits for an hour, like The Beatles, or fewer, like Jerry Lee Lewis, exactly sixty minutes. I was like an artist given a piece of canvas on which to paint. I had to fit the dimensions of the surface regardless of my subject. I had to distill the career of The Beatles and their dozens of classic cuts without diminishing the scale of their social and musical importance or the expanse of my admiration. I had to build on the four key hit records of Lewis, with a total running time of ten minutes, to fashion a programme as suffused with energy and rebellion as they were, even though it was six times as long.

After the first two in the original series, Smokey Robinson and Bruce Springsteen, had been broadcast, the Controller of Radio 1, Derek Chinnery, asked if I could provide a second set of thirteen. I obligingly replied affirmatively, pleased that the Smokey and Springsteen had been so well-received.

The impulse to respond favourably to flattery must always be resisted! I was committed to researching, writing and delivering an hour-long programme every week for half a year. I could not decide I did not want to do one some week because the transmission time was already listed in the *Radio Times*. I got into a cycle where I would make the broadcast Thursday night, start gathering my research materials on Friday morning, worry over the weekend, and write like a demon on Monday and Tuesday. Only on Wednesday did I really rest. (I did get one week off when a John Lennon interview was re-run.)

When the series was over the twenty-five scripts were published as the book *Masters of Rock*, in the introduction of which I wrote 'I can't imagine doing anything quite like it for some time. You have to be a Daley Thompson of the brain to go through so many events in so short a time.'

I was cajoled out of this extremely early retirement to do fourteen more profiles in 1982. At least by then I had learned that I was more likely to preserve my sanity if I reduced the number of consecutive weeks I worked. In 1984 I was approached to do a few more, and I brashly suggested only nine new ones to follow a repeat of the previous fourteen. My proposal was accepted though in the end, and to the disappointment of the Gene Pitney fan club, I only did eight. The great sixties star, writer of 'He's a Rebel' and 'Hello Mary Lou', performer of 'Twenty-Four Hours From Tulsa' and 'I'm Gonna Be Strong', was the ninth on my list, a final favourite on a list of more obvious candidates like Michael Jackson and Elvis Costello. The names of a few of the feted were leaked in John Craven's column in the *Radio Times* and Pitney's was among them. I received countless letters from his devoted fans, promising they would be listening to their radios at the appointed hour. Alas, the executive producers had miscalculated and there were only eight free Sunday afternoons for my series. The ninth, the Gene Pitney, had to go. To be whipped into ecstasy at the prospect of a Pitney programme, then dashed to disappointment, must have been, as Gene himself sang, 'Half Heaven Half Heartache'.

Knowing months in advance that my new appreciations were forthcoming I undertook to write a few of them up front to avoid the hideous deadline pressure I had inflicted on myself in the first series. A resort to rudimentary mathematics let me know how many days I had to devote to each script, and I was able to finish the set without once running around the house screaming.

I must thank Teddy Warrick, my mentor on the first fourteen programmes herein, and Stuart Grundy, producer on the last eight.

Pauline Smith and Alison Hunt, their respective secretaries, had the unenviable task of typing my scripts for transmission, timing the records and logging the copyright data on each disc. The reader of this volume cannot hear the music alluded to, though he or she is invited to hum along if it pleases them, so I have deleted the references to records played in the programmes and smoothed over the transitions in and out of each piece. These are the only alterations made to the original scripts.

Thank you for sticking with me this far. You've sung the songs and heard the programmes. Now read the book.

ACKNOWLEDGEMENTS

The author and publishers would like to thank the following for permission to use copyright photographs in this book: p. xii, p. 92, p. 102, p. 126 The Photo Source; p. 8 John Timbers; p. 16, p. 22, p. 30 Pictorial Press; p. 38, p. 46, p. 62, p. 110 London Features International; p. 154 London Features International/Pennie Smith; p. 54 Adrian Boot; p. 70, p. 84, p. 144 David Redfern; p. 118 A&M Records; p. 136 Dezo Hoffmann; p. 170 George Hurrell.

John Lennon

MILLIONS MOURNED the murdered John Lennon as they had reacted to no other pop star's passing, and indeed no celebrity's death since the assassination of John F. Kennedy. The sudden and violent nature of Lennon's demise explained part of the feeling, but only part. More than any other former Beatle and any other rock hero, John Lennon was a personal pop star, writing not about the life and loves of a fictitious or faraway individual, but about himself. In his songs listeners could hear cries of pain, words of love, and hope for a better world – a world where they as well as Lennon wished they could live.

When Paul McCartney announced on 10 April 1970, that he was leaving The Beatles, it was important international news. I heard the flash while driving south on Interstate Highway 89 near Amherst, Massachusetts. The only ones who weren't really shocked were the Fab Four themselves and those who knew them. The group had been disintegrating for some time, and all had pursued solo activities.

John Lennon had done more recorded work apart from the group than any of the others. Notice the words 'work apart from the group' rather than 'solo work'. For reasons that were partly sexist, partly racist, and partly logical, no one could believe that the founder of the world's most popular musical act could choose to ally himself with an older, oriental, female avant-garde artist. Yet from November 1966, when Lennon met Yoko Ono at her art exhibition in a London gallery, and certainly from the making of their first record together in 1968, she was the single most important figure not only in his daily life but in his music. The two can not be separated.

Her influence on him was so profound that even the occasion of their first meeting found its way into his work. He had climbed a ladder to look into a spyglass suspended from the ceiling. There, through the glass, was the single word 'yes'. Seven years later, on his song 'Mind Games', he sang 'Yes is the answer'. His 1972 title 'Woman Is The

1

Nigger Of The World',was a direct Ono quotation, and many of the lines in 'Imagine' were inspired by Yoko's book *Grapefruit*. Indeed her co-production credits on many Lennon hits make Yoko Ono the most successful female producer in chart history.

Of course, it was Lennon's sense for singles and an occasional memorable melody that helped the records sell. He could record three albums of experimental material with Yoko – *Two Virgins, The Wedding Album* and *Unfinished Music No. 2: Life With The Lions* – and then consciously write a song for the anti-war movement that was no less avant garde but was commercial, so much so that it went to No. 2 in the charts and overtook 'We Shall Overcome' as the anthem of peace protestors through and beyond the Vietnam War.

'Give Peace A Chance', the first hit song ever performed in a bed, was written by Lennon and Ono, though the label credited Lennon and McCartney because John was still honouring his boyhood agreement with Paul that they would credit each other for their compositions. The listed artist was The Plastic Ono Band, which didn't really exist. Friends and visitors had sung along with John and Yoko on the track, and the precise membership of the group was as difficult to determine as it was unimportant.

The Plastic Ono Band was intended to be what Lennon called 'a conceptual band'. 'It's just an idea,' he said. As he later told *Playboy*, 'So *we* are The Plastic Ono Band, and the *audience* is The Plastic Ono Band. There is no Plastic Ono Band.' Reporters invited to the launch of The Plastic Ono Band saw themselves on a video screen.

It made the papers. So did every unusual move John and Yoko made, from posing nude for the sleeve of *Two Virgins* – John said Ono's art was so pure he couldn't clothe her on the cover – to the bed-ins for peace they held in Amsterdam and Montreal.

Lennon was so accustomed to mass acceptance that when one of his singles didn't make it big, he was furious. 'Cold Turkey' reached the top twenty in Britain and the top thirty in America, but to the Beatle who had just scored big with both 'Get Back' and 'The Ballad of John and Yoko', this was an insult. He couldn't understand that neither the musical bleakness of the single nor the experience of heroin withdrawal could be appreciated by his usual audience. 'Cold Turkey' was understandably a relative flop but it remains one of the most powerful and frightening records ever made. Marc Bolan said it was the first new musical sound since The Beatles themselves had arrived in the early sixties and it boasted as brave a lyric and vocal performance as pop music had heard. In short, it was a single to be proud of, a fact lost in the carnival atmosphere Lennon himself created when he returned his MBE medal to the Queen in protest at Britain's role in Biafra and support of the American involvement in Vietnam, and the chart failure of 'Cold Turkey'.

Exactly two months later John wrote and recorded a more obviously commercial single in one day. The lyric was an expansion of a fashionable late sixties idea that what you had done in the past was catching up on you now, and what you were doing now would affect your fate in the future. Lennon thought, true, but what you do also affects how you feel and think immediately thereafter. The result was 'Instant Karma'.

Lennon performed this single on *Top of the Pops*, the first ex-Beatle to appear on the show. Yoko was alongside his piano, knitting. Fans who thought solely in terms of John, Paul, George and Ringo were astounded. Why was this woman, who already had to bear a good deal of the blame for breaking up The Beatles, sitting on stage knitting? Years later John told Radio 1 interviewer Andy Peebles that the appearance was an event, they wanted to be together and Yoko's contribution this time was . . . to knit.

They'd married, making their bond official, and they wanted to be together. They'd made two live appearances together, in Toronto and London, the Canadian concert being made into a live album. Now they each released an LP called *Plastic Ono Band*. The discs came out at the same time and had nearly identical covers. The writing and vocalising were individual, and it is on *Plastic Ono Band* that John Lennon is best heard as a solo artist.

It is on *Plastic Ono Band* that John Lennon is best heard, period, for this album was a masterpiece. Influenced by the primal therapy he had recently undergone, in which the patient remembers important moments past and feels his reactions to them, Lennon expressed all the pain he felt from his personal and professional life in a collection of songs that are articulate both in what they say and how they say it.

'Mother' was a reference to his beloved Julia, who when she was deserted by her husband let her sister Mimi raise John and who was killed in a road accident while he was still a teenager. In the track 'God' Lennon listed idols no longer useful in his life, including such human deities as Zimmerman – a reference to Bob Dylan by his real name – and The Beatles. He concluded his sad litany with the words 'The dream is over'. In yet another classic track he railed bitterly against those who would exploit the champion more important than the celebrity, the 'Working Class Hero'.

The last named track, conspicuously denied airplay on some American stations because of its single defiant four-letter word, seemed sincere support for the masses. However, there were times when it appeared Lennon was condescending. He admitted he would back causes out of guilt, writing 'Power To The People' after a conversation with revolutionary Tariq Ali because he wanted 'to be loved by Tariq Ali and his ilk'.

Plastic Ono Band was intentionally sparse instrumentally and direct verbally. Lennon continued this approach in his notorious *Rolling Stone* interview, an extended talk with editor Jann Wenner that was as silly as it was sensational. Caught while still undergoing primal therapy and adjusting to the break-up of The Beatles, the star came out with fascinating revelations and ludicrous temper tantrums. Most regrettably, his disparagement of Paul McCartney demanded a response, prompting an occasional exchange on vinyl and in print that was beneath both of them.

There was no doubting, however, that Lennon was still at the peak of his creative powers. His next album, *Imagine*, was another masterpiece, despite its unworthy belittling of McCartney in an inserted photograph and on the number 'How Do You Sleep?' *Imagine* is best remembered for its haunting title track, an evocation of distant utopia, for 'Oh Yoko', a jolly declaration of dedication that demonstrated the writer's mood had improved after a year, and 'Jealous Guy', an expression of regret for the way he felt he had treated women and, in particular, Yoko.

The haunting melody of 'Jealous Guy' had been written in India. Its beautiful arrangement led Lennon to call *Imagine* 'Plastic Ono with chocolate coating'. It certainly appealed to consumer taste around the world, becoming his first solo No. 1 in both Britain and America. Through the years, the title track became his best-loved single song, though it was bizarrely not issued as a 45 in the UK until 1975. 'Jealous Guy' *never* became a single, and it was up to Roxy Music to take it to No. 1 as a tasteful tribute in 1981.

The mellowing of the bitter Beatle seemed complete with a song recorded in the last week of October, 1971, just over a fortnight after the release of *Imagine*. He and Yoko recruited the Harlem Community Choir to join them for a Christmas song. Producer Phil Spector recreated his Wall of Sound and topped even his own wonderful Christmas album with 'Happy Xmas (War Is Over)'. Released in the States for the 1971 holidays and a Christmas later in Britain – there was no time to get it out in time the year it was made – 'Happy Xmas' remains one of the best songs of the season rock music has yet produced. Its good greetings and fond wishes are always timely, guaranteed to warm the heart of even the stingiest Scrooge.

Lennon seemed restored both in his emotional stability and in his uncanny sense of combining message and music in a way that was both artistically satisfying and commercially successful. The appearance was an illusion. His very next project, *Sometime In New York City*, was a full-scale collaboration with Yoko that was a massive miscalculation. Every cut was a political or social statement in which the balance between education and entertainment was lost. The music was buried beneath the message, and while it was true that the single, 'Woman Is The Nigger of The World', received resistance from radio because feminism was not fashionable and 'nigger' was not a word usually broadcast, it was also true that it was only mildly interesting as a record. *Mind Games*, the next set, was also below par. It fell short of the top ten in Britain and has since been relegated to a budget price. Some of the lines seemed quaintly dated for 1973. But what bothered John Lennon late that year was not the reception to a record. He was suffering from the twin traumata of his continuing battle with US immigration authorities, who wanted him out of the country, and a mutually agreed separation from Ono. The legal persecution was clearly political and based on flimsy grounds, and Lennon eventually won his right to stay in the States. The parting from his wife was more hurtful than any court proceeding. Lennon started drinking heavily, and made a sad spectacle of himself in a California club.

His personal and professional return to grace came in a series of happy coincidences. Tony King, a friend from Beatle days, introduced him to Elton John, then the most popular star in America. They played on a track for each other, Lennon on Elton's version of 'Lucy In The Sky With Diamonds' and Mr John on John's 'Whatever Gets You Through The Night'. Elton asked if Lennon would perform the latter with him on stage if it got to No. 1. The Liverpudlian, who had never had a No. 1 solo single, jokingly agreed. To his amazement, the single went to the top in the States, and so did the album it came from, *Walls And Bridges*. Lennon had to keep his promise to play on stage with Elton John. He went to Boston to see Elton's live show and then set the date: Thanksgiving night, 28 November 1974, Madison Square Garden. I have never seen an audience react as those New Yorkers did when Elton announced his surprise guest. Surely no roof could resist such an upward surge of energy and affection, yet somehow it managed to stay in place as the friends offered the two hit singles plus, poignantly, 'I Saw Her Standing There', which Lennon introduced as being by 'an old fiancé of mine named Paul'. The fans were beside themselves with ecstasy, but Yoko Ono, who was in the audience, thought John looked lonely. She sought him out later, and they agreed to re-unite. A few already recorded tracks were still to be released, including the beautiful single 'Number Nine Dream' from *Walls And Bridges* and the partly successful package of favourite oldies, *Rock And Roll*. But Yoko told John that just as he didn't have to be a Beatle to be happy, he didn't have to make records. For nearly six years he didn't.

He spent his time raising their son, Sean, and performing the duties of what he called a 'househusband', while Yoko attended to their many business affairs. He let his contract with EMI run out and, except for the occasional visit from friends like Elton, David Bowie and McCartney, lost touch with the music business. Life doesn't end, he told a reporter, when you let your subscription to *Billboard* expire.

In 1980, he and Yoko decided to return to recording, and launched their album *Double Fantasy* with a series of major interviews: *Newsweek*, *Playboy*, *Rolling Stone*, the last British interview with Radio 1, the last of all with RKO radio. '(Just Like) Starting Over' had made the British top ten and was on course to be an American No. 1 when a man who was deeply unhappy with his own life murdered a man who was very happy with his.

The injustice of it all was clear in the new music. A decade earlier *Plastic Ono Band* had been the voice of a soul plagued by demons within. *Double Fantasy* testified that the soul had now found peace in a way that seems easy but looks terrifying when you have a lot to lose: to be a person, loving and living with those closest. In 'Beautiful Boy' John unashamedly sang of his love for son Sean in a way that struck home with all parents. Paul McCartney chose it as his single most treasured Desert Island Disc. For his wife Lennon expressed similar tenderness, without reservation or embarrassment, and all lovers found their feelings eloquently expressed in 'Woman'.

The sales surge that followed the death of John Lennon, taking first 'Starting Over', 'Woman' and then 'Imagine' to No. 1 in Britain, was a way of keeping him alive as long as there was a record to buy. An entire generation found it difficult to believe that the man who had made them happier than any other entertainer, a man who meant more to them personally than any mere entertainer, no longer existed. Even more horrible to face was that he had been taken in violence. He had said 'All You Need Is Love' and 'Give Peace A Chance', sentiments that in moments of cynicism seemed trite. His death was conclusive evidence that they are never trite. What John Lennon stood for will be of the highest value and greatest urgency until all weapons are destroyed and all killing ceases. Anyone who would follow him must first face the reality that the evil he wanted to eliminate genuinely exists. Facing that reality awakens one from the fun-filled fantasy of the early sixties. The dream really is over.

Elton John

HE CLAIMED he had an unhappy childhood, that he was a regimented and inhibited youngster. A lot of people are like that. He regretted that he was overweight and wore glasses. A lot of people are like *that*. He was part of a musical group that was going nowhere, a frustrated soloist whose only work on his own was singing in a pub. There are a few of those, too. The thing that separated Reg Dwight from all the others was that he decided to become someone different. There is only one Elton John.

Elton John was born Reginald Dwight on 25 March 1947, and that is the last time we will mention his original name. There is something particularly obnoxious in pretending to be overly familiar with a star by constantly referring to his real name, his birthplace, or an obscure mutual childhood friend. As a matter of fact, Elton would maintain he didn't have many childhood friends anyway, but records – they were different. His parents collected them, and the lad heard their Guy Mitchell, Tennessee Ernie Ford, and Kay Starr and then their Bill Haley 'ABC Boogie' and Elvis Presley 'Hound Dog'. The last two changed his life. When he heard Jerry Lee Lewis and Little Richard, he knew there was only one thing he wanted to do.

Piano was a rock and roll instrument in the late fifties and Elton joined his first group, The Corvettes, when he was thirteen. Rock and roll always meant more to him than his classical studies at the Royal Academy of Music and his first professional band, Bluesology, played blues and rock numbers. They backed touring American soul stars and the white blues singer-turned-cabaret-celebrity, Long John Baldry. It was from Baldry's first name and saxophonist Elton Dean's Christian name that Elton John got his own monicker.

John wanted to be a songwriter, but could only compose melodies. Replying to an ad in the *New Musical Express*, he was teamed with lyricist Bernie Taupin by Liberty Records executive Ray Williams. Their first collaborations were, in Taupin's words, 'pseudo-intellectual pre-

Shown with Elton at a party for the second edition of *The Guinness Book of British Hit Singles* are, from left to right, Bob Geldof, a bearded author, Kate Bush, Tom Robinson and Paula Yates. It was at this event that Elton first met Robinson, who became his occasional lyricist flower power trash'. Their first LP for DJM Records, *Empty Sky* contained one attractive ballad, 'Skyline Pigeon', and a not-so-attractive imitation of Mick Jagger.

At least Taupin and John were prolific. Each writing half the song, they came up with twice as much material as the standard singer-songwriter. They accumulated enough for two albums, a ballad-based set simply called *Elton John* and a country-influenced collection titled *Tumbleweed Connection*. It was while in Los Angeles promoting the former that Elton played a song from the latter. He captivated the critics by kicking away the piano stool and playing the upright upright on 'Burn Down The Mission'. It was a style that became a sensation. Elton's hands would keep on the keys while his fleet flew through the air. Years later, the French songstress France Gall had a hit in her homeland with a song whose title translates as 'He Plays The Piano Standing Up'. In 1970, the critics were delighted. *Los Angeles Times* columnist Robert Hilburn raved in a famous review. Never was the phrase 'overnight sensation' more appropriate. 'Your Song' went top ten. *Elton John* went gold. The American success rebounded home, and the pianist was popular on both sides of the Atlantic.

For a man who would become known as the flamboyant showman of the seventies, Elton's first hit LP, sometimes called 'The Black Album' because of the darkness that surrounded his face on the cover, was a distinctly muted beginning. The top tracks were almost all beautiful ballads: 'Sixty Years On', about aging, 'The Border Song', a plea for racial harmony, 'The Greatest Discovery', a boy's first marvellous meeting with his baby brother. Taupin touchingly tackled some of the sensitive subjects of everyday life, and John gave his words suitably soothing substance. 'The Black Album' remains emotionally affecting listening, a reminder that for all the costumes and clowning there was a heart behind the hijinks.

The world almost never saw the costumes and the clowning because right after they broke with *Elton John* and *Tumbleweed* Elton and Bernie nearly blew it. They had four albums issued in little more than a year. Admittedly, their contract with DJM did call for two LPs every twelve months, and *Tumbleweed* and *Madman Across The Water* fulfilled that obligation. They couldn't be blamed that bootleggers were issuing illegal copies of their WABC-FM radio concert, necessitating the release of the live album *17-11-70*. And they hadn't foreseen when they agreed to score the film *Friends* that they would be popular when the soundtrack was finally released. But all four albums were out nearly simultaneously and, naturally enough, sales suffered.

It took a brief break of a few months and a strong single to get them back on the beam. Taupin had been driving his car when suddenly two lines came to him. As soon as he got home, he wrote down these words, which rejuvenated Elton John's career: the beginning of 'Rocket Man'.

As a single the song reached No. 2 in Britain and No. 6 in America. The team of John, Taupin, producer Gus Dudgeon and mentor Steve Brown had brought Elton to a take-off point for a four-year voyage as spectacular as any space shuttle, a journey co-captained by one of rock's most memorable managers, John Reid. The album containing 'Rocket Man', *Honky Chateau*, spawned a string of seven consecutive American No.1 LPs. 'Honky Cat' was another US top ten single, 'I Think I'm Gonna Kill Myself' an unexpected highlight of the Royal Command Variety Performance. 'Salvation', originally assumed to be a single, never became one, but it and 'Mona Lisas And Mad Hatters' are still two of Elton's classiest cuts.

The contractual obligation to turn out two albums a year was a blessing in disguise. It forced a flow of material that enabled Elton to be the singles star of the early and mid-seventies. Every three months, a new EJ single was there. It almost always made the American top ten. It often made No.1. 'Crocodile Rock' was the first of six American chart-toppers for Elton John. It was intended to be a salute to some of his boyhood favourites including 'Oh Carol' by Neil Sedaka and 'Little Darlin'' by The Diamonds. Ironically, it outsold all the originals, and helped propel the album *Don't Shoot Me, I'm Only The Piano Player* to No.1 in both the UK and US. It was the most straightforward package of pop the songwriters had yet produced, even including a tribute to Marc Bolan called 'I'm Going To Be A Teenage Idol'. Yet lying alongside the ultra-commercial tracks like 'Crocodile Rock' and 'Elderberry Wine' were sensitive songs like 'High Flying Bird', a tragic track about a girl Taupin had known, and 'Daniel', the story of a one-eyed war veteran who could only find peace in Spain. Because it seemed so solemn, DJM resisted its release as a single, only consenting when Elton agreed to pay the promotional costs if it proved unpopular. He never had to pay.

The early seventies were dominated by two separate schools – the singer-songwriters and the glam rockers. Elton John dominated the decade by being both. Whereas an artist like Carole King or Don McLean would have one massive album and a couple of less successful sets, Elton and his team kept producing strong songs. Where someone like Gary Glitter or The Sweet looked androgynous, John appeared outrageous. At 5ft 8in, he felt short, and compensated by wearing platform shoes. He could play 'Your Song' at Disneyland wearing Mickey Mouse ears and shorts, come on to an English stage in an outfit he called his Cadbury's Chocolate Box suit, or wear so many feathers he likened himself to a giant chicken. Unlike most early seventies artists who had substance but lacked style or vice versa, Elton John boasted both in bucket loads.

His outstanding 1973 double album *Goodbye Yellow Brick Road* was perfect proof. Mixed in with the working boy's anthem 'Saturday Night's Alright For Fighting' and the all-for-fun 'Your Sister Can't Twist' were the solemn 'Funeral For A Friend', the first evidence of Elton's love of doomy instrumentals, and 'Candle In The Wind', Bernie's tribute to Marilyn Monroe that got its title from record executive Clive Davis' remark about Janis Joplin. 'Candle In The Wind' was a moderate hit in Britain, but its flip, 'Bennie And The Jets', became an American No.1 and, to Elton's even greater delight, his first hit on the soul chart.

'Bennie And The Jets' was a million-seller. *Goodbye Yellow Brick Road* sold in excess of seven million. Even a B-side from the LP, 'Harmony', got more requests at radio level than many other artists' A-sides. Elton John was on top of the entertainment world, especially in America where he was the biggest star in all show business. He made television newscasts as no pop singer had done since the sixties. The John juggernaut was even able to cruise through a mediocre album, *Caribou*, and rode into a phenomenal period from late 1974 to late 1975.

His *Greatest Hits* sold five million in the States alone in a matter of months. Two singles not on any album, 'Lucy In The Sky With Diamonds' and 'Philadelphia Freedom', both went to No. 1. He helped friends John Lennon and Neil Sedaka on two tracks of theirs, 'Whatever Gets You Through The Night' and 'Bad Blood', and both of them went to No. 1. To mark his first solo summit scaler Lennon guested at Elton's Madison Square Garden show on Thanksgiving Night 1974, the former Beatle's last concert appearance and one of the historic occasions of rock. Sedaka's success came on Rocket Records, the label Elton had started with four business colleagues, and gave him his first certified gold disc. Another project Elton touched turned to platinum when the soundtrack to *Tommy* was powered into the top three by John's version of 'Pinball Wizard', which received saturation airplay and eventually became a British top ten single.

Despite his omnipresence on American radio, he wasn't yet overexposed because every track was different. 'Lucy' was a Beatles tribute, 'Philadelphia Freedom' an affectionate greeting to Billy Jean King and her tennis team sung in the style of Philadelphia soul groups The Spinners and Stylistics. (Indeed, Elton had considered recording The Stylistics' 'Rockin' Roll Baby' until he realised there was a line about an orthopedic shoe.) 'The Bitch Is Back' was straightforward rock and roll, 'Don't Let The Sun Go Down On Me' a deeply dramatic big ballad. Elton John, who had accumulated and assimilated perhaps the most comprehensive record collection of any pop star, was demonstrating both his affection and ability by proving himself master of several styles, never releasing two singles in a row in the same mode. He won the easy listening audience *and* the hard rock brigade *and* the soul crowd. His massive sales figures were the proof of his mastery of multiple markets.

His personality cult found a natural peak in the autobiographical album *Captain Fantastic And The Brown Dirt Cowboy*, which became the first LP to ever enter the *Billboard* chart at No. 1. It did so without the benefit of a previous smash single, though a powerful piece did emerge as the most sensational true confession to ever grace the top ten. 'Someone Saved My Life Tonight' was the story of what happened the night John Baldry convinced Elton he didn't really want to marry his fiancée. Elton, Bernie and Baldry talked into the early hours. When the struggling songwriters got home Taupin rolled around the basement floor somewhat the worse for wear and Elton tried to kill himself. 'It was a very Woody Allen type suicide attempt,' he later recalled. 'I turned on the gas and left all the windows open.' Taupin told the tale in the first person, making Elton sing a potentially painful lyric. The vocalist didn't mind. He said the episode was long over and for him no longer tragic but amusing.

Captain Fantastic was a major achievement. To record an album about two men's still-young lives and not bore everybody else, to make them listen and make them care, indicated considerable skill. This autobiographical album and the *Greatest Hits* seemed to naturally bring to a close a period of Elton's career and he certainly did abandon the niche he had established. He cut a predominantly up-tempo album, *Rock Of the Westies*, because he wanted to, but lovers of the emotive Elton weren't interested. After a quick No. 1 single, 'Island Girl', and another LP chart debut at No. 1, *Rock Of the Westies* actually went through a period of losing sales. Stores which had ordered too many were returning their excess stock. The man made another seemingly masochistic move by releasing a second live album, the unnecessary *Here And There*. Elton had issued it to fulfil his obligations to DJM so he could go on his own Rocket label but in so doing he shortchanged his fans and forfeited his place in the sun. *Here And There* broke his string of American No. 1 albums, and he never regained the position.

He decided he didn't want it anyway. When the leader of a top American group crawled to his doorstep suffering from his own excesses, and when an old guitarist friend died of a drug overdose while on a jet plane, Elton realised his suspicion was correct: the rock and roll lifestyle is for short-lived suckers. While recording his 1976 double LP *Blue Moves* he decided to go off the road and bade the business a temporary goodbye with that ambitious album and a piece of inspired self-indulgence, a Marvin-and-Tammi-type duet with Rocket Records mate Kiki Dee. 'Don't Go Breaking My Heart' was more than just a throwaway. It was the No. 1 record in the world for 1976.

John took a sanity break for a year and a half. It was a case of almost clairvoyant timing. This was the precise period when punk rock and New Wave swept the British scene. When Elton did return to recording in 1978, he humbly wondered if there was a place for him in the new order. Did he have the right to assume he would be automatically welcomed back?

The question wasn't simply a case of being polite. During the extended interval his old team had disbanded. Though he had never broken with Elton, lyricist Taupin was in Los Angeles, working on other projects. Producer Dudgeon had new artists' sessions to supervise and the old musicians had other engagements, though the loyal and lovable percussionist Ray Cooper was still on hand. In many ways Elton was truly *A Single Man* for his comeback, so it was appropriate that the smash single from the album, 'Song For Guy', was his first hit instrumental.

This opus was written and recorded in one day. At first it had no title. The following day, Elton learned that Rocket Records messenger Guy Burchett had been killed in a motorbike accident while he had been working on the song. He instantly knew what to call the number. 'Song For Guy' reached No. 4 in Britain, his biggest home hit in five years. Elton John was back, big.

But not in the United States. 'The thing that crucified me most', he told disc jockey Andy Peebles, 'was that in America the record company said "Song For Guy" wouldn't be an instrumental hit, because "Music Box Dancer" by Frank Mills was already in the charts and there wasn't room for two instrumentals.' The unpromoted single failed to penetrate the Hot 100, his first flop.

Elton carried on without catering to the Americans and certainly not to MCA Records, whom he would shortly leave. He concentrated on other territories, becoming the first rock superstar to tour the Soviet Union and one of several to spend a good deal of time in France. But whereas most of the others were merely there as tax exiles, Elton expanded his career. Though he had recorded three LPs at the Château d'Herouville, the so-called 'Honky Chateau', he had never sold many records in France until *Blue Moves*. *A Single Man* had continued the sales surge, and when France Gall had her hit about him, Elton decided to duet with her on a French No. 1, 'Les Aveux', that was never released in Britain. Elton John stepped off the Anglo-American superstar track and did whatever he fancied – recording the duet in French with France Gall, adapting a French hit, 'Nobody Wins', into the English language and cutting a quickie disco album, the commercially catastrophic *Victim of Love*, with old friend producer Pete Bellotte of Donna Summer fame. He re-mixed old sessions cut with the legendary soul mentor Thom Bell to issue an EP that generated an American top ten single, 'Mama Can't Buy You Love'. He mixed songwriters Gary Osborne, Tom Robinson and Judie Tzuke with Bernie Taupin for a motley mélange, *21 At 33*, that at least featured Osborne's touching tune 'Little Jeannie', Elton's return to the top three of the *Billboard* singles chart. From pleasing everyone in the early and mid-seventies John had moved on in the late seventies and early eighties to pleasing himself. It wasn't until *Jump Up*, his 1982 long player, that he once again got two hits from one album, the John Lennon tribute 'Empty Garden', penned with Bernie, and what was a more dramatic departure, the adult ballad 'Blue Eyes'. It was his first top twenty hit in both Britain and America for six years. He continued to enjoy worldwide success with several singles taken from *Too Low For Zero* and *Breaking Hearts*. In the words of one of these famed 45s, he was 'still standing'.

But more impressive than any feats Elton John has recently been achieving is the fact that he is performing them on his own terms. During his self-imposed exile he had solidified his strengthening ties with Watford Football Club, the team he had supported since boyhood and of which he became Chairman, finding something whose fortunes meant as much to him as his own career. He could be a pop star without being a slave to a way of life that had claimed some of his friends, and which had almost claimed him when he made a second silly suicide bid in 1975. In 1984 he happily married. And having been talented enough to invent the superstar Elton John in the first place, he has now been strong enough to re-invent him as a man. Elton has learned and proved that a better life can lie beyond the yellow brick road.

Curtis Mayfield

CURTIS MAYFIELD is a careful and considerate lover. He's a deeply religious man, not a fire-and-brimstone repent-or-be-damned preacher but a celebrant of God's goodness. And he's an optimistic man who feels that a positive approach is the best way to face problems he only too keenly perceives. I can say this about Curtis Mayfield not because I know him or because I'm his publicist, but because he has revealed it in his music. In the songs he has written for himself, his long time group The Impressions, and numerous other artists, he has let me know that he is about as humane a man as *I* have ever known. And, somehow, he has managed to communicate his concerns in entertaining, commercial songs.

Curtis Mayfield was born in Chicago on 3 June 1942. He first sang in a gospel group called The Northern Jubileers that were affiliated with the Travelling Soul Spiritualist Church, of which his grandmother was a minister. Fellow Chicagoan Jerry Butler was another Northern Jubileer and when he and Curtis met The Roosters they joined forces to become The Impressions. They recorded a single that Vee Jay Records head Ewart Abner thought was too slow to release. Promotion man Red Schwartz thought otherwise and took it to his friend Dick Clark, host of the nationally broadcast afterschool viewing must, *American Bandstand*. In his biography, *Rock, Roll and Remember*, Clark relates how he thought the teen dancers would come to a dead halt when they heard the plodding piece. Schwartz, however, convinced him to give the song one spin at a time arranged to give Vee Jay executives a chance to see the kids' reaction. Vee Jay didn't have a television set, so they had to borrow one from Chess Records down the street. Red Schwartz was right. The kids loved the record. It was released on Vee Jay's Abner label and became one of the big ballads of 1958. It was called 'For Your Precious Love'.

The classic clincher was both a top twenty pop hit and a top ten rhythm and blues number that summer. But the artist credit wasn't

15

quite what the group had expected. Abner gave the lead singer top billing, and listeners thought the tune was sung by Jerry Butler and The Impressions or simply Jerry Butler. It was inevitable that Jerry exploit the circumstances and launch a solo career, a career which provided some of the most deeply satisfying soul sounds of the sixties. His first R&B No. 1 was the 1960 release 'He Will Break Your Heart', co-written by Curtis Mayfield. It became a pop No. 1 in 1975 when recorded by Tony Orlando and Dawn under the title 'He Don't Love You (Like I Love You)'.

The rest of The Impressions, however, found themselves without a recording deal when Abner Records were taken over by Vee Jay, and for a short while Mayfield made ends meet by playing guitar in Butler's band. But he didn't have to make it a long-term proposition as in 1961 The Impressions signed with ABC Records and exploded on both the R&B charts and the Hot 100 with their first issue, a Mayfield composition that managed to maintain a mood of mystery and mysticism as befit the tale of the 'Gypsy Woman'. It was an unexpected delight: an immaculately produced, cleverly arranged romance with obvious vocal contributions by all three Impressions – lead singer Curtis Mayfield, bassist Sam Gooden and tenor Fred Cash. There had been other members before and would be others later, but for the historic sequence of hits The Impressions scored in the sixties, the membership of the trio was constant.

'Gypsy Woman' revealed not only their skills at close harmony singing, particularly in the higher part of the register, but also Mayfield's writing prowess. The tune has enjoyed a series of notable covers, ranging from Brian Hyland's top three remake in 1970 to Ry Cooder's version in 1982. Even Mayfield himself could not resist having a second go when he became a soloist in the seventies.

Hyland and Cooder are, of course, white artists and one noteworthy aspect of The Impressions' success is that it was nearly as constant in the pop field as it was in R&B. It wasn't in Mayfield's nature to be a moaning blues singer nor an energetic screamer like some of the sixties Stax stars. He did not lose in integrity compared to those great soul artists, but did gain an element of wide appeal merely by delivering his vocals in a cool, controlled style. Curtis simmered rather than boiled. Adding the precise, ordered arrangements of Johnny Pate to the mixture gave The Impressions major Hot 100 hits like 'It's All Right'. The biggest pop hit The Impressions ever had, 'It's All Right' reached No. 4 in the autumn of 1963. It was also their first R&B No. 1. What was it that, in the face of adversity, was all right? Religious guidance? Civil rights leadership? Or simply the love of a man for a woman? Mayfield wasn't being specific at this point, but he was definite on two matters:

that thinking positively will make the going easier, and that the power of music will help see one through. These themes would recur in his work, and so would the contributions of arranger Pate, who gave The Impressions a crispness that many other R&B productions lacked. His use of brass became associated with the so-called 'Chicago sound', as did the coolness of Mayfield's vocals. Jerry Butler was even called 'The Iceman'.

The Impressions were off and running on a streak of seven consecutive top twenty hits. Another artist from the Windy City, Major Lance, was enjoying four straight similar successes, and all from the pen of his high school friend, Curits Mayfield. 'The Monkey Time' introduced Lance to the top ten and the monkey to dancers across America, but the Mayfield song sung by Lance that was heard round the world had one of the strangest titles in chart history, 'Um, Um, Um, Um, Um, Um'. Wayne Fontana and The Mindbenders outranked the Major version in the British charts, taking the tune to the top five. They were only one of many acts to achieve a UK placing with a Curtis Mayfield song. Gene Chandler entered with 'Nothing Can Stop Me' and The Fascinations visited with 'Girls Are Out to Get You'. In sixties America the charts were full of his compositions for fellow Chicago artists like Walter Jackson, The Five Stairsteps, and Jan Bradley, who had made the top twenty with the touching and truthful 'Mama Didn't Lie' even before 'It's All Right'. Mayfield wrote more hits than he's generally given credit for and had he been in Detroit rather than Chicago he might have had far more publicity. He wasn't particularly distinctive in his physical appearance either, so he and his fellow Impressions had to settle for hits without heroics.

In the spring of 1964, at the height of Beatlemania, 'I'm So Proud' fitted into American top forty playlists, somewhere between 'Can't Buy Me Love' and 'She Loves You', or maybe between 'I Want to Hold Your Hand' and 'Love Me Do'. It was a tender ballad and it stood out from every other hit of the time precisely because it *was* so slow, so reflective, so contemplative. He and Johnny Pate surrounded sweet sentiments with an appropriately gorgeous gossamer backing track. Love is beautiful, they seemed to be saying, let's make it sound beautiful.

During 1964 Mayfield's message remained uplifting. 'You Must Believe Me', he told his girl in the song of the same name. In 'Talking About My Baby', he sang directly about the lover who filled him with pride. 'Keep On Pushing', he said in The Impressions' top ten single with that title. Here he spoke more openly of life's tribulations than before, but this made it even more urgent than ever to confront and overcome obstacles.

At the year's end, the three friends made their first openly religious 45. Sidney Poitier was starring in the movie *Lilies of the Field*, about a black man who helps nuns build a chapel. It was a critical and commercial success and, even though a bit cute, presented an affectionate view of both the Poitier character and the female religious order. The Impressions achieved one of the rare gospel top ten hits when they released the film's theme, 'Amen'. Its success inspired Mayfield professionally, just as the subject matter had impressed him personally, and he wrote two religious tunes for singles in the first half of 1965. One was the soul-stirring 'People Get Ready', perhaps the best synthesis of pop and gospel yet made. The other was 'Meeting Over Yonder'. But when the latter fell short of the top forty, it became clear that The Impressions had blurred the focus of their commercial career and it took two and a half years to make a complete recovery. If not more devotional singles, how about more up-tempo sides? 'Amen' had been their first fast smash, how about the speedy 'You've Been Cheating', 'Can't Satisfy', or 'You Always Hurt Me'?

The tempo tactic didn't work. Those three were all enjoyable tracks but they weren't classic pieces. More to the point, they weren't big hits. Perhaps because Curtis was concentrating on his two new record labels, Windy C and Mayfield, he wasn't giving The Impressions his full attention. If that was the case, it explains the timing of his group's famous comeback. It was shortly after the two companies floundered as a consequence of the financial difficulties of distributor Cameo-Parkway that The Impressions returned to the No. 1 spot on the R&B chart. 'We're a Winner' lived up to its title.

Sam Cooke had written the first anthem of Negro awareness, 'A Change Is Gonna Come'. The civil rights movement of the sixties called for development of his theme, and the first major artist to address the subject was Curtis Mayfield. 'We're a Winner' was an appeal to black consciousness that exhorted Americans of his race to follow their leaders, aspire to and achieve that distant and indistinct goal of which Martin Luther King and others spoke. 'Say It Loud, I'm Black and I'm Proud' James Brown would sing later in 1968. 'I Am Somebody', Johnny Taylor would cry. Curtis Mayfield beat them both to the punch with 'We're a Winner', in a way that thrilled his people – witness its No. 1 R&B placing – and also satisfied white folk. The target of the tune was integration, not separatism, so it was a top twenty pop hit as well.

It was an important theme for Mayfield. He had hinted at it before, but now he was being completely forthcoming about his racial beliefs. In the next two years, The Impressions released three more important singles concerning race relations. Their last major ABC hit, 'We're

Rolling On', was an obvious derivative of 'We're a Winner'. But two singles for their new Curtom label, owned by and named after Curtis Mayfield and his manager Eddie Thomas, were major works. 'This Is My Country' and 'Choice of Colors', The Impressions third No. 1, managed to combine cries for togetherness and declarations of black pride with memorable melodies and arresting arrangements. Mayfield's message contained some bitterness, particularly in 'This Is My Country', but his delivery lacked the harshness of the black power rhetoricians of the era. Some critics have suggested these race records were naive and simplistic, but they forget that pop singles are rarely subtle, the point having to be made clearly in three minutes. After all, 'Say It Loud, I'm Black and I'm Proud' was pretty direct too.

Just as they had with their religious songs, The Impressions had gone down a road to riches that turned into a career cul-de-sac. The subject matter was not lucrative in the long term, and re-definition was required. It was 1970, the year when The Beatles broke up, Simon and Garfunkel split, John Fogerty exited Creedence Clearwater Revival, and Diana Ross left The Supremes. It seemed as if all the writers or front persons of famous groups were trying it on their own in the new singer-songwriter era. This was the best time for Curtis Mayfield to bid goodbye to The Impressions. It wasn't a bad choice. He scored immediately in the States with '(Don't Worry) If There's a Hell Below We're All Gonna Go', and in 1971 made his ludicrously overdue British chart debut with 'Move On Up'.

The solo sound of Curtis Mayfield, as exemplified by that top twenty hit, had indeed moved on from The Impressions style. He was taking the tempo at a faster pace on many tracks, forsaking a few degrees of the coolness of the Chicago sound for elements of the funk-rock mixture Sly Stone had popularised. Without the anchoring of Sam Gooden's bass, Mayfield's tenor voice seemed to soar above the instrumental track. Mayfield and The Impressions were two different entities, and the group continued to record on Curtom without any confusion as to what track was by whom.

In December 1971, Mayfield performed at the Philharmonic Hall in New York City. At a post-concert party he was offered the chance to score a film directed at the black audience which tradesters would refer to without irony as 'the black market'. It was an action picture about drug dealing in the big city, a plot that seemed to be another so-called 'black exploitation' movie. So it might have merely been had not Curtis Mayfield written the music for *Superfly*. The soundtrack album was a multi-million seller. It spawned two gold singles, the title song and 'Freddie's Dead'. It was also the first work to receive a gold tape award for over one million tapes sold. This commercial peak of Mayfield's career put him in a class with Isaac Hayes and Marvin Gaye as one of the three most important black artist/composers. The new vitality of his music, combined with the ever-present perceptiveness and humanity of his lyrics, gave Mayfield a distinctive sound for the seventies. But he now gave his greatest energies to other artists in new big screen projects. While his own records did less well in the mid-seventies, he turned out a string of hits for great black stars singing the soundtracks of not-so-great movies. Gladys Knight and The Pips had a top five single, 'Claudine', from the forgettable film of that name. Aretha Franklin had an extended return to the top of the soul chart with the scintillating 'Something He Can Feel' from the less-honoured motion picture *Sparkle*. And The Staple Singers went all the way to No. 1 in America with a Mayfield song and production, the title track of *Let's Do It Again*.

With The Staple Singers going to No. 1 mere months after Tony Orlando did with 'He Don't Love You (Like I Love You)', Curtis Mayfield the writer bagged a brace of Hot 100 chart-toppers fifteen years after his first R&B No. 1. For Curtis Mayfield the executive, Curtom was doing fine, especially with The Staples, The Impressions, and, soon afterwards, Linda Clifford. But Curtis Mayfield the artist had peaked. He didn't fit into the disco movement of the late seventies, where the beat and the bass were more important than the words and the vocal. He has continued to record, but whether there will ever again be a prominent place for the songwriting ace is as debatable as it is unimportant.

Mayfield had a great gift not just for a melody or a lyric line but for self-expression so loving and emotionally persuasive that he could seduce you into wanting to be something you couldn't. He could make you love a woman you'd never even met. He made being Negro so exciting a white boy could momentarily wish he were black. And when confronted with a testimony of faith like 'People Get Ready', Curtis Mayfield could make even a confirmed agnostic wish he could believe.

From left to right, Danny Kirwan, Mick Fleetwood, Peter Green, John McVie, Jeremy Spencer

Fleetwood Mac

THEY LED two lives. No, they weren't double agents, nor were they schizophrenics. Mick Fleetwood and John McVie were the constant rhythm section in a group whose membership changed so radically that it managed to epitomise two different kinds of music from two different countries in two different decades. In the late sixties it was the top popular blues band in Britain. In the seventies it was the top soft rock group in America. Its name came from the surnames of its two founding and long-serving members: Fleetwood Mac.

The British blues movement of the sixties didn't die when first The Rolling Stones and then Eric Clapton went on to be mass audience superstars. The man who had nurtured Clapton, John Mayall, kept the fire burning with further editions of his Bluesbreakers. It was in the spring 1967 incarnation of the group that Peter Green, Mick Fleetwood and John McVie first played together.

Guitarist Green and drummer Fleetwood had met earlier in the short-lived 1966 Peter B's Looners, Peter B being Peter Bardens of subsequent Camel fame. It wasn't the only imaginatively named ensemble in which Green had toiled. His first semi-professional band, which he joined when he was fifteen, had been called Bobby Denim and The Dominoes.

An instrumental foursome, Peter B's Looners only needed a couple of months to realise they weren't going to make a fortune. They feared they weren't even going to make ends meet so Rod Stewart and Beryl Marsden were recruited to provide both a male and a female voice. The new group was called Shotgun Express but it lasted less than a year. Peter Green left quickly to join The Bluesbreakers, while Fleetwood stayed on several months before leaving the music business to become an interior decorator.

It's difficult now to think that Mick Fleetwood might be doing up the inside of your house rather than leading America's bestselling band of the late seventies. But whitening the walls he might be had he not received a summons from John Mayall, who was so respected his invitations were taken as virtual commands. For a little over a month, The Bluesbreakers were Mayall, Green, Fleetwood and bass player John McVie. They recorded five numbers, including an instrumental they called 'Fleetwood Mac'. Fleetwood however was ousted from the band, supposedly for drinking too much, before it had a chance of being released and with Green, Jeremy Spencer and Bob Brunning he formed the first Fleetwood Mac. They only recorded one track, Peter Green's 'Rambling Pony', before bassist Brunning left in favour of John McVie. He had known he would have to go if McVie wanted in, and departed to form his own well-received Sunflower Brunning Blues Band. It sounds as if every English blues musician of the sixties played in at least sixty groups, but we should remember that John McVie has only ever been in two bands – The Bluesbreakers and Fleetwood Mac.

The first Fleetwood Mac made a much-discussed debut at the Windsor Jazz and Blues Festival in August 1967. One month later, *Melody Maker* called Peter Green 'the newest, toughest and meanest of the guitar cowboys'. It's hard to imagine a nineteen-year-old from the East End of London as a tough and mean cowboy but he certainly did know how to patrol his own territory. It was Green who negotiated the group's deal with Blue Horizon Records, who invited singer and slide guitarist Jeremy Spencer to join at the suggestion of label head Mike Vernon, and who wrote their first hit, 'Black Magic Woman'.

This spring of 1968 success was Fleetwood Mac's second single. The first, 'I Believe My Time Ain't Long', had been written by Jeremy Spencer, a Buddy Holly and Fabian fan who had heard Elmore James in 1964 and become a fervent follower of the Chicago bluesman. He loved performing James material and writing in his style.

The combined talents of Green and Spencer provided their quartet with enough good and varied material to make their album première, *Peter Green's Fleetwood Mac*, a top five hit. It stayed on the LP chart for thirteen months, a spectacular success for a small label and an early indication of how an independent could compete with the majors.

It wasn't just the size of their record company that was unusual however. There was also the matter of their appearance. More than a foot in height separated their shortest and tallest members. Jeremy Spencer was a diminutive 5ft 4in, while Mick Fleetwood measured 6ft 4½in. Furthermore, an early press release boasted that 'Like cavemen, they dress for comfort, rather than effect'.

'Need Your Love So Bad', Fleetwood Mac's second British hit single, was written by Little Willie John. The legendary American singer had scored a top five rhythm and blues hit with it in the States in 1956, so the Yanks didn't need a version by English upstarts. Indeed, as long as Fleetwood Mac concentrated on blues inspired by or in homage to American blacks, their records meant little in the US, although this didn't stop them going on tour there. Not unexpectedly, the group didn't know what to expect when they crossed the Atlantic. Peter Green reported his reaction when a black policeman approached him after a concert on the West Coast. 'I thought he was going to arrest us for swearing on stage', he shuddered, 'but he came up and complimented us. He said it was one of the best bands he'd ever heard.' This was the type of review that meant most to Mac. Black musicians responded favourably, and they were the people the band wanted to reach.

1968 was a year of fast developments for the group. After the second single came the second album, *Mr Wonderful*. Consumers didn't consider it quite as wonderful as the debut disc, but it still made the top ten. And there was a fifth member for the group, guitarist and vocalist Danny Kirwan. After sorting through three hundred replies to a pop paper plea for musicians to play with, he rejected them all and accepted Peter Green's offer to join Fleetwood Mac. The quintet was in the unusual position of having three front men, all of whom played the guitar and all of whom sang. Kirwan dismissed the suggestion that this combination caused chaos. 'We don't get in each other's way at all', he said. 'I do my number and they do theirs. And, of course, Jeremy plays piano as well.'

Danny's early recording sessions with Mac were devoted to tracks intended for release on LP. One of them turned out particularly well. 'We thought it would be a good idea to release it as a single', Kirwan recalled. There was an understatement. 'Albatross' was a No. 1. Peter Green remembered he was thinking of something 'very peaceful' when he composed 'Albatross', though not about the seabird who plagued the Ancient Mariner in the famous Samuel Taylor Coleridge poem. 'Very peaceful' it must have been, for in 1968 and in years since 'Albatross' has transported millions of listeners into their own flights of fancy, far from the cares of everyday life, far even from the realities of the surroundings. Far, far away ... to be brought back into the present only by a jarring jockey's jabbering.

'Albatross' went to No. 1 in late January 1969. Fleetwood Mac had gone where no blues group of their seriousness had gone before. Peter Green was delighted the success had happened gradually and with his own song. The act he thought was far more likely to have staying power than any one-hit wonder.

They proved the point immediately by getting to No. 2 with the follow-up, 'Man Of The World'. It was in the same vein as 'Albatross' but a vocal. Green was quite clear as to how he felt about it: 'It's a sad

song so it's a blues, but people will say it's not because it's not a 12-bar
... It's very sad, it was the way I felt at the time. It's me at my sad-
dest.' At the time it wasn't obvious what Peter had to be sad about,
though dramatic evidence that something was wrong would appear in
less than a year. Record sales were unaffected by any old fan's disappointment at the popularisation of Fleetwood Mac. In late 1969 the
quintet enjoyed yet another smash, 'Oh Well'.

'Oh Well' was the vocal classic of the early Fleetwood Mac, just as
'Albatross' was the instrumental masterpiece. In the early eighties it
was still in the revamped group's set sung by Lindsay Buckingham
even though *his* legs are not as thin as the lyric states. 'Oh Well' was a
perfect party platter, the third top two hit the five had fostered in 1969.
The magnitude of this success became clear when *Melody Maker*'s
annual chart tabulation showed that, using a points system, Fleetwood
Mac had been Britain's top act of the year, outdistancing The Beatles.

It was all too much for Peter Green. How much of his decision to go
was based on an aversion to commerical pressure and how much was
due to the judgment-distorting effects of drugs will never be known.
The simple fact is that, after honouring his commitments to the group
in the spring of 1970, he left for an uncertain future, a future that is no
more certain now than it was then. Unlike many stars of the late sixties
who died before they could fulfil their promise, it was Peter Green's
tragedy to survive and not fulfil his promise. He has never been able to
exorcise his personal demons and produce work of the high standard
he himself set, even though he has had an occasional helping hand
from his old work mates.

An instant reminder of the impact of his music came when, shortly
after he departed, the previously recorded track 'The Green Manalishi'
became a top ten single. Producer Martin Birch shuddered when
recalling the making of it. 'The weirdest session I've ever taken part
in', he called it. 'Peter wasn't communicating very much and Jeremy
was well into this Children of God thing. The whole atmosphere was
very, very, strange.'

After Green left, Fleetwood Mac went into quick and near total
eclipse. The addition of John McVie's wife, the former Christine Perfect, did not immediately help even though she had starred with Chick-
en Shack, particularly on 'I'd Rather Go Blind', and had been voted
Female Vocalist of the Year by *Melody Maker* readers. Things instead
got worse with the defection of Jeremy Spencer, who turned to John on
a plane flight and said 'Why do I have to be here if I don't want to be
here?' McVie had heard pop stars complain before and didn't take the
remark seriously, but it was the last time he spoke with Spencer for
two years. Jeremy joined the Children of God – a religious sect, not a

rock group, though years later he did make music with fellow be-
lievers.

You need a diagram or Pete Frame's invaluable book *Rock Family
Trees* to follow the changes in the line-up of Fleetwood Mac during the
early seventies. Out went Danny Kirwan, an uncertain young man
who was the first member of the group to be asked to go. He was
replaced by Bob Welch, previously a Las Vegas lounge white soul
singer, who lasted nearly four years. Former Savoy Brown singer Dave
Walker and Long John Baldry guitarist Bob Weston also came and
went during a period that saw the group fade into history in their
homeland while they gradually developed a following in the States
through a sequence of tours and a series of albums. Fleetwood and
McVie almost despaired when the re-issued 'Albatross' went to No. 2
in the UK. It was their old sound, and they would not perform it on
stage. They complained, quite reasonably, that their new single, 'Did
You Ever Love Me?' was being overlooked.

That beautiful ballad revealed a hidden strength of the group. Christine McVie had given the group an instrument, the keyboard, and a
woman's voice. Her songwriting provided a lyrical and female perspective.

An infusion of musical excitement and production discipline was all
that was lacking to make Fleetwood Mac a new and commercial ensemble. That infusion came in the form of Lindsay Buckingham and
Stevie Nicks, who helped make the group's eponymous 1975 album a
million seller.

The way they were discovered was bizarre. That word is over-used
these days but that doesn't make the genuinely bizarre event less
bizarre. Mick Fleetwood was in a Californian supermarket when a
fellow shopper recommended he record in Sound City Studio. When
he visited the place engineer Keith Olsen played him a sample of the
studio's work, an album called *Buckingham-Nicks*. Mick was so
impressed he soon despatched Olsen to invite the duo to join Fleetwood Mac.

At this point Buckingham and Nicks were doing their equivalent of
Fleetwood's interior decorating. He was an ad man and she was a
waitress. When Keith Olsen arrived at their New Year's Eve party and
announced they were wanted in Fleetwood Mac, it took them longer to
believe he was serious than it did to decide to say yes.

Fleetwood Mac climbed the US charts slowly but surely for a year,
ultimately reaching No. 3 and selling over a million copies. It just kept
going. 'It's good to have finally gotten away from questions like
"Whatever happened to Peter Green or Jeremy Spencer?"' sighed
John McVie. The success of the next LP changed the question around

as millions of new buyers asked 'Who were Peter Green and Jeremy Spencer?' *Rumours* was the No. 1 album in the world in 1977. Britain finally woke up and made it No. 1 in early '78. But chart positions alone do not tell the entire tale. Until *Thriller*, *Rumours* was the best-selling single long-player of all-time. (The double-album *Saturday Night Fever* was overall No. 1.) It has sold over twenty-five million copies and still makes periodic appearances in the chart. No product sells this many copies without reason. *Rumours* was an excellent piece of work, with almost every song strong, but that's not a sufficient explanation. Mick Fleetwood observed it was like a soap opera. 'Every track was written about someone in the band.' Since the romantic couples, the McVies and Buckingham-Nicks, had been tiffing, this suggested that the album was full of interpersonal tensions and dramas. This *is* what the public want, at least what they can relate to. Finally there is the right-place-at-the-right-time factor: in the United States the original rock and roll audience was now in young middle age and wanted a softer and smoother sound, though it still wanted it rooted in rock. *Rumours* gave it to them.

'Dreams', written and sung by Stevie Nicks, was Fleetwood Mac's first American No. 1 single eight years after 'Albatross' had paced the pack in Britain. One says 'in Britain' rather than 'at home' because, to all intents and purposes, this was no longer a British band. The sensibilities and strengths of Lindsay Buckingham, who has had the greatest effect on the production and instrumental sound, are very American, as are the delicacy and demeanor of Nicks' vocals. More than this, the group all live in the States and seem to be happy doing so.

Rumours generated four US top ten singles, including Buckingham's 'Go Your Own Way' and Christine McVie's 'Don't Stop' and 'You Make Loving Fun'. Its success gave the group the money for any experiment, no matter how outlandish. That included renting Dodger Stadium for a day and booking the marching band of the University of Southern California to make a guest appearance on one track. It sounds preposterous, but it made for their first UK top ten hit in nine years. Lindsay Buckingham took the quintet's warm-up jam, added words, and called it 'Tusk'.

'Tusk' got its title from conservationist and photographer Peter Beard, a friend of Buckingham. Stevie Nicks told Mick Fleetwood that if he named the new album after that track, she'd quit. He did, and she didn't. 'He knew I loved the band too much to leave over a stupid name', she observed.

What hurt more than her objection to the title was listener reaction to the music. 'Only' five million copies of the *Tusk* double album were sold, compared to the more than twenty million of its predecessor.

Lindsay Buckingham in particular had dared to experiment on the package, and felt keenly disappointed. 'I don't think we were aware of how much of a chance we were taking in terms of business', he admitted. 'You realise people aren't getting the message. You wonder whether you've been deluding yourself or what, especially when the rest of the band start telling you it's time to get back to the standard format.'

That's what happened after a double live album marked time. Having gotten some of their personal musical desires satisfied on their solo sets, Stevie's phenomenally successful *Bella Donna* and Lindsay's quite well-received *Law And Order*, Nicks and Buckingham subsumed their own identities in that of the band on the 1982 issue, *Mirage*. The result was a highly acclaimed platinum album, their second US No. 1. 'Hold Me' became their first top five single in five years. In 1984 Christine McVie became the third member of the quintet to achieve a solo top tenner.

It may have seemed they were light years and lifetimes away from their initial incorporation as Britain's best blues group. But Mick Fleetwood saw a certain symmetry. 'Right now there are three definite front-line people,' he related. 'We've come back to how the band was at the beginning with Peter, Danny and Jeremy. People could enjoy different aspects with the band.'

'Now, with Stevie, Lindsay, and Christine, we've come full circle.'

Neil Young

AT THE fifteenth birthday party of Radio 1, David Jensen was approached by a representative of the World Service. 'How is it', the guest asked, 'that you are so big and yet so unimportant?' Jensen was flabbergasted at what seemed a gross insult. The visitor continued. 'Especially when you have so many natural resources?' The deejay suddenly realised it wasn't himself the questioner was referring to, but his homeland, Canada. It's a remark applicable to his country's role in rock, too. How can it have so many people and be so close culturally to the United States and yet have spawned so few rock stars?

It's to the disadvantage of Canada that many of its musical heroes are not associated with their native country. In the case of Neil Young, he's considered Californian. He's spent almost his entire adult life there and the laid back quality of many of his famous numbers suggests the West Coast sound.

But Young started in Canada. He was born in Toronto on 12 November 1945, the son of a well-known sports journalist. When his parents split, ten-year-old Neil went with his mother to Winnipeg and it was in the cafeteria of the Calvin High School there that he first sang before an audience. The song was The Beatles' 'It Won't Be Long'.

It's impossible to know what impact Young's voice had on his schoolmates, who were probably too busy eating their cheeseburgers and ice cream wafers to pay much attention anyway. But that voice is one of the most distinctive in popular music. It could be described as a high-pitched whine, which sounds slanderous though it isn't meant to be. Young has always sung in an unfiltered tone in that part of the register baritones can only dream of reaching. It is an eerie, ethereal noise, which when infused with emotion sounds as if the singer is either suffering greatly or spending a holiday in a haunted house. I first heard it while in the basement of my college fraternity and I shall never forget it. It was late, the lights were out and most of my so-called 'brothers' were asleep. Where the intoxicated Buffalo Springfield fan on the top floor got the nerve to turn the volume all the way up I'll never know, but I do know that when that mournful voice reached me from far away on that cold dark night it chilled me to the bone. Appropriately enough, the track was called 'Out Of My Mind'.

Buffalo Springfield was Neil Young's first American group. He'd played in a couple of bands in Canada, including The Mynah Birds, who also featured Rick James, the early eighties punk funk Motown man. (Imagining James and Young together now stretches brain tissue.)

In 1966, Young drove to Los Angeles with his friend Bruce Palmer in a thirteen-year-old hearse. He hoped to meet up with Stephen Stills, whom he'd met playing folk clubs in Toronto. Neil and Bruce were motoring in Los Angeles, about to leave to look for Stills in San Francisco, when Steve and Richie Furay got stuck behind them in a traffic jam. Realising that not many people would be driving a hearse with Ontario licence plates on Sunset Boulevard, Stills yelled 'That has just got to be Neil!' He leapt out of the car, as did Furay, and a joyful re-union took place three thousand miles from the site of their original meeting. The three guitarists and bassist Palmer decided to form a group, recruiting Dewey Martin to play drums. They named themselves after the steamrollers which were re-surfacing the street they lived on. Each carried the brand name 'Buffalo Springfield'.

Before they released any records the quintet played live dates, including the Hollywood Bowl, and television shows, including the networked *Hollywood Palace*. They reportedly received over twenty offers from record companies before settling with Atco. Stephen Stills wrote the hits on the *Buffalo Springfield* album, the group's own top ten single 'For What It's Worth' and The Mojo Men's cover of 'Sit Down I Think I Love You'. Neil wrote nearly half the songs but his composing contributions to the second LP were more substantial. *Buffalo Springfield Again* boasted Young's 'Expecting To Fly', 'Broken Arrow', and 'Mr Soul'.

The second album they recorded, *Stampede*, was never released. The cover and title suggested a Western connotation to 'Buffalo' that had never been intended by the steamrollers who provided the group's name. The bass player on the rejected sleeve was hiding his face since the original bassist, Bruce Palmer, was recurrently deported for drug and immigration violations. The remaining members of the group had to live with Stills and Young's occasional rows and though they would always be resolved to the advantage of the group, the musical differences provided some anxious moments. Anxiety was something Neil Young couldn't handle well in those early days; in his words, he was 'going crazy' and suffering 'many identity crises'. He left the group only to return and leave again. Buffalo Springfield gave their last concert on 5 May 1968, though engineer Jim Messina collected enough old material to fill a summer album release, *Last Time Around*.

Looking back, Young told *Rolling Stone* reporter Cameron Crowe 'I just wasn't mature enough to deal with it. I was very young.' He retired to a house overlooking Topanga Canyon and wrote the songs for an album, which because of its multi-tracking and re-mixing he called 'overdub city'. The record company called it *Neil Young*. Its first track, 'The Loner', perfectly described his personal life at the time. He never developed a reputation for putting his heart on his sleeve and his love life in his lyrics like fellow Canadian Joni Mitchell did, but that's only because his words were slightly more veiled. They were about him, but almost a full step farther away than Joni's were to her.

In what must have been a grave disappointment to a young man who had so recently been in an important group, Neil's debut disc failed to chart. He asked friends from the group Crazy Horse to help him record some new material and liked the feeling of playing together so much he invited them to stay with him. Unbelievably, they cut three great tracks in one day – 'Down By The River', 'Cowgirl In The Sand', and 'Cinnamon Girl'. The resultant album was called *Everybody Knows This Is Nowhere*, but it certainly was somewhere. It was in the charts at No. 34, higher than any Buffalo Springfield set. 'Cinnamon Girl' was a first-class short rocker and 'Down By The River' a top-notch extended piece, creating a feeling of suspense and regret that, for some unexplained reason, the first person character had shot his lover down by the river.

It wasn't just critics and consumers who were captivated by *Everybody Knows This Is Nowhere*. Stephen Stills made a personal visit to invite Neil to join Crosby, Stills and Nash, who had just released their celebrated collection. Young told interviewer Elliot Blinder that CS&N wanted a bigger instrumental sound and needed him on guitar. At first Stills didn't want to give him equal billing, saying 'Everybody'll know who you are'. The Canadian evidently held out because when the expanded group began its tour in the summer of 1969 they were known as Crosby, Stills, Nash and Young.

The Crosby, Stills, Nash and Young album *Deja Vu* was an American No. 1 that took approximately eight hundred hours to record. Neil joked that 'Helpless' was laid down at four in the morning, 'when everybody got tired enough to play at my speed'. Eight hundred hours in the same room sounds like a new dimension in togetherness, but it wasn't quite like that. Only three tracks on *Deja Vu*, 'Helpless', 'Woodstock', and 'Almost Cut My Hair' were recorded with all four lead artists present. The other tracks were cut in combinations. Young's only composition credits were for 'Helpless' and the wistful trilogy 'Country Girl', though he received a co-writer's listing with Steve Stills for 'Everybody I Love You'.

Neil's real high point with Crosby, Stills, Nash and Young, often referred to as the leading law firm in rock, came in the spring of 1970. Richard Nixon's Vietnam policy had taken an ominous turn with the American invasion of Cambodia. When students protested on campuses across the country, the National Guard shot four dead at Kent State University in Ohio. In the student strikes and emotional outbursts that followed, no one managed to articulate the fury as effectively as Neil Young. 'Ohio' was a shattering experience, certainly to hear and evidently to record. David Crosby wept after it was finished. It remains one of the great protest songs in pop history. Young himself realised the irony in making money from the misfortune of others, but to his credit didn't try to cash in as much as he could. 'Ohio' was a top twenty US hit, but there was no studio album to follow. Neil instead finished his third solo LP, and with the exception of a live double, *Four Way Street*, another American No. 1, there was no more from Crosby, Stills, Nash and Young.

Stills did guest on his friend's new work, *After The Gold Rush*, which also featured Crazy Horse, Greg Reeves and Nils Lofgren. Here was a top ten success on both sides of the Atlantic that critics fell over themselves praising. *Los Angeles Times* scribe Robert Hilburn used the adjectives 'lovely, beautiful, romantic, delicate and fragile'. The title track, supposedly inspired by a Dean Stockwell–Herb Berman screenplay called *After The Gold Rush*, was a piece so refined that Prelude have had an a capella hit in Britain with it twice. 'Only Love Can Break Your Heart' was a chart single in the States for Neil himself. But the lasting track was the inevitably controversial one, 'Southern Man'.

Young wrote his anti-Confederate sentiments in the dressing room of the Fillmore East; he admitted he'd never been on a civil rights march. Lynyrd Skynyrd certainly thought he was being a bit cavalier with his opinions, and in their 'Sweet Home Alabama' reminded him that the southern man doesn't need him around, anyhow.

Though he preferred *Everybody Knows This Is Nowhere*, Young knew *After The Gold Rush* was strong. But he delayed releasing his next solo set until March 1972. He wasn't being moody, he simply wasn't well. At times he has suffered from epilepsy and diabetes; in 1971, however, it was a bad back that kept him on the sidelines. Able to stand only four hours a day, Young recorded what he called 'a mellow album' wearing a brace. The physical condition of the artist set the low-energy level of some of the music, but this was just what the market, if not the doctor, ordered. *Harvest* was a No. 1 album in both the US and UK and 'Heart Of Gold' an American No. 1 single. Other outstanding tracks were 'Old Man', a reflective slow song prominently featuring harmony singers James Taylor and Linda Ronstadt, and 'A Man Needs A Maid', a number recorded in England with the London Symphony Orchestra. The last title refers to Carrie Snodgress, the actress Neil fell for when he saw her in the film *Diary Of A Mad Housewife*, who became his real-life lover.

Harvest specialised in big ballads, but Neil Young tired of them. As he said in 1977, '"Heart of Gold" put me in the middle of the road. Travelling there soon became a bore so I headed for the ditch.' A better analogy might be that he took a swan dive from the heights of his profession – everyone knew he would go splat on landing, but they didn't know quite where. He made a movie, *Journey Through The Past*, which featured many obscure images, and generated a poor double album soundtrack which included a full side of a mediocre song, 'Words', some curious chatter and an odd version of part of Handel's *Messiah*. The sleeve was a still of a dozen black-hooded men on black horses, rather like a Ku Klux Klan emerging from a soot storm, chasing a man with a pick-up truck on a beach. Young said he couldn't explain what it meant, and if he didn't know, he couldn't expect others to comprehend it. The album didn't even make the top forty, a shocking setback coming off a No. 1.

The artist's next three albums showed a developing despondency that culminated in the 1975 release *Tonight's The Night*. It was recorded quickly with little attention to hitting the right notes. Young was reacting to the drug deaths of guitarist Danny Whitten and former roadie Bruce Berry. He and the musicians would drink for several hours a night before entering the studio, getting, as he put it, 'high enough, right out there on the edge where we felt wide-open to the whole mood. It was spooky.' These unusual conditions and Neil's nearly-obsessive state of mind produced an album as disturbing as it was disturbed. As critic Dave Marsh observed, Young had reached so far into himself that hearing the record was like witnessing a murder or a suicide. Neil Young so believed in *Tonight's The Night* he broke his usual silence to do a round of promotional interviews. He knew it would fail commercially, but as he bluntly pointed out, he didn't need the money and he didn't need the fame. 'I just appreciate the freedom to put an album like *Tonight's The Night* out if I want to.'

He didn't want to often, fortunately for his sanity as well as his bank balance. His subsequent albums, while not up to his early standard, often included at least one excellent lengthy piece, such as 'Cortez The Killer' from *Zuma* and 'Like A Hurricane' from *American Stars And*

Bars. Young was a fine guitar player as well as a singer and writer – incidentally, he credited Hank B. Marvin as a great inspiration – and on 'Like A Hurricane' his guitar work is outstanding.

The track signalled a comeback of sorts for him in the late seventies. His 1978 issue, *Comes A Time*, featured the lilting 'Lotta Love', which his back-up singer Nicolette Larson took to the American top ten, and his own moving version of the unofficial Canadian national anthem, Ian Tyson's 'Four Strong Winds'. In 1979 he returned to the LP top ten with his controversial *Rust Never Sleeps*. Commenting on the recent death of Elvis Presley and the break-up of The Sex Pistols, he wrote that it was better to burn out than it was to rust. A friend from Devo mentioned that a rust inhibiting product in Akron, Ohio had the advertising slogan 'Rust Never Sleeps'. Young liked it. 'It relates to my career', he said. 'The longer I keep on going the more I have to fight this corrosion.'

With the prominent mention of Johnny Rotten in 'Hey Hey, My My (Into The Black)', and his friendship with Devo, it was apparent that Young had managed to stay in touch with late seventies trends, an ability that had eluded many of his Californian mates. He demonstrated this dramatically in 1982 when he used the vocoder and synthesizer on two fine tracks. Sadly, the year saw the release of his third flop film. After *Journey through the Past* and *Rust Never Sleeps*, a mediocre movie with some good concert footage, came *Human Highway*, delayed for years before its 1982 release and panned by *Variety*. It was now obvious Neil would never make a motion picture masterpiece.

After forays into rockabilly and country, fans still care enough to wonder what Young will do next. One reason he is still welcome is that he has never over-exposed himself. Though each album has been, as he put it, a musical autobiography, each piece has also been very much of its moment: he's off somewhere else next time around. And because he's never cultivated a physical image, no one has tired of seeing his face or his form. He's a classic case of how to find longevity in the music business: don't consciously seek it. Make good records, and people will buy them. It sounds so simple. Why can't more Canadians do it? Why can't we all do it?

Aretha Franklin

SOME GEMS are flawed. Not all their facets are smooth. From certain angles they may even appear ordinary. But from a selected perspective, they appear perfect, shining as luminously as the brightest star.

So it is with Aretha Franklin. She's not good looking like Diana Ross, and this has caused her anguish. She gives dull interviews, and this has caused us anguish. And her live performance can be, in the recent words of *Variety*, 'downright embarrassing'. But put her in a recording studio and she is transformed into the most beautiful, articulate and exciting person on this planet. When she gives full vent to her great gift, she gives us the music of heaven, and commands our attention, our awe, our respect.

Aretha Franklin's successful synthesis of gospel and rhythm and blues was made possible by her early experience in religious music. Her father, the Reverend C. L. Franklin, was America's bestselling preacher. His spoken sermons won several gold discs. His New Bethel Baptist Church in Detroit featured fine gospel singing, and his home was a haven for stars in the field like Sam Cooke, Mahalia Jackson and Clara Ward.

Perhaps it was inevitable that the clergyman's daughter should take up the form, and tour with him across America. But there was no certainty that she would sound as good as she did. At the age of fourteen, Aretha made her first record, *The Gospel Sound Of Aretha Franklin*, which included a spine-tingling version of 'Precious Lord'. She was still a teenager when she journeyed to New York City to audition for John Hammond. The CBS executive was renowned for discovering or at least cultivating the careers of Bessie Smith and Billie Holliday, perhaps black music's two greatest female stars to date. Aretha Franklin also wanted to be famous.

It wasn't as easy as just taking a trip to the Big Apple. Columbia, the American recording division of CBS, didn't know how to harness the young girl's abilities. The histrionics and hysteria associated with

gospel, even if controlled, were not the stuff of the singles chart, and in an effort to turn her into an entertainer Aretha was recorded on a variety of popular material. Sometimes a session man played piano, ignoring the artist's own exciting keyboard style.

Aretha made ten albums in six years for Columbia. It has been fashionable in recent years to denigrate this material for not showing her off at her best, but she did achieve several moderate R&B hits, beginning with 'Today I Sing The Blues' in late 1960. She also made a good LP tribute to another former guest to her father's home, Dinah Washington, and scraped into the top forty of the Hot 100. The latter feat was achieved in a slightly bizarre fashion, with Aretha recording 'Rock-a-Bye Your Baby With A Dixie Melody', a tune already popularised by Al Jolson, Judy Garland and Jerry Lewis. It reached No. 37 in the US pop chart at the end of 1961, but instead of being the beginning of a string of hits, it seemed a curious one-off, for Aretha Franklin did not visit the top forty again for six years.

Admittedly she was only twenty when she had her first chart success. But even in adulthood she showed a strange inability to distinguish between what she could do brilliantly and what she was only reasonable at. She would show equal enthusiasm for a track that allowed her to display unmatched strengths and another that she could handle only adequately.

Columbia certainly didn't discern the difference, and as the years went by Aretha floundered. Looking back she has showed no animosity towards her mid-sixties mentors, but if she was unable to sense that something was wrong the record industry wasn't. Competitive bidding started for the contract of the mishandled Miss and the contest was won by Atlantic Records, whose ace producer Jerry Wexler had masterminded Ray Charles' transition from jazz to the pop and R&B charts.

Atlantic's immediate success with its new signing owed as much to luck as to talent. Wexler had gone to Muscle Shoals, Alabama to record Aretha in Rick Hall's Fame Studios but, because of disagreements, they returned to New York with only one and a half numbers. The complete one happened to be a song Aretha had found herself – 'I Never Loved A Man'. It was a historic find. 'I Never Loved A Man' is a genuine classic, a record so full of commitment and passion it had to be a spontaneous performance. It was. There were no overdubs, except for a section of double-tracked vocals. It was impromptu in another sense, too, because Aretha played the song to the musicians in the studio. The rhythm section worked it out then and there while the horn parts were written in the office.

All record people strive for the ultimate approval from radio programmes, airplay, without which there are no sales. Their worst nightmare is to win airplay before stock is in the stores. The public is won over to the single before it can be bought. By the time the disc is available, the audience may have tired of it. This was the dilemma Jerry Wexler faced when he gave acetates of 'I Never Loved A Man' to friends in rhythm and blues radio. They went straight on the record, but Aretha wasn't available to finish the B-side for another week. One can imagine Wexler's feelings as he listened to the radio those fateful seven days, the producer in him delighting that his charge was winning hearts, the record executive in him agonising that she may be losing sales.

In the end it didn't matter. 'I Never Loved A Man' was a No. 1 rhythm and blues hit and a top ten Hot 100 smash in the spring of 1967. That B-side Aretha finished off with her sisters Carolyn and Erma, 'Do Right Woman-Do Right Man', also won considerable airtime.

So began one of the greatest strings of hits in all of popular music. Within a year and a half Aretha Franklin accumulated ten top ten R&B hits, including six No. 1s and two No. 2s, and nine top ten pop charters, including the No. 1 classic, 'Respect'. No female artist since Connie Francis had done so well in the Hot 100. Franklin outflanked Francis by scoring on the R&B and LP charts, too. *I Never Loved A Man* was the first of six gold albums for Aretha on Atlantic. The singer was saying 'Baby I Love You' and America was reciprocating the sentiment.

'Baby I Love You' was Aretha's third million-selling 45, after 'I Never Loved A Man' and 'Respect'. It featured on the second Atlantic LP, *Aretha Arrives*, which also included '(You Make Me Feel Like) A Natural Woman'.

Her albums weren't just collections of singles padded out with filler. From the first set programmers immediately jumped on 'Respect', which the song's writer, Otis Redding, happily admitted was superior to his own hit version. They also showcased 'Do Right Woman-Do Right Man' and gave heavy attention to 'Dr Feelgood'. The latter song gives insight into what Aretha was doing that was so right. She was invoking the Lord, singing with the fervour and aspects of the style of gospel music. The interplay between Aretha and her backing vocalists on 'Respect' is a fine example of the call-and-response technique of gospel applied to secular music.

The combination of the sacred and the profane was irresistible. What man could resist the suggestion that his heathen love was holy? What woman could pass by the opportunity to issue the invitation? The righteous rhythm ruled the charts again in the winter of 1968 as

Aretha Franklin became a link in Don Covay's 'Chain of Fools'.

She may have made herself sound like a loser in love, but Aretha Franklin was a winner in the year's Grammy Awards. 'I Never Loved A Man' earned her the first of an almost unbelievable eleven Grammy Awards. There was no doubt she'd deserved it. But as she cemented her reputation as the world's foremost soul singer, the trophy for Best Female R&B Vocal Performance became hers almost automatically, and she sometimes won in the seventies when she didn't merit the victory. It was a measure of how clearly she dominated her field in the late sixties and early seventies that when Grammy voters saw her name they ticked it instinctively. With Otis Redding gone, Aretha Franklin *was* soul music.

Her right to the claim was formalised with the 1968 album *Lady Soul*. It sounded like Aretha was fending off all challengers to her throne like she was swatting away flies. 'Chain Of Fools' was included. So was 'Good To Me As I Am To You', featuring a marvellous guitar line by Eric Clapton. And then there were the two tracks that constituted Aretha's greatest double-sided single, two cuts that illustrated how she was simultaneously ruler of rhythm and boss of the blues. Both sides were major hits. On the A-side, 'Since You've Been Gone', she established the mood of the piece in an amazingly quick three seconds. The stratospheric high notes on the flip, 'Ain't No Way', were provided by Cissy Houston of The Sweet Inspirations. Sweet indeed was the fate of the twin smash, with both sides reaching the R&B top ten and the pop top twenty. 'Since You've Been Gone' also made the singles list in Britain, which had previously scandalously resisted Franklin fever. Only 'Respect' had even touched the top ten.

It would seem that an artist as expressive on vinyl as Aretha would have something to say in print. Certainly many peers had political or social statements to make in the late sixties, and there was no shortage of requests for interviews with her. But she quite conspicuously had little to say. Perhaps it was because in major media pieces that did appear, such as a lengthy profile in *Time*, the all-too-human side of the life of this musical goddess was being paraded before the public. It was loudly rumoured that her husband, Ted White, beat her. But even years after she separated from the man her press sessions were non-events. *Record Mirror* suffered humiliatingly when in one phone interview Aretha kept breaking away to catch up on her favourite soap opera and in another year when the star's mother answered the phone to say her daughter was too busy to be disturbed. Radio 1 conducted a lengthy dialogue with the living legend that couldn't be used: it was too much of a monologue, with Aretha answering mostly in simple statements or monosyllables. Perhaps the most intriguing audience she did grant was with America's leading black publication, *Ebony*. She had lost weight and wanted to model some new clothes.

In a publicity-conscious business, it seems inconceivable that Aretha could act so unexcited about her thrilling career. Her policy was to say what she had to say in her music.

In 'Think', a powerful song co-written with Ted White, she seemed to be asking for more than just consideration as a lover. It felt like she was demanding equality as a black person and as a woman. In an era when black consciousness was at its peak and the feminist movement was just stirring, this was an urgent message. Aretha was vital to her time, and for this reason, no matter how many hits she may have in the future, she will always be associated with the late sixties.

The flip side of 'Think' was a touching tribute to Sam Cooke, one of the earliest artists to make the transition from gospel to pop. Aretha's reading of his first mass appeal hit, 'You Send Me', started with a delicate piano introduction and built to a vocally frantic conclusion. It gave her another two-sided winner.

Her next release was an even mightier double-header. 'The House That Jack Built' raced into the R&B and pop top tens, but deejays quickly noticed the slower side, and it, too, climbed to both top ten lists. And, wonder of wonders, that big ballad, 'I Say A Little Prayer', went to No. 4 in the United Kingdom, the biggest British success of her career. The Bacharach–David composition had been a top ten tune for Dionne Warwick in America the year before, hence the slightly less spectacular fate of Aretha's interpretation in the States.

'I Say A Little Prayer' was none the less Lady Soul's biggest hit for two years. She continued to chart, but fell short of the pop top ten with a series of singles that either combined deep, almost mystical feeling with unmemorable melody, such as 'Call Me' and 'Spirit In The Dark', or were clearly inferior cover versions, like 'Eleanor Rigby' and 'The Weight'. 'I'm Eleanor Rigby', she began her Beatle number. She didn't convince. Not only Paul McCartney but Ray Charles had previously offered more moving vocals on this song. 'Don't Play That Song', Aretha reprised Ben E. King's hit in 1970, and her fans began to wish their heroine would play any song that allowed her full flight.

Almost magically, the covers started to work for Aretha, first with 'Don't Play That Song', a British top twenty entry, and then Simon and Garfunkel's 'Bridge Over Troubled Water' coupled with Jerry Butler's 'Brand New Me'. This dual remake sold nearly three million in the States alone. Its successor, 'Spanish Harlem', was both an American and British smash in the second half of 1971. Aretha Franklin was restored to her full powers as she issued mighty singles like 'Rock Steady' and 'Day Dreaming'. 'Rock Steady' was one of

America's earliest important tributes to Jamaican music.

The preacher's daughter also released an excellent album, *Young, Gifted And Black*, but it was her last great long playing effort. After this her LPs became uneven. *Hey Now Hey*, her 1973 collaboration with producer Quincy Jones, yielded the exquisite 'Angel', but little else of worth. Only occasionally did Aretha make even a sublime single. 'Until You Come Back To Me', a US and UK pop and soul hit in the winter of 1974, was one such side. It was co-written by Stevie Wonder, who had cut the song in the late sixties but never released it himself. When he gave it to Aretha and she did it proud, Motown placed it on an anthology of Wonder's old material.

The mid and late seventies were a great time for Stevie, but not for Aretha. She would occasionally top the soul chart, as with Curtis Mayfield's 'Something He Can Feel' or the 1977 effort 'Break It To Me Gently' but she wouldn't cross over to pop, much less to Britain. When disco dominated the black music scene in the late seventies, Franklin was totally lost, making an awkward token effort to follow the trend and seeming out of touch with her regular style.

When she left Atlantic Records to join Arista in 1980, it seemed heresy, just as when Diana Ross left Motown. Seeing their names on different labels just wasn't right. But in Aretha's case, it had to be right. She needed an infusion of energy and new producing and promotional finesse to get her off the ground. Arista gave it to her. She returned to the British charts with a version of the Doobie Brothers 'What A Fool Believes', scored a moderate American success in a duet with George Benson, 'Love All The Hurt Away', and won another Grammy, admittedly inexplicably, for a re-make of Sam and Dave's 'Hold On I'm Coming'. Most importantly, she was teamed in 1982 with the masterful producer Luther Vandross, himself a major artist. Vandross got Aretha to 'Jump To It'.

'Jump To It' gave Aretha Franklin her unprecedented eighteenth No. 1 on the black music chart. More importantly, it showed that with proper guidance she could record for a new era. Her stimulating scat singing, her rapping with fellow members of her sex, her unpredictable and enthralling flights into the upper register – all thrilled listeners in the early eighties as her soulful material had enchanted fans in the late sixties.

It would be foolish to pretend that her performance, no matter how contemporary, doesn't come from the same source that gave us 'Respect' or even 'Rock-A-Bye Your Baby With A Dixie Melody'. Somehow, as a child in her father's church, Aretha Franklin learned to talk in a language that only a few great artists can speak. Other humans can hear it, and they can appreciate it, but they can only listen in wonder. It is the sound of the most basic passion and inspiration expressed in music. It is an affirmation of the love of God and the love of life, which become one and the same. When one sings of the glory of God's world, one sings of His glory. It is a broad but basic form of prayer.

The Doors

IN ADDITION to its well-known charts of current bestsellers, *Billboard* has a weekly list of the most purchased mid-price albums, LPs that have passed their sales peak and are being marketed by their record companies at a budget price. In the last week of October 1982, The Doors had three of the top seven on this chart. All three were over ten years old, and one of them, their debut disc, was a recent economy No. 1 even though it was released in 1967.

Americans weren't buying Doors' albums just because they were inexpensive. A full-price compilation of the group's greatest hits issued in 1981 went gold. Furthermore, a biography of lead singer Jim Morrison was a bestseller for weeks in the *New York Times* book section.

There is something about The Doors' work which has had lasting relevance to American youth. That something has a lot to do with the mystique that has surrounded the life and death of Jim Morrison, who supposedly passed away in 1971, but who many fans expect to walk through the door some day and say hello.

Jim Morrison was born on 8 December 1943. He never could recall a specific moment when he first wanted to be a performer. He told interviewer Jerry Hopkins 'When it finally happened, my subconscious had prepared the whole thing.' Indeed, Morrison, whose teenage years coincided with the early days of rock and roll, had written the lyrics for several songs on a Californian beach long before he joined a group. One of them, 'Hello I Love You', became an American No. 1 in 1968. It was inspired by a beautiful black girl walking towards him in the sand.

Morrison met keyboard player Ray Manzarek at the film school of the University of California at Los Angeles. Manzarek, eight years older than his new friend, had combined classical training with professional experience in Chicago blues clubs. It was in his group Rick and The Ravens that Morrison got his first stage experience. Manzarek's group were due to back up Sonny and Cher at a high school

dance, but one of their members quit. To supply the contracted number of musicians, Ray had Jim sit on stage and pretend to play the guitar. The instrument wasn't even plugged in.

Neither was Morrison for a while. After leaving UCLA he drifted around the Californian community of Venice, Los Angeles' answer to San Francisco's hippie haven Haight-Ashbury. Jim ran into Ray Manzarek again on the beach one day. When he recited some of the lyrics he'd written in his considerable leisure time, Manzarek uttered the legendary words, 'Those are the greatest song lyrics I've ever heard. Let's start a rock and roll band and make a million dollars.' They did, and they did.

The first single by The Doors, a quartet composed of Morrison, Manzarek, and two instrumentalists from Ray's meditation group, guitarist Robby Krieger and bass player John Densmore, was 'Break On Through'. (Krieger and Densmore had previously laboured in a group called The Psychedelic Rangers.) The group got their name from William Blake's line, 'There are things that are known and things that are unknown; in between are doors'. Jim Morrison told a friend, 'I want to be the door'. He also was fond of Aldous Huxley's book *The Doors of Perception*.

The world Jim Morrison's Doors opened on to may not have been that different from the world in which the listener turned the doorknob. As the late lamented rock critic Lester Bangs wrote, 'The Doors were *dread*, and . . . dread is the great fact of our time'. But the dread that hangs over everyone's head every day is general. The worst, if it comes, will happen to everybody. The dread The Doors dreamt of was purely personal. The worst, if it comes, will happen to *you*, or to an individual like you.

What was Jim Morrison doing starting a song like 'The Crystal Ship' with a line like 'Before you slip into consciousness, I'd like to have another kiss?' It made your flesh crawl, or at the very least tingle in a way it hadn't done since The Rolling Stones sang 'Paint It Black'. Morrison was a master of menace. His husky voice half sang, half narrated lines that were part poem, part lyric, full of disturbing images and opaque phrases that sounded theatening even if they didn't mean anything specific. His stage appearance disquieted. Often in tight leather trousers, he would shout, grunt, and scream when words weren't enough. His often vulgar behaviour in performance suggested a man who was not only playing at being out of control, but who was.

Morrison was a fright to promoters, who feared losing their audience, their licence, their reputation – whatever they were most afraid of forfeiting. The Doors were fired several times from their very first residency at the Whisky A Go Go in Los Angeles, though they came back every time except the last. The final sacking came when Jim introduced the latest and most sensational set of lyrics to 'The End', a piece that began as a two-verse number about lost love and wound up being the most shocking song in rock. The group gradually extended the musical framework of 'The End' while Morrison recited self-written poetry. On the night The Doors were finally shut out of the Whiskey he had borrowed from the saga of one of history's most unfortunate kings, Oedipus. Taken from his parents as an infant, Oedipus learned as an adult that he had killed his father and made love to his mother. His reaction was to pluck out his eyes; Morrison's was to utter an unearthly primal scream.

In the summer of 1966, when 'Hanky Panky' by Tommy James and The Shondells and 'Wild Thing' by The Troggs were No. 1s in America, this was pretty strong stuff. It still is. When Francis Coppola was looking for music to convey what the Marlon Brando character called 'the horror' of the Vietnam War in his film *Apocalypse Now*, he chose 'The End'.

'The End' may have terminated the residency of The Doors at the Whiskey A Go Go, but by that time it didn't matter. Jac Holzman, President of Elektra Records, had been to see them and though he didn't think they had it the first time around was sufficiently impressed to offer them a deal after his fourth visit. Elektra had until recently specialised in folk music, but realised that it had to get in on the young people's music of California. The label had signed Love, whose leader, Arthur Lee, recommended The Doors. At first Morrison's group wanted to be as big as Love. Later, Jim would claim the world and demand it now.

Deciding to go with Elektra wasn't too difficult. The only other two offers came from White Whale Records, whose big act was The Turtles, and a company fronted by Doris Day's son, Terry Melcher. The Doors were produced by Paul Rothchild, who reported amazing scenes in the studio. The first night he tried to record 'The End', Morrison was so drugged he could not perform and wound up doing serious damage to the room. The following evening, the experience was so enthralling that both Rothchild and engineer Bruce Botnick stopped twiddling dials and sat astonished as Morrison went into his murderous rap. Fortunately, they had set the controls at the proper levels and the performance was captured for posterity.

In two slight concessions to commercial reality, Morrison agreed to drop a famous four-letter word from 'The End' and edited the lyrics of 'Break On Through' to remove the word 'high'.

'Break On Through' and the album *The Doors* were released in January, 1967. The single was an appropriate one for a disc debut, but it didn't make the Hot 100. This failure was of more than slight concern, since the label had erected a billboard promoting the LP on Sunset Boulevard. 'The Doors: Break On Through With An Electrifying Album' was the slogan on the very first rock music advertisement on the Strip. In later years, if drivers on Sunset had tried to conceal their eyes from signboards plugging records, they would have had multiple accidents.

Sales salvation came in the form of a lengthy track written predominantly by Robby Krieger, whom producer Rothchild considered a grossly underrated guitarist. The studio mentor pointed out that Krieger's training had been in flamenco music, where he had learned to use *rubato* – being able to sustain on one note and then move over very smoothly and easily to another note without a lot of flamboyance. He consequently wasn't noticed on many Doors numbers, though his contributions were invaluable. 'Light My Fire', which was finished with a marvellous organ riff from Manzarek and slight lyrical additions by Morrison, provided a rare opportunity to hear Krieger on a solo.

None the less it was Ray Manzarek's organ flourish and Jim Morrison's exotic delivery of erotic lyrics that made 'Light My Fire' most memorable. When The Doors couldn't work out a shortened version themselves, they allowed Elektra to cut the track simply by chopping out the middle.

With the thoughtful instrumenal interlude and the dramatic build-up to the final verse removed, 'Light My Fire' was non-stop excitement. It reached No. 1 in America in late July, staying there for three weeks until 'All You Need Is Love' replaced it. The Beatles were The Doors' nemesis that summer: the Californian quartet got to No. 2 in the album chart with *The Doors* but were kept out of the top spot by *Sergeant Pepper's Lonely Hearts Club Band*, only finally getting a No. 1 placing on the *Billboard* Mid-Price chart fifteen years later.

The album from Morrison's men was one of the first mainstays of progressive FM radio during the summer of 1967. 'Light My Fire', 'Break On Through', 'The Crystal Ship' and even 'The End' were firm favourites. So, for the more adventurous stations who didn't mind a single obscenity, was 'The Alabama Song', the only non-original on the set. This tune had originally appeared in Bertolt Brecht and Kurt Weill's *Mahagonny*. As producer Rothchild put it, 'I guess Brecht was saying in the thirties what Morrison is trying to say in the sixties . . . it's sort of The Doors' tribute to another time, another brave time for some other brave men.' In 1980, David Bowie charted in Britain with a single of the same song, no doubt as influenced by The Doors in this particular case as he was by Brecht and Weill.

'Light My Fire' was the first top ten single Elektra Records had enjoyed in its eighteen-year existence, so expectations must have been high when The Doors began recording their second album while their first was still in the top ten. Sadly, *Strange Days* was a comparative disappointment. Though the last track on this collection was, like 'The End', an extended piece, 'When The Music's Over', lacked the same power and passion. The two singles from this package, 'People Are Strange' and 'Love Me Two Times', fell short of the top ten, though the first was at least properly morbid and mysterious. The highlights of the album were the courageous and colourful cover, which showed a troupe of circus performers with only a wall poster of The Doors to suggest the recording artist, and the spoken track 'Horse Latitudes'. Here *was* something completely different.

Jim Morrison had been writing poetry since he was a child. He loved the form, considering it eternal. He told *Rolling Stone* 'Nothing else can survive a holocaust but poetry and songs. No one can remember an entire novel. No one can describe a film, a piece of sculpture, a painting. But so long as there are human beings, songs and poetry can continue.'

Those off-the-cuff words are pretty poetic themselves. The merits of Morrison's verse will be left to others to discuss, though it should be pointed out that volumes were published and an album of his readings with posthumously added music was released. Still, 'Horse Latitudes', written while he was a high school student, sounds the most interesting of the lot, if only because of the fascinating sound effects the band Rothchild and Botnick created to accompany it.

Jim got the chance to use another of his artistic interests in his work on the early 1968 single 'The Unknown Soldier'. He made one of the earliest rock promotional films to illustrate the text of the terrible tale in which an anonymous warrior was executed by a firing squad. Because of its violence, the clip was not used on television, but it was sometimes shown in concert. The song was a brilliant coupling, depicting the needless and random tragedy of war and then resurrecting the victim in a unilateral declaration of peace. The effect on live audiences preoccupied by America's involvement in Vietnam was electric. 'The Unknown Soldier' became The Doors' fourth top forty hit and helped their third album, *Waiting For The Sun*, achieve their first LP No. 1. The chart-topping singles success of the set's second single, 'Hello I Love You', was an even greater aid.

None the less the evidence was there that The Doors had perhaps peaked on their first album. That classic collection had been recorded quickly; 'The Unknown Soldier' had required 130 attempts. Jim Morrison was, in the language of the time, not together. Even 'Hello I Love You' was an old composition recorded only because the marathon 'Celebration Of The Lizard' didn't work out in the studio.

Morrison went through a three-year period of personal and professional misadventure exhaustively chronicled in Jerry Hopkins and
Danny Sugerman's biography *No One Here Gets Out Alive*. The
authors did one of the best researching and reporting jobs in the
history of rock and roll journalism. Bizarrely, however, Sugerman
reached the conclusion that 'Jim Morrison was a god'. The evidence he
presented suggested that the singer was not only obviously tremendously talented but also a tormented human being. Anyone who urin-
ates on friends' floors, ruins studios, abuses women who love him and
runs his own body down through excessive drinking is a man who
never learned self-respect as a boy and could not find it in artificial
crutches while a man.

From late 1968 through 1969 Morrison made headlines for his
arrests in New Haven and Miami, the first for obscene language and
starting a riot, the second for several offences including indecent
exposure on stage, but he didn't make much good music. The disappointing *Soft Parade* album did contain one cracker, though, the inno-
vative and amusing 'Touch Me'. 'Stronger than dirt', the three words
at the end of 'Touch Me', comprised the slogan of a washing powder
commercial well-known at the time. The brass and strings also suggested an element of self-parody, as well as being a welcome extension of
the group's limited instrumental sound. The two live performances of
this number on the CBS network *Smothers Brothers* show stay in the
mind over a decade later as outstanding examples of rock vocalising on
television. Jim Morrison had the most dynamic live singing style of any
late sixties groups shown on TV. Anyone who has seen the sequence
where The Doors performed 'Light My Fire' on the *Ed Sullivan Show*,
refusing to censor the lyric, will remember the exciting effect created
by Morrison screaming the word 'fire' into the microphone.

Tragically, he could not convey this control in concert by the time
the *Morrison Hotel* album won the group back some critical approval in
1970. Morrison was dissipated personally and disappointed professionally. When *LA Woman* was released in 1971, completing contractual obligations to Elektra Records, Morrison went to stay for a
prolonged period in Paris. He was surprised to hear from the States
that the album had been rapturously received. Initial response had suggested that the LP's lengthy 'Riders On The Storm' might be rejected,
but this cool flirtation with jazz proved a hit single on both sides of the
Atlantic. In the best Doors' tradition, it combined the twin themes of
sex and death.

By the time 'Riders On The Storm' was a hit, Jim Morrison was not
around to enjoy it. He departed this world in July, 1971, in Paris.

That's a clever way of saying that either he died or disappeared. His wife claims she found him dead in his bathtub and produced a death certificate illegibly signed by a doctor saying he'd died of natural causes – a heart attack. She was the only witness; no autopsy was ever performed. As Doors' manager Bill Siddons stated, 'There was no service, and that made it all the better. We just threw some flowers and dirt and said goodbye.'

To this day, some fans are suspicious. Since widow Pam Morrison died of a heroin overdose in 1974, there has been no one alive who actually saw Jim's corpse, unless the never-deciphered scrawl on the certificate really was the signature of a physician. It would certainly be understandable if Morrison had wished to avoid imprisonment in Miami; you can't incarcerate a coffin. It would be believable if he wanted to escape the pressures of being the front man of The Doors, and he had sometimes speculated about assuming a totally different identity. Unfortunately, it is also completely consistent with his lengthy history of physical self-abuse that his body simply gave up the ghost.

The craziest of his cult think he will return. They adore his image as 'The Lizard King', a phrase from 'Celebration Of The Lizard'. This is rather like worshipping Peter Noone as King Henry VIII because Herman's Hermits once recorded 'I'm Henry VIII, I Am'.

Nevertheless, the popularity persists. As Morrison said 'The lizard and the snake are identified with the unconscious and the forces of evil.' When an artist's repertoire emphasises the bad and the ugly at the expense of the good, and more successfully than any other rock songwriter makes one fear for one's life and one's wife, he is going to attract a loyal fan following and a lot of strange people.

Bob Marley

IMAGINE BEING the top pop star in your country. You tour abroad – and every interviewer asks you to explain the origin of your music and to justify its popularity. Imagine being a fervent believer in a minority religion – and in every one of those interviews you are asked to rationalise your belief as if you worshipped the man in the moon. Imagine wearing your hair and maintaining personal habits consistent with your faith and culture – and having that brought up every time like a broken record.

You might well get a bit hostile. But with the exception of occasionally lapsing into Jamaican patois, Bob Marley always answered with patience and humility. He may have been the Third World's greatest musical hero and one of the planet's best songwriters, but he didn't flaunt it. He had no time for negativity, whether in a room with a reporter or when singing about his land and Lord. From a tiny island in the Caribbean, Bob Marley got the whole world jamming.

Many rock fans are under the impression that Bob Marley and The Wailers were launched by Island Records in 1973 with the release of the album *Catch A Fire*. Island founder Chris Blackwell, friend and fan of Marley, provided the funds for the group to be recorded and promoted in the traditional Anglo-American music business way. The sound of reggae, previously confined to its native Jamaica and to occasional one-offs in the singles charts, had arrived to stay in Britain.

That much *is* true, but there's a great deal more to Marley's career than the phase known in the UK. The artist had been recording in Jamaica since 1961. That gave him a longer span of disc making before his British breakthrough than after it. *Record Collector* tabulated forty-seven different singles issues on eleven different labels – and that's just the total put out in the UK before 1973. Quite a few more Jamaican releases were not distributed in Britain. It's enough to make a collector ecstatic and depressed at the same time, ecstatic because there are so many rare records to track down, depressed because the supply is

scarce and the values high. There's an estimated £30 price tag on a mint copy of Bob Marley's 1961 debut disc, 'Judge Not'.

Bob Marley was born on 6 February 1945, in the Jamaican parish of St Ann's. He was the son of a British sailor and a Jamaican woman, but as happened to another musical pioneer, John Lennon, his father had gone away before the boy's birth. When the young Marley started playing music in the late fifties, calypso was the local music best known around the world. Harry Belafonte had popularised the style around the globe, and though the form is no longer in fashion, the contribution of Belafonte should never be underestimated. His album *Calypso* was the first LP by a solo artist to sell a million copies in the United States and his 1957 Christmas No. 1 'Mary's Boy Child' was the first record of any kind to sell a million in Britain alone. In the following quarter-century he performed many humanitarian works and worked for the rights of his race, as Bob Marley came to do.

Still, Belafonte had been born in New York City. Marley was the genuine article. He made his records in Jamaica. It was Desmond Dekker, a fellow welder, who introduced Bob to his first label, Beverleys. Dekker had suffered an eye injury on the job and during his recuperation had cut a hit called 'Honour Thy Father and Thy Mother'. On a visit to Beverleys with Dekker, Marley met Jimmy Cliff, who arranged an audition. Bob recorded 'Judge Not'. In about as much time as it takes to say 'Get Up, Stand Up', Bob Marley had met two men who would have international hits within a few years and made his own disc debut.

The glory story stops there. 'Judge Not' sold not, though it was released in Britain on Island. The follow-up, 'One Cup of Coffee', written by the American black balladeer Brook Benton, bombed. Bob Marley's solo career was over before it had really begun.

He went to Trenchtown, an area that journalist Vivien Goldman called 'the zinc shack shanty town ghetto side of Kingston'. The teenager lived in the home of Bunny Livingston's father. Bob and Bunny and a neighbour named Peter McIntosh formed a group with Junior Braithwaite and Beverley Kelso. They named themselves The Wailing Wailers.

'Simmer Down' was the first Wailers single, 'It Hurts to be Alone' the first issued in Britain. The backing track was a clear example of the ska sound. The Wailing Wailers were just vocalists at this time, and the instrumentalists played the ska beat. On a succession of hits they were backed by The Skatalites, a band best known in Britain for their own 'Guns of Navarone'.

The head of the Wailers Studio One Label, producer Coxsone Dodd, supposedly liked Marley so much he let him sleep in a room behind the studio. But his affection did not manifest itself in a financial fashion. Bob recalled to writer Carl Gayle that when he expected a handsome royalty cheque for Christmas 1966, Dodd presented him with a mere £60. Anyone who has seen the legendary Jimmy Cliff film *The Harder They Come* knows that Jamaican record executives had a notorious reputation for not paying their artists. Having failed to make a fortune despite several major hits, Marley left for the United States to live with his mother. Junior Braithwaite and Beverley Kelso had already quit The Wailers; it looked as if the group was finished.

Even if they had never made another record, they would have left the legacy of the Rude Boy. Their singles 'Rude Boy' and 'Let Him Go (Rude Boy Get Bail)' were among the first to celebrate the renegade from Kingston's shanty town who would become a common character in Jamaican music.

Bob Marley's residence in the United States was brief. Working in a chemical factory couldn't have been too inspiring for a singer-songwriter but according to Vivien Goldman's biography *Soul Rebel – Natural Mystic*, it was having to register for the American draft during the time of the Vietnam War that finally convinced the lapsed musician to return home.

When he got there he, Livingston and McIntosh, who were now called Bunny Wailer and Peter Tosh, decided they would make sure they weren't deprived of their rightful record royalties. They formed their own label, Wailing Soul. Unfortunately, they overlooked another aspect of musical monetary misconduct, piracy. They lost significant sales when their Jamaican No. 1, 'Bend Down Low', was bootlegged, and Wailing Soul was wound down.

In 1968 Marley developed a valuable relationship with the American actor-singer Johnny Nash. The Texan was one of the few men in pop history who genuinely deserved to be a massive star, but never became one, partly because he pursued a dual career and partly because he never followed through on his occasional periods of hit singles. Every few years he would have a couple of successes and then vanish. 1968 saw the beginning of three consecutive British top ten hits for him, 'Hold Me Tight', 'You Got Soul' and 'Cupid'. These were among the first worldwide smashes using Jamaican rhythms. In 1972, Nash's next batch of biggies included the Bob Marley song, 'Stir It Up'. This cover version was a top twenty hit in Britain in 1972 and America in '73. Johnny's reading of his friend's 'Guava Jelly' was sufficient to inspire Barbra Streisand to record the song, the ultimate proof that a songwriter was being accepted across the lines that normally divide musical forms.

In 1968 Nash's assistance came in the form of taking Marley to

Sweden to help score a film in which he was appearing. It helped make ends meet until The Wailers could begin recording again. Three important ingredients helped make this row of releases a memorable success. First, they worked with producer Lee 'Scratch' Perry, who gave them studio direction and ideas that put Wailers records in a distinctive class. Secondly, they added a rhythm section of bassist Aston Barrett and his drummer brother Carlton, making The Wailers a tight, self-contained unit. Thirdly, Marley and his mates were able after their first hits on Perry's Upsetter Records to finally form their own long-lasting label, Tuff Gong.

The Wailers were the toast of the Caribbean when they were signed to Island. As Aston Barrett, nicknamed 'Family Man', explained to *Black Music* magazine, The Wailers had been the best vocal group, The Barrett brothers the best backing band. They reasoned that together, they could 'smash the world'.

'Concrete Jungle', the opening track on *Catch A Fire*, was the first reggae album cut many rock reviewers had heard. They may have run into Jimmy Cliff's 'Wonderful World, Beautiful People' or Dave and Ansil Collin's 'Double Barrel' on the radio, but *Catch A Fire* was the first reggae LP given the rock promotional campaign by an important label. It even had a gimmicky sleeve, a mock cigarette lighter which flipped open to reveal the LP. Unfortunately, on many copies it eventually flipped off, requiring an arduous re-assembly every time the album was played.

By the time they made *Catch A Fire*, The Wailers were incorporating elements of their Rastafarian religion in their music. The faith, and the new reggae beat, gave reviewers plenty to write about. Anyone who believed that Haile Selassie, the Emperor of Ethiopia, was the living God, was inviting insult, particularly after Selassie left this world. Marley never deviated. 'These newspapers don't understand', he told interviewer Tim White, 'or they want to crush my thinking into the dust.'

The Jamaican would not be crushed. He even dealt with the departure of his friends Tosh and Livingstone-Wailer, Peter before the release of *Catch A Fire* and Bunny after it. The leaving of Tosh was leavened by use of several of his songs on *Catch A Fire* and its late 1973 successor, *Burnin'*. The latter LP commenced with the inspiring Marley/Tosh collaboration, 'Get Up, Stand Up', in which the oppressed of the world were urged to stand up for their rights. It's a track that inspires action and touches the soul, and it was the kind of Wailers music that began to make the band critical favourites. Another track from *Burnin'* won Marley more widespread attention when Eric Clapton went to No. 1 in America with his version of 'I Shot the Sheriff'.

With Tosh and Livingstone gone, it seemed only logical as well as good commercial sense to name the group with their musical replacements Bob Marley and The Wailers. The 1974 debut of this ensemble, *Natty Dread*, contained all Marley compositions, though, as usual with the Island LPs, not all the songs were new. 'Bend Down Low' was included in an updated version, and throughout the seventies Marley found opportunities to recycle some of the Jamaican Wailers hits on his Island albums. The man from St Ann's was still in his ascendancy on *Natty Dread*, an LP named after the Rastafarian who kept his hair in long plaited dread locks. The songs mingled reggae, religion and revolution as if all three were vital parts of life. Listening to Marley made them seem so. In the midst of misery there may yet be moments free from care.

A beautiful ballad from *Natty Dread* gave The Wailers their first British hit single in 1975. Marley and his men played two dates at the Lyceum in London with the female vocal trio The I-Threes, who included Bob's wife Rita. These concerts have become myth with the passage of only a few years. They seemed to certify the simultaneous arrival at last of a new form of music and the first Third World superstar.

But these shows were more than just symbolic. They deserve their historic reputation simply as the events they were – joyous nights of communal partying. I was there on the first evening, and I shall never forget it. The weather, warm and fine so the sliding roof of the Lyceum could be opened. The crowd, truly multiracial, oblivious to their own skin colours and paying attention only to the mutual experience they were enjoying. The music, exciting and flawless, posing the implicit question that many who had been present at Woodstock must have asked: is this the beginning of a new age of fellowship?

The special feeling that Bob Marley and The Wailers generated that night created a self-contained world: it only feels like this in here, together, listening to this music. Miraculously, it was captured on *Live at the Lyceum*, which managed to convey the deep humanity and spirituality of 'No Woman No Cry'.

The album and single began the band's British breakthrough in earnest. Those who thought reggae could never sell in the States, where the indigenous black population had their own music, were confounded when *Rastaman Vibration* reached the US LP top ten in 1976. The UK top ten debut came with the 1977 album *Exodus*, which contained no fewer than three hit singles, 'Waiting In Vain, 'Jamming', and the title track, 'Exodus'.

Bob Marley was an international star, but he wasn't selling out. 'Exodus' talked plainly of the trek of 'Jah people', his religious folk who looked forward to a return to Africa. 'Punky Reggae Party', the flip of the top ten single 'Jamming', noted the natural alliance between the outcast groups, Rastafarians and punks. Reggae was a favourite form of the original punks; Johnny Rotten played it on the radio in a celebrity's choice programme and the Clash played it in person. A public demonstration of Marley's courage came when, shortly after he had escaped an assassination attempt in Jamaica, he returned to the island to play at the One Love Peace Concert. He called Prime Minister Michael Manley and Leader of the Opposition Edward Seaga to the stage and had them clasp hands with their arms raised over Marley's head. It was an astonishing moment, the ultimate testimony to the musician's stature in his homeland. He had become the greatest unifying force in Jamaica, supplying an affirmative answer to the question he was then posing in the British hit parade: 'Is This Love?'

Bob Marley wasn't just a charismatic figure in his home country. He was an inspiration to the entire black world. In the same year as the One Love Peace Concert, 1978, he was awarded the Third World Peace Medal at the United Nations. The presentation was made by Senegal on behalf of all African countries. The following year a track called 'Zimbabwe' appeared on his album *Survival* – it was a measure of his personal emergence around the world that record people had inadvertently started referring to 'Marley's new album' rather than 'The Wailers' latest'. Robert Mugabe must have heard the number, for he invited the Jamaican group to play at the official Zimbabwe Independence celebrations. It was the greatest possible evidence that Marley had become identified with the fight against oppression around the planet.

Bob Marley will be forever associated with the independence of Zimbabwe for three reasons: his song bearing the country's name as its title, which became a single as well as an album cut, The Wailers' performance at the Independence Celebrations, and Stevie Wonder's marvellous 'Master Blaster', which linked peace in the nation and Marley's music as two great reasons for joy and jammin'.

Though the graphs of Wailers' album sales and chart positions were erratic, the general trend was upward. After *Exodus* had been their British top ten debut, *Kaya* had peaked at No. 4 and, in 1980, *Uprising* outsold all previous packages except *Exodus*. From the new set came one of the most necessary dance ditties of the year, the top five single 'Could You Be Loved'.

Marley seemed at the peak of his prestige and prowess in 1980. But that September he collapsed jogging in Central Park. Doctors told him he had cancer. He died within a year, on 11 May 1981. A month before his death he was honoured with Jamaica's Order Of Merit, a distinction collected by his son Ziggy. The Honourable Robert Nesta Marley was given an official funeral by the Jamaican people. Edward Seaga and Michael Manley were again in attendance, this time their roles as Prime Minister and Leader of the Opposition reversed.

Reggae wasn't rock and roll after all. Instead of wasting himself on drink or hard drugs, or being killed instantly in a plane or car crash, Marley died a gradual natural death, like the ordinary people he sang about. It was a tragically young passing, especially considering there was so much good he could yet have achieved in a world that unfortunately needs good men and women. The only virtue of his going as he did was that it contributed to his canonisation: he can be forever preserved in the mind as an always young, always vital street saint.

Those who mourned him could do so on several levels. The people of Jamaica had lost their greatest national figure. The Third World were deprived of their outstanding musical spokesperson. Show business missed a fine songwriter and exciting performer. Bob Marley managed the musical mission impossible: he spoke for his people and talked to the world. To all he left the message, 'Get Up Stand Up, Stand Up For Your Rights'.

The Who

THERE ARE some movements in pop music that can be summed up in one single. Either the record was the first definitive statement of a social group's goals or it managed to capture attitudes and lifestyle so accurately it became an anthem. Think of the original rock and rollers and you think of 'Rock Around The Clock'. Pause for punk and you've automatically got 'Anarchy In The UK'. The Mod manifesto was and still is 'My Generation'.

The difference between The Who and the artists who made the other two discs is that the four West Londoners went on to make other statements to other people, first talking to a wider audience of their own age and then appealing to another generation altogether. Their career was like a mountain range: the profile went up and down, the going was always rocky, but there were some glorious peaks.

'My Generation' sounds the work of people who could not see the possibility of another point of view, whose commitment to their way of life was so complete they could not entertain even the notion of being different. Though that may have been so at the moment, Pete Townshend has stated that the late seventies heirs to The Who, The Jam, were truer to the Mod lifestyle for a longer time than his group was. The Who are associated with the Mods because they were with them when they were fashionable and because they made the definitive Mod music, but they didn't stay Mods.

Indeed, they weren't to begin with. When Roger Daltrey invited John Entwistle to join his group The Detours in the summer of 1962, and when a few months later the bass player successfully suggested his friend Pete Townshend be brought in on rhythm guitar, the band's repertoire knew no single style. They re-created instrumental hits by The Shadows and Ventures, performed current chart records, and even threw in a little trad jazz. Entwistle and Townshend were well-suited for the latter, having played together at Acton County Grammar School in an amateur trad group called The Scorpions. Coincidentally

enough, that would also be the name of a school group in South London who played Kenny Ball type jazz. Those Scorpions would become Status Quo.

In early 1963, lead guitarist Daltrey frequently feuded with The Detours' lead singer, Colin Dawson. When the front man left the group Roger, who had done some vocalising, moved into the singing spotlight, and Townshend moved from rhythm to lead. One night Pete, who was studying at Ealing Art School, asked a group of his mates for new names for the group. As each ludicrous suggestion was offered, someone would say, 'The *who*?' Then a friend named Richard Barnes asked, why not try 'The Who?' Townshend did.

This should be where the band begins its famous string of hits, but it isn't. First they changed their drummer and then, again, their name. Doug Sanden, who had been with Daltrey in the early Detours, was approximately a full decade older than Roger, John and Pete. For the sake of image and energy level they replaced him. An intoxicated seventeen-year-old named Keith Moon presented himself for an audition and during the course of one violent number managed to damage the drum kit. The Who loved it. As Moon recalled, 'Nobody ever said "You're in". They just said, "What're you doing Monday"?'

Another new addition to the team was short-term mentor Pete Meaden. He thought the group needed an identifiable image, chose modernism, and changed the quartet's hairstyles, clothes, and name. For a brief time in 1964, The Who became The High Numbers.

Meaden wrote the lyrics for their first single 'I'm The Face' and 'Zoot Suit', both tracks clearly concerned with the clothes consciousness of the Modernists, or Mods as they were better known for short. The image and the idea were right; the songs weren't. 'I'm The Face' didn't chart, at least not until its re-release in 1980 late in a mini-Mod boom, when it crawled to No. 49. An original copy on Fontana TF 480 would today earn its owner around £80.

By revamping the right R&B records in the Mod meeting place, a club called The Scene, The High Numbers became the main men of the Mods. A pair of fledgling film directors named Kit Lambert and Chris Stamp saw them play one night at the Railway Hotel in Harrow, the next night at Watford Town Hall. Lambert and Stamp decided they had to manage these young men. Fortunately for them, the young men agreed.

The new managers engaged expatriate American Shel Talmy to produce the foursome for Brunswick Records. It seems unbelievable, but no other producer and no other label wanted the group, which was once again called The Who. Many companies had already rejected the demo tape of the song that became their first hit, and even when it was recorded audiences didn't snatch it up instantly. It took considerable television exposure to successfully promote 'I Can't Explain'. The disc finally reached No. 8 in the spring of 1965. It *can* be explained – it was a classic single blessed with a crisp production. It also had an unbilled guest appearance by rhythm guitarist Jimmy Page, then a top session player booked for the recording by Shel Talmy. The producer was so unsure of the untested Who he had The Ivy League sing backing vocals.

I first heard the single on radio station CKLW, broadcasting to Detroit from across the Canadian border in Windsor, Ontario. At night you could just pick it up in New England, and it was as exciting to me to hear the new hits played first by this 'barometer' or try-out station as it was for British kids to hear the latest American discs fading in and out on Radio Luxembourg.

The lead guitar and drum playing grabbed me immediately, and I bought the single as soon as possible, though I had no idea who the players were. Perhaps it was my purchase that pushed 'I Can't Explain' to its peak American position of 93.

I mention the distinctive drum style because it's important. Keith Moon never worked more energetically or excitingly than on that first hit. He later polished his playing, but the rock and roll revelation he was, was there from the start. Like many of the greatest records in rock, Moon the artist offered passion without restraint. Somehow he could channel this fury into a musical form that communicated contagious chaos. If he could have controlled the other aspects of his life as skilfully, he might have been a happier and longer-lived man, but if he had been able to intellectualise and rationalise his talent, he probably would have lost the naiveté that fuelled him. In his innocence, Moon was the instrumentalist most loyal to the spirit of pure rock and roll. His power propelled all of The Who's first four singles, all top ten hits: 'I Can't Explain', 'Anyway Anyhow Anywhere', 'My Generation' and 'Substitute'.

The Who did indeed substitute for their first release of 1966 – themselves for Shel Talmy. They feuded with the strong-minded American and ceased working with him after their first album, *My Generation*. The partnership ended with a perfect record: one classic LP in one attempt.

My Generation replaced a projected platter of predominantly American rhythm and blues songs. This would have been in the style of the Mod movement, but would not have led it. With the title song and the affectionate 'The Kids Are Alright', The Who spoke both to and for their fashionable fellows.

Pete Townshend's early lyric writing seemed as direct and natural as

Moon's drumming. As he told journalist Griel Marcus fifteen years later, 'I was completely and totally alone. I had no girlfriend, no friends, no nothing – it was me addressing the world. That's where the power of that early stuff comes from.' In later years Townshend would become reflective and self-questioning, but in the mid-sixties he was forthright and unaffected, telling everyone what it was like to be a young man. One single was even called 'I'm A Boy'. This fell just shy of the No. 1 spot, topping out at No. 2. 'My Generation' had also peaked there. It remains a source of disbelief that for all their historic hits, The Who never had a No. 1 single.

Still, chart-toppers aren't everything. Live performance counts just as much if a group intends to persevere, and The Who did survive. Granted, there were many rows through the years, to be expected since Daltrey had been the original group leader and Townshend emerged as the man who put words in his mouth. On stage both were charismatic characters. Roger was a natural visual focus, a keep-fit fanatic who evolved from cute to handsome. He was a master of the microphone, which he would swing around on its lead and manage to catch in time for the next verse, though there always remained the tantalising prospect that it would slip out of his control and bean somebody.

What Townshend lacked in looks he compensated for in style. That's not being cruel, it's simply re-stating something he often said. Nearly obsessed by the size of his schnozz, which drew taunts from schoolmates, Townshend vowed to turn his body into a machine to distract attention from his nose to the rest of him. Through the years his guitar technique, including his windmill arm spins and chopped chords, was as distinctive as Chuck Berry's duck walk. And, of course, there was the *coup de grâce* that for years capped all live Who gigs, the ritual destruction of Townshend's guitar, smashed to pieces in assumed rage. This stunt started by accident when the top of the instrument hit a low club ceiling and broke off. Angry that the audience didn't seem as concerned as he by this loss, he proceeded to smash what was left. The word quickly spread that this musical mayhem had to be seen, and what was once spontaneous became a set piece.

They loved it in America, where The Who went for the first time in 1967. Immediately they had their first Stateside success, 'Happy Jack'. That Easter The Who appeared on Murray The K's package show in New York City. WINS disc jockey Murray Kaufman had been assembling his holiday revues for years, and this time had on the same bill Smokey Robinson and The Miracles, Wilson Pickett, Mitch Ryder, The Who, Cream, The Blues Project, and folk singers Jim and Jean. The Who performed four shows a day for five days and destroyed their instruments each time. Biographer Chris Charlesworth reported a casualty list of twenty-two microphones, five guitars, four speaker cabinets and a sixteen-piece drum kit, and that's excluding the items that were repaired. I was present at this last Murray The K extravaganza. The Who were a flash fire before our eyes. In the blink of an eye an extraordinary event occurred, and ended. You had to see more of them. Americans got more later that year, with the first proper US tour and a scene-stealing appearance at Monterey. The quartet were rewarded with dramatically increased record sales, and The Who's only American top ten placing. That star single was 'I Can See For Miles'.

It's strange to hear Pete Townshend remember 'I Can See For Miles' as a failure, when it was a top ten single in both Britain and America. But it was 'only' No. 10 in the UK, where The Who were accustomed to better. They'd had five consecutive top five 45s (not counting releases by their former record company) until a salute to the imprisoned Rolling Stones, a cover of 'The Last Time', and 'I Can See For Miles'. Perhaps even more distressingly, the album that contained the new track, *Who Sell Out*, had fallen short of the top ten LP list, when the first two long players, *My Generation* and *A Quick One*, had both been top five.

A Quick One got its title from a series of song fragments at the end of the album, 'A Quick One While He's Away', that received the designation of a 'mini-opera'. There was another such piece on the second side of *Who Sell Out*, an album whose alternation of tracks with commercials and pirate radio jingles was a provocative if lightweight concept.

No one should have been surprised, then, when the next Who effort was both a concept album and a rock opera. But no one could have expected what a great work *Tommy* would be. The first track to be released from the album, 'Pinball Wizard', was written in honour of journalist and pinball fanatic Nik Cohn, who later wrote the short story that became *Saturday Night Fever*. The idea of a deaf, dumb and blind boy who becomes a table king has never sounded as ludicrous as it really is, and few fans ever seriously questioned the logical soundness of the premise behind *Tommy*. The notion that someone deprived of most of his senses could only be reached from the outside world by touch and that his energies would be expressed in fantastic and fabulous music, proved attractive rather than asinine, probably because the music played by The Who was fabulous.

The double album *Tommy* is one of the watersheds in rock music. Townshend admitted he'd been influenced by The Pretty Things concept album *S. F. Sorrow*; now many more groups tried their hand at concept LPs, many of them not worth the effort. It's like any artistic

breakthrough in rock: the imitations are almost always inferior, probably because they lack the inspiration. Certainly Townshend, who had
become a devoted follower of the guru Meher Baba, had plenty of that.
A lengthy interview in *Rolling Stone* in which he had previewed *Tommy*
had showed that he was not only head of The Who for press purposes
but the philosopher of pop.

It was to the great credit of his three colleagues that they tolerated
both the length of time it took to assemble the album and the unusual
nature of Pete's piecemeal demos. A fine example of how fragments
could unite to make a single strong entity comes when Tommy, cured
of his afflictions, becomes a Messiah figure. He pleads for their sensory
input saying 'See Me, Feel Me', even though they reject his movement
by saying 'We're Not Gonna Take It'.

'Tommy' changed lives – at least those of The Who. The international multi-million seller ended for ever the chronic financial problems they incurred with their instrument smashing and, one might
add, hotel room smashing. Public expectations forced them to include
large segments of *Tommy* in their live act for years, and their energies
were further expended on it in the seventies via Lou Reizner's stage
show and Ken Russell's film.

Townshend was pressured by the anticipation he would come up
with another gem in short order. Cleverly, The Who cut a concert
classic, *Live At Leeds*, not just to prove they were still hard rockers but
to give themselves time to work out another studio set. Pete Townshend had to shelve his proposed piece *Lighthouse*, but several pieces
were saved for the new LP. They showed an extraordinarily intricate
knowledge of synthesizer programming.

They also showed Townshend still at the peak of his powers. 'Won't
Get Fooled Again' worked on two levels, as an intelligent anti-
revolutionary comment on revolution and as a no-holds-barred rocker.
The liberation in the number comes not from an uprising that replaces
one bad leader with another but from Roger Daltrey's soaring,
unearthly concluding scream.

'Won't Get Fooled Again' was another masterpiece, but it wasn't the
only top track on *Who's Next*. 'Baba O'Riley' and 'Behind Blue Eyes'
were other outstanding offerings, and John Entwistle's 'My Wife' may
have been the best yet in his series of one or two songs an album, many
of which revealed his sly sense of humour. Indeed, 'The Ox', as he had
been nicknamed as early as the *My Generation* album, was marvellous
at understatement. While the other three members of the group all
competed for visual attention, Moon flailing his limbs, Townshend
flaying his guitar, and Daltrey floating his microphone through the air,
Entwistle just stood there. Watching him as the anchor of the band was

sometimes funnier than looking at the others' acrobatic antics.

Who's Next was not only a critical favourite but the act's only No. 1 album. In the 1970s the recorded output was both less prolific and less proficient. *Quadrophenia*, a double album tale of a typical mid-sixties Mod, worked better as a film than on record and stage. *The Who By Numbers*, a 1975 issue, was a low-key effort that reflected the concerns of being ageing rock stars and maturing men.

The theme got another airing on the 1978 release *Who Are You*. The title track had been inspired by Townshend's meeting with a couple of star punks, an instant identity crisis. Another track that directly addressed changing fashion was 'The Music Must Change', on which no drummer appeared. It proved ironic, as did the cover photo showing Keith Moon in a chair labelled 'Not to be taken away', which he was by an accidental drug overdose shortly after the LP came out.

Initially the surviving trio had the wrong response for the right reasons. The Who should be kept going with former Small Face and fellow West Londoner Kenney Jones taking the seat but not the place of Moon. The group would continue as an adult rock band. The only problem was that Pete Townshend's musical musings about his life and times were better expressed on his next two solo albums, especially the wonderful *Empty Glass*, than on the following two Who works.

Miraculously they courageously called an end to touring. Finally Townshend announced it was all over. This was a tremendously tasteful voluntary retirement by the group that was, year in and year out, with Moon and with Jones, the best live rock and roll band in the world. They showed they knew that circumstances do change and lives do evolve. It is better to halt part of one's career before it becomes less special, and The Who were special.

Jimi Hendrix

THERE ARE some moments you cannot forget. Such a moment occurred on a rainy night in Bridgeport, Connecticut, on a small football pitch temporarily re-converted to an open air concert hall. Jimi Hendrix was supporting Herman's Hermits, which is rather like serving caviar as an hors d'oeuvre for a quarter-pound cheeseburger. Hendrix was definitely not happy in his circumstances and surroundings, but had resigned himself to his task and played an exciting set. Finally he said, 'Well, I suppose this is what you all came for', and proceeded to play a blistering guitar solo with his teeth.

This kind of dental dexterity had never been seen in Bridgeport, but for Hendrix it was only too common. His was the dilemma of the artist who is both great musician and great showman. He was torn between his desire to experiment with his craft and his audience's expectation that he would burn his guitar or play with his teeth or pretend to make love to his instrument. Only such a one-man circus could make some people overlook the most important thing about him – his music.

Sometimes the child knows. When he was ten years old, James Marshall Hendrix picked up his family's broom and started strumming it like a guitar. He told his father he was 'learning how to play it'.

Without any external encouragement, the young Hendrix had gravitated to the instrument for which he had an extraordinary innate ability. His father, a landscape gardener, got the message, and presented his son with an acoustic guitar the following year and an electric model the year after that.

James was born on 27 November 1942, in Seattle, Washington. His mother was of Red Indian descent, his father was black, but Hendrix found himself in a mostly white neighbourhood going to mostly white schools. James was dissatisfied with Seattle, and enlisted in the army. One would have thought this event would be well-documented, but for some reason *Rolling Stone* dated it as 1959, the *New Musical Express* 1961, and biographer Chris Welch 1963. Hendrix has been plagued by historical inaccuracies: the sleeve notes of his first album list his year of

birth as 1947, a full five years out, and a mistake that would have made him not just a great star of 1967 but a prodigy.

Suffice it to say that Hendrix was in the paratroopers, got injured in a jump and was discharged. He toured as a back-up musician for numerous rhythm and blues stars, including Little Richard and The Isley Brothers and, because the work was there, with Joey Dee and The Starliters, the 'Peppermint Twist' group. The guitarist didn't begin to develop his own style until he formed Jimmy James and The Blue Flames, a guise under which he began to attract the attention of other artists. He backed Curtis Knight for a series of recordings that would never have been well-known had they had not been reissued after he was famous. He impressed John Hammond Jr, white blues singer and son of a legendary record executive, who gave him his first major engagement as a lead guitarist. He staggered guitar hero Mike Bloomfield, who told *Guitar Player* magazine: 'I can't tell you the sounds he was getting out of his instrument . . . I didn't even want to pick up a guitar for the next year.' And he won over former Animal Chas Chandler who, tipped off by a female friend of Keith Richard, saw him play in Greenwich Village. The two men came to England and, under Chandler's direction, James – now Jimi – recorded 'Hey Joe'.

'Hey Joe' was a song the American Tim Rose had recorded that both Hendrix and Chandler liked. The new version was cut by Jimi and two Englishmen, drummer Mitch Mitchell and bass player Noel Redding. Mitchell came via Georgie Fame's Blue Flames, a great irony since Hendrix had named his first group The Blue Flames – 'not very original', Jimi admitted. Redding had travelled an equally unusual route. He'd shown up to audition for The Animals as lead guitarist, but the slot had already been filled. Chas Chandler recommended he see Hendrix and try bass. When Noel did see Jimi, he declared 'I don't see anybody else playing lead guitar with this bloke' and, for the first time in his life, became a bassist.

Hendrix, Redding and Mitchell were The Jimi Hendrix Experience, and an experience it was for both the trio and their fans. They were precisely right for 1967, the banner year of peace, love and psychedelia. The first week of the year Hendrix and Chandler were down to their last two pounds. By the end of the twelve months The Experience had scored four top twenty hits, a No. 2 album, and an American breakthrough at the Monterey Pop festival.

Their second single, 'Purple Haze', is the definitive Jimi Hendrix track. Its very structure suggests the artist was an instrumental genius. The first guitar chords are vertical rather than horizontal, static posts around which the lengthy introduction is woven. That intro was highly melodic and, with the rhythm section working at full tilt, highly exciting. By the time the vocalist came in, it didn't really matter if he could sing or not.

'Purple Haze' was more complex than the average top forty record, but then Hendrix's music was more than just rock. As critic Mikal Gilmore pointed out, there was a further element in the sound. 'By assigning Noel Redding's bass to a role more rhythmic than harmonic', he wrote, 'Hendrix afforded drummer Mitch Mitchell the mobility to explore and colour his surroundings in much the same way jazz drummers . . . did . . . the Experience trio formulated a musical vision that melded the verve of rock to the nerve of jazz.'

And that wasn't all. Hendrix was capable of producing a sensitive slow song, as he did on the band's third single, the beautiful ballad 'The Wind Cries Mary'. 'I just wish I could sing really nice, but I know I can't sing', Jimi told Chris Welch. 'I just feel the words out.' He certainly felt them out all right on 'The Wind Cries Mary', but the sad fact is that, though an adequate if not outstanding vocalist, Hendrix always considered his singing inferior. He only began to sing when he saw Bob Dylan perform and realised that the great writer was not letting an imperfect voice prevent him from delivering his own songs. If Dylan could be brave enough to face flack, so should he.

'The Wind Cries Mary' was high in the singles charts when The Jimi Hendrix Experience went to America to play at the Monterey Pop festival. Paul McCartney had told the organisers of the event that they simply had to have Hendrix. The young man who had grown up on the same coast in Washington state was still unknown in his home country, but with the Beatle's recommendation and Brian Jones' willingness to introduce him on stage, this was an offer that could not be refused.

From The Mamas and Papas to The Grateful Dead, a wide range of counterculture music was displayed at Monterey. Ironically, the two artists who stole the show in the eyes of the largely white audience were black men, Otis Redding and Jimi Hendrix. The Experience's version of 'Wild Thing' stopped the show. It had been in Jimi's set since being a No. 1 for The Troggs. If anyone suggested it was a bit unsubtle for the new guitar hero's style, they were overlooking an important point. Despite his own virtuosity, Hendrix was not a musical snob. On his first major tour of Britain, a package show that included Cat Stevens, The Walker Brothers, and Engelbert Humperdinck, he expressed great admiration for the vocal power of Humperdinck, and he would watch his set from the wings. Part of this may have been further recognition of his own singing shortcomings, but part was surely genuine respect for Engelbert's ability to hold the high notes loud and clear.

The first Jimi Hendrix Experience album, *Are You Experienced*, was climbing the charts while the group was in California. It ultimately reached No. 2, kept out of the No. 1 spot only by *Sgt Pepper's Lonely Hearts Club Band*, which stayed on top for twenty-three weeks. It was just Hendrix's luck to run up against the longest-running No. 1 LP since *Please Please Me*. But rather than milk the album for a single to encourage further sales of the package, a tactic which would almost certainly be used today, the band offered the fans a completely new 45, 'Burning Of The Midnight Lamp'.

This came into the singles charts in the last week of August, 1967, the same week 'Purple Haze' became The Experience's first Hot 100 entry in America. It was the burning of another appliance for which Jimi Hendrix was even better known. On the opening night of his tour with Engelbert Humperdinck, Hendrix and Chas Chandler were thinking up new stunts for the act. Journalist Keith Altham suggested setting fire to the guitar, since the tune 'Fire' was already in the show. As Chandler recalled, a roadie was dispatched to get a tin of lighter fuel. The instrument was soaked in the liquid. It took five minutes of striking matches on stage to get the beast to burn, but when it did it was a terrifying sight, so frightening the compere ran on stage to try to extinguish it. He burned his hand.

The trouble with a stunt like that, as with The Who's destruction of their instruments, is that the public expects to see it every performance. Hendrix grew annoyed with this anticipation, and also the expectation that he would play with his teeth, something he first tried in Tennessee. He gradually began to resist these demands. Towards the end of his life, when confronted by calls for his first few single hits, he would shout 'I'm not a jukebox'.

In early 1968, *Axis: Bold As Love* was a top five success in both America and Britain, even without the benefit of a hit single. One had to be more than a hippy hero to reach such heights, but there's no doubting that Hendrix was a special star to the progressive pop pundits, who loved what he was doing.

What *was* he doing? To this day nobody really knows how Hendrix achieved all his famous effects. The liner notes of the posthumous compilation *The Essential Jimi Hendrix* lists his instruments and the elements of his sound system, but they don't say how Jimi got these pieces to make those noises. Sheer volume was one simple but crucial part of the process. So were fuzz-box and wah-wah pedals, and a machine which rotates speed and sound direction called the Univibe. Hendrix used feedback to distort and disport. But whereas John Lennon had tried tape reverse on 'Rain' and distortion on 'Tomorrow Never Knows', and Pete Townshend employed feedback on 'My Generation', Jimi Hendrix utilised multiple tricks on his tracks.

He also knew when to step back a bit, as on a well-loved cut from

Axis: Bold As Love, 'Little Wing'. A song this reflective could be enjoyed in sedate surroundings, and many Hendrix buffs increased their sedation by the use of drugs.

Jimi was one of the leading acts to get high by, and I must admit that my last experience of hashish was heightened by Hendrix. My college roommates told me you had to smoke to fully enjoy The Experience's version of Bob Dylan's 'All Along The Watchtower'. Under the spell of that stuff, I listened in awe as Jimi began a guitar line in one speaker, broke it off somewhere between it and a second speaker, and resumed it in the second one. It was the ultimate sensory experience – or at least, so it seemed.

'All Along The Watchtower' was a re-working of a number from *John Wesley Harding*, Bob Dylan's 1968 acoustic album. The Experience version was so different one could hardly recognise it – an essential feature of an imaginative cover. It wasn't Hendrix's only tribute to the man who had convinced him he should sing; 'Like a Rolling Stone' was a concert favourite, and he also did 'Drifter's Escape'.

'All Along The Watchtower' returned The Jimi Hendrix Experience to the top five in late 1968. It was the highlight of *Electric Ladyland*, a double album that alongside some disappointing extended pieces boasted bits of brilliance including 'Burning Of The Midnight Lamp' and 'Voodoo Chile'. The latter song appeared in two versions, a lengthy blues jam and a short version suitable for release as a single. The tight take was ultimately issued on 45, but in sad circumstances, after the artist's death in 1970. It would be Britain's fourth posthumous No. 1, as Jimi Hendrix joined Buddy Holly, Eddie Cochran, and Jim Reeves. Coincidentally, he had expressed the wish that songs by Cochran, his favourite rock and roller, be played at his funeral.

Electric Ladyland, an American No. 1 album, marked the end of The Jimi Hendrix Experience as a recording unit, and the leader disbanded the trio for good in early 1969. It was perhaps inevitable. With the exception of a few tracks, all Experience recordings had been Hendrix compositions. In the studio Jimi had been so dominant Noel and Mitch were sometimes annoyed. The last album had featured a gatefold sleeve with a giant colour picture of Hendrix and tiny sepia snaps of Redding and Mitchell. The credits read: 'Produced and directed by Jimi Hendrix.' Produced, doubtless. But directed? This cinema term, meaningless when applied to discs, could only be interpreted as an indication that Hendrix was in total control.

But he wasn't, really. He couldn't assemble the large group of musical giants he wanted. Perhaps the best sample of work with a different set of musicians is, strangely, a live recording, the no-holds-barred demolition of 'The Star Spangled Banner'. The American national anthem would never be the same again for rock fans after Hendrix's historic hatchet job at the Woodstock Festival, where he took the Francis Scott Key composition by the neck and throttled every metallic nuance out of it. Perhaps this performance might suggest a new direction, but it instead led only to a reading of 'God Save The Queen' at the Isle of Wight Festival in 1970.

Jimi floundered through 1969 and into 1970. A trio called The Band Of Gypsies, with Buddy Miles on drums and long-time personal friend Billy Cox on bass, recorded a live album at the Fillmore East on New Year's Eve 1969, but it wasn't outstanding. His live appearances in the last year of his life were mostly lacklustre, a problem blamed on drink, drugs, jet lag, or having his drink spiked, depending on who was doing the explaining, and when. A drug bust and heavy police surveillance did not lighten his load.

Hendrix suffered from the pressure of all men who are asked by their worshippers to be gods. And he felt the stress of the artist who wants to grow but doesn't quite know how. He went back to the studio with Mitch Mitchell, taking Billy Cox with them, and nearly completed a fine album, *Cry Of Love*. Just before it was finished, he suffocated on his own vomit in a London apartment.

The date of death was 18 September 1970. Tests showed he had experienced barbiturate intoxication, but there was insufficient evidence to either suggest suicide or rule it out, so the coroner returned an open verdict.

Hendrix re-issues, repackagings and live albums flowed like a flight of locusts to plague the public. The only required purchase for the collector was the finally finished *Cry Of Love*. This posthumous album release earned top three placings on both sides of the Atlantic, and suggested that the artist might have been entering the second great period of his work.

But this sort of speculation is useless. There's another track on *Cry Of Love*, which definitely, not tentatively, points towards a conclusion. The song is called 'My Friend' and the finding is that Jimi Hendrix was very much a man alone, for the friend in the song is the man in the mirror in the morning. Only those with terrific talent know what it is like to walk that way alone. Those who have found great success know how isolating it can be. As an American who had lived for a couple of years in Europe, he may well have felt the displacement the lack of a permanent home can bring. And, as a black man in a white man's world of rock guitar heroes, he must have felt in a singular minority. For many, if not all of these reasons, Jimi Hendrix was far out on a limb, and couldn't come back.

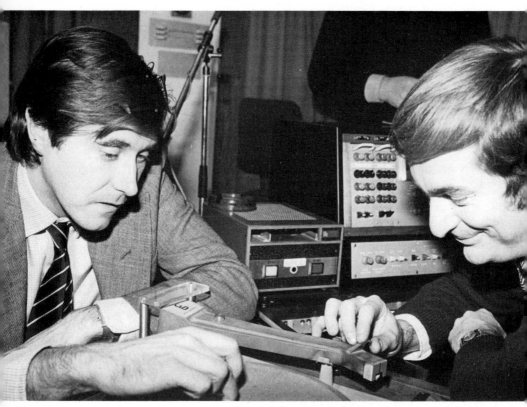

Bryan Ferry in the studio with the author

Bryan Ferry and Roxy Music

WHAT BEGAN as a pose became a way of life. Bryan Ferry, lead singer of Britain's leading experimental group, Roxy Music, tried on a tuxedo and found it fit. In searching for the latest in a series of costumes, Ferry stumbled on a visual image that seemed to suit his temperament. He had always aspired to taste, manners, refinement; now he looked the role. He was too gentlemanly to sing of love's pain like the soul singer he loved. Roxy Music spoke of angst, not agony. Ferry's songs were delicate, delicious and decadent.

Bryan Ferry was a miner's son from County Durham who from his adolescence loved both the visual arts and rock-and-roll. To him, they were difficult to distinguish, both being part of artistic expression. In the mid and late sixties, he toiled first in The Banshees, beating Siouxsie to the name by a full decade, and then in the soul group The Gas Board. All the while he was fascinated by fashion, making sure while in The Gas Board that he was wearing hip American attire.

Ferry acquired a degree in Fine Art from Newcastle University, where he studied under the pop art pioneer Richard Hamilton, and came to London, where, though he knew little about the subject, he taught ceramics in a Hammersmith girls' school. In 1970 he was dismissed for letting his classes degenerate into record-playing sessions.

The future didn't look overly bright. Ferry had failed an audition for King Crimson, and when he began to take demo tapes of his new group to record companies, he only succeeded in learning a variety of ways of saying 'I don't like it', including 'This is the worst tape I've ever heard'. But the band won two important champions, Richard Williams of *Melody Maker*, then the leading pop paper, and John Peel, then as now the champion of the new and novel. 'One of the most exciting demo tapes ever to come my way', Williams praised in print. 'May well be at the head of the field in the avant-garde stakes.' Peel proved a pal by offering Ferry and friends a session on Radio 1. Now things were looking up. The band linked with a management company, ironically the same firm that handled King Crimson, and signed a deal with Island Records. After a handful of triumphant personal appearances, Roxy Music hit the top ten with their very first single.

'Virginia Plain' faded in, the bane of every deejay. Bryan Ferry loved being in a club when the disc jockey turned the volume up at the beginning of the single, only to be blasted out of his headphones when the full sound level was reached.

The record was a delightful debut, and an unusually successful one, soaring to No. 4 in the charts. Roxy Music were vocalist and keyboard player Ferry, synthesizer star Brian Eno, saxophonist Andy Mackay, guitarist Phil Manzanera, and drummer Paul Thompson. They would have been named Roxy, but a minor American group had beaten them to the title. Still, Roxy Music suggested what they were about, a rock group with the glamour of the cinema (Roxy being a favourite movie theatre name in America) and a consciousness of pop art (film houses of the name tended to be built in the heyday of art deco). 'Virginia Plain' was full of lyrical allusions to the silver screen and the pop culture crowd, with references to *Flying Down to Rio* and Baby Jane Holzer. Its very title was a take-off on a brand name of cigarettes. Ferry also worked in the name of his lawyer: the very first lines, about making a deal and taking it to Robert Lee, are simply the story of a new band making their legal as well as musical start.

All the members of Roxy Music made important contributions to the immediately distinctive sound of 'Virginia Plain'. Their first album, simply named after themselves, was also a top ten success. The music was readily recognisable for two reasons: Ferry's emotionally distant and doom-heavy vocals and Eno's experiments with the synthesizer. Hearing a track like 'Ladytron', one quickly came to realise it could only be Roxy Music.

Roxy Music went top ten in the autumn of 1972. It was a great sales success for the members of the band who hadn't been thinking of conventional pop stardom. Mackay and Eno had been devotees of avant garde music while at university, and though Andy was at Reading and Brian at Winchester Art School they became firm friends. At one point they considered doing a two-man act with much of the music played on pre-recorded tapes, but in the late sixties and early seventies such an idea was hopelessly *outré*. A decade later, Marc Almond and David Ball of Soft Cell found international success doing precisely what Mackay and Eno had dismissed.

For Manzanera, the fabulous fortunes of the first two Roxy Music issues were also more than he could recently have hoped for. He had spent nearly two years in a group called Quiet Sun, and had been bypassed in the original Roxy Music auditions by David O'List. Manzanera became Roxy's sound mixer, graduating to guitarist when O'List left in early 1972.

Drummer Paul Thompson was Ferry's Geordie connection in the ensemble. He had come in when American Dexter Lloyd left. Graham Simpson, a bass player who had been a friend of Ferry's at university, had been his original musical partner, but left not just the band but the business. After his departure Roxy began a policy of hiring a different bass player for each album.

'Virginia Plain' was the first of three consecutive top ten singles. The second, 'Pyjamarama', also did not appear on album. In the early seventies it was considered unhip and unfair to fans for purveyors of progressive pop to put their 45s on their 33s. This attitude altered, and accordingly the third Roxy Music single, 'Street Life', led off the third album, *Stranded*.

Stranded was decorated with a sumptuous sleeve showing Playmate of the Year Marilyn Cole lying listless on the jungle floor. She was the latest in the succession of top models who adorned the covers of Roxy records. Keri-Ann had posed provocatively on the first album, while Amanda Lear had held a leopard on a leash on the jacket of *For Your Pleasure*, with Bryan Ferry making a cameo appearance as her chauffeur.

Stranded was the strongest set to date from the Ferrymen. It was clearer than ever that Bryan was boss, or at least outfront, because Eno had exited. His contributions had become considerable, greater than originally expected, and he had also succeeded in projecting a personality that not only complemented but competed with Ferry's. Eno was an extrovert on stage, Ferry an introvert. The synthesizer star assumed an adrogynous appearance that was luscious rather than ludicrous. Some visual attention and gradually some musical attention shifted from the centre of the stage to the side. This band wasn't big enough for the both of them. One had to go, and, since it couldn't be the lead singer and lyricist, it was Eno. Happily, the remaining years of the seventies vindicated both men. Eno went on to make a historic trilogy with David Bowie and notable works with several other artists. A critic's poll named him one of the two dozen most influential men of the rock era.

For Ferry and Roxy Music, the loss of the most mysterious aspect of their sound resulted in greater commercial success. *Stranded*, hailed by critics from the first, went on to become first – No. 1 in the LP list. It was a completely satisfying set, a celebration of the possibilities of progressive pop. The stage show was a smash, too – the potted palms brought in at great expense for concerts at the Rainbow Theatre created a complete self-contained environment. Years later, Adam Ant would try to make his live shows as exciting an experience for the concertgoer as Roxy at the Rainbow had been for him.

For each tour, the group would wear different outfits. Ferry was foremost in consciously creating a character. It's difficult to recall now, but he had first appeared as a cross between a Teddy Boy and a motorbike maniac, with slicked back hair and a leather jacket. The latest look each year became as much a cause for critical comment as the music itself, but Ferry faltered only once, in 1975, when he got gaucho gear that led one daily paper to liken him to 'a refugee from the Horse of the Year Show'.

In 1973, Ferry found a suit that fit. He wore a tuxedo and was immediately nicknamed the 'lounge lizard' of rock. The image particularly suited his sophisticated and startling solo album, *These Foolish Things*. 'A Hard Rain's A-Gonna Fall' was its staggering first single. Rarely had an album of cover versions sounded so unlike the originals, especially in the case of the Bob Dylan classic of thermonuclear paranoia. Dylan had written the song hurriedly during the Cuba Missile Crisis of 1962 and had thrown all the powerful images he had into the one number, fearing there might not be time left for anyone to write anything else. Ferry illustrated each of Dylan's mind pictures with appropriate sound effects or musical punctuation. To reinforce that the rain about to fall was 'hard', an expression that means contaminated but sounds like it means heavy, Ferry drove the song with sledgehammer force to the finale. This approach earned the open praise of many of Britain's top drummers, including Led Zeppelin's John Bonham, Black Sabbath's Bill Ward, and Ringo Starr, who sent Ferry a congratulatory telegram.

In one sense Bryan could have stopped his solo career with this track. It proved perfectly that a classic cut could be re-interpreted with complete success; he didn't have to do so again and again. Working on reworkings, his string of solo singles in the mid-seventies included a ruefully reflective 'Smoke Gets In Your Eyes' and a wild workout on 'Let's Stick Together'. Both were delightful. He even earned four top ten singles and three top ten albums. But in applying his aloof, arty stance to familiar material, Bryan was serving an extremely rich dessert to someone else's more substantial main course. The main reason he never caught on in the States was that, in the context of American radio, he didn't sound sincere. Whether he was surrounded by heavy rock on an album oriented station or a soul ballad on top forty, he sounded frivolous. What worked on album and in concert seemed silly on the air, and it is through radio plays that records break in the States. Without it, Bryan didn't catch on in America, the only considerable disappointment in a glorious career.

His style always seemed more at home within the framework of Roxy Music, where an accomplished musical backing balanced his quirky neurotic erotic vocals. A perfect example was the 1975 No. 2, 'Love Is The Drug'. It was a worldwide hit, becoming the band's only top thirty US entry. This glorious group, with Eno replacement Eddie Jobson now at the peak of his crowd-pleasing prowess, seemed on the verge of new break-throughs. Instead, they broke up.

The press had carried rumours for months, nay, years, ever since Ferry's initial solo success. It was one of those stories that, repeated often enough, would one day turn out to be true. In the summer of 1976, it became so.

It was a serious loss for a field where the content in the craft was rarely as thoughtful or as educated as it was in Roxy. But the main members of the band proved they could do important work on their own. Ferry's solo career reached its peak, and he proved on the album *In Your Mind* that he could sing original material on his own as well as covers. Mackay had a spectacular success with *Rock Follies*, which he co-wrote with American playwright and lyricist Howard Schuman. The soundtrack of the television series, starring Julie Covington, Rula Lenska and Charlotte Cornwall, went to No. 1, the first chart-topping TV album in British history. Phil Manzanera, who had previously issued the majestic *Diamond Head*, teamed with Eno and other musicians for a memorable short series of concerts and a live recording that included a brain-bending version of The Beatles' 'Tomorrow Never Knows'. They could all survive on their own. But once the point was proved, it didn't have to be proved any more. There was no real reason why, at least for occasional recordings and tours, the nucleus of Roxy Music couldn't come together again. Happily, it did.

The Roxy reunion momentarily seemed an embarrassment when the first single from *Manifesto*, 'Trash', peaked at forty, It had been released mainly because it was finished first, always a sign of record company haste. 'Dance Away', put out less than two months after 'Trash', was quite a contrast. From their least successful single Roxy went to their most profitable. It outsold all their other 45s, and though kept out of the top spot by Blondie was none the less one of the top ten best-selling singles of 1979.

The disco craze was in full swing, and Roxy Music had inadvertently found a new outlet. 'Dance Away' was a club smash, a perfect change of pace from the beats-per-minute-menu dished out by deejays. Another track from *Manifesto*, 'Angel Eyes', was re-mixed to provide another disco smash and another top five single. Ironically Abba had a top five record of the same title the same season. Chartologists fondly remember the weeks both discs were in the chart at the same time.

Roxy Music were back and in full gear. Their sound was in one sense more clearly commercial, as they played shorter numbers rather than the extended experimental pieces that had made the early albums so exciting. On their 1980 LP, *Flesh And Blood*, they included two cover versions, 'In The Midnight Hour' and 'Eight Miles High', hoping these might be more accessible to Americans.

But in one sense they were making definite progress. In the eighties Roxy developed a way with quiet, sophisticated ballads, songs like 'Oh Yeah'. Subtitled 'On The Radio', this was one of two top five hits from *Flesh And Blood*. 'Over You' was the other. Proving Roxy could still work at full tilt was the almost unbearably exciting 'The Same Old Scene', which featured in the flop film *Times Square*.

The constant radio play that resulted from three hit singles kept the album near the top of the charts for months. Indeed, *Flesh And Blood* had two separate stints at No. 1 totalling four weeks between them. Four different LPs sat at the summit during the seven weeks that separated *Flesh And Blood* and *Flesh And Blood* – a highly unusual, though not unprecedented, circumstance.

After a second No. 1 album, it was surely time for the group's first No. 1 single. It had eluded them for so long it was obvious it was something that couldn't be planned. It turned out to be a complete fluke. When John Lennon was murdered, Roxy were in Germany for a television show. Their natural instinct was to include a Lennon number as a tribute. Bryan Ferry suggested 'Jealous Guy' from the *Imagine* album. It went so well a German executive raved that it must be a single. At first the group declined, but on return to Britain they realised it might be a tasteful salute after all. They cut the tune at Phil Manzanera's studio in Chertsey. In the middle of March, 1981, they got their No. 1.

'Jealous Guy' was the only John Lennon song not performed by the writer to reach the top during the Lennon fever that followed his death, a time in which he himself had three posthumous No. 1s. The bass player on 'Jealous Guy', Gary Tibbs, had his own three No. 1s in 1981, going on to play with Adam and The Ants on 'Stand And Deliver' and 'Prince Charming'.

Though a Lennon song, 'Jealous Guy' was the quintessential Roxy record. Great emotion was conveyed tastefully, not excessively. Only Bryan Ferry could portray passion so dispassionately. Manzanera and Mackay once again demonstrated they knew what not to play as well as what to play. The spaces they left by refraining from cluttering the record allowed the listener to enter and get involved personally.

These are hallmarks of all the best recent Roxy. On *Avalon*, their third No. 1 LP, the slow style was taken to further lengths, with the title track being performed as if inside the haze of the dazed character's mind. Whether they remain in this mode will be told in time, but it certainly is an appropriate avenue for middle-aged musicians to explore. It's not so much that they're too old to be frantic any more but that experience and expertise can be called to play in an area so long dominated by the disinterested and unadventurous. And the style certainly suits the singer. Ferry now almost always appears in some sort of jacket and tie. He is one of those few performers, like Sid Vicious or Ted Nugent, who has become their own image. He has acquired the class he sought, both in the American sense of taste and refinement and in the British sense of being one of the proper people – dare one say it, the in crowd. He has married happily and acceptably, and though there is no way his fans can really tell, it would appear that he has found his own personal paradise, his Utopia, his Avalon.

In 1985, Bryan told Paul on The Other Side of the Tracks *there would be no further Roxy Music recordings.*

Marvin Gaye

EVERY CHILD checks to see what famous people share his or her birthday. It's an easy early way of earning some vicarious glory. Among the greats born on my birthday are Hans Christian Andersen and Sir Alec Guinness. But there's another star who shares my natal day who can not only tell a tale and invest it with emotion but sing it, too, better than almost anybody born on any day: my birthday mate, Marvin Gaye.

Gaye was born on 2 April 1939, many years after Hans Christian Andersen and quite a few before me. The son of a minister, Marvin played organ in his father's church and sang in the choir. He joined the orchestra in high school and served a brief stint in the army before enlisting in The Rainbows in 1955. That wasn't another service corps, it was one of Washington's top vocal groups, not surprising when one considers it also featured Don Covay and Billy Stewart. The Rainbows cut several singles, including 'Mary Lee', 'Shirley', and 'They Say', but none made the national charts. In 1957, Gaye and two other former Rainbows became The Marquees, and briefly backed Bo Diddley.

It was Harvey Fuqua who played the catalyst in Marvin's career. In Washington looking for new Moonglows, Fuqua found The Marquees. They recorded two singles with him on Chess Records in 1959. While playing in Detroit Harvey and The Moonglows were spied by fledgling record executive Berry Gordy, who invited Gaye and Fuqua to join his new organisation. The singers had their eyes open, too. Both of them married sisters of Gordy, Fuqua finding Gwendolyn and Gaye grabbing Anna.

Marvin was heard on some of the earliest Tamla hits, but not as the vocalist. For several months he was drummer for The Miracles on disc and on tour. As he put it succinctly, 'I needed money'. His own solo career got off to an inauspicious start in May, 1961, when Tamla released the Berry Gordy song and production, 'Let Your Conscience Be Your Guide'. There was almost no indication of Marvin Gaye's poten-

85

tial in this first single. Writer-producer-label-owner Gordy seemed to be casting his charge as a jazz balladeer. Indeed, when he co-wrote his own fourth single, Gaye set his song in a jazz mode. Gordy, listening in the control booth, suggested changes. He didn't want a fourth flop. Marvin's mentor altered some chords, and the commercial prospects of the number became apparent.

Three young women who worked at Motown were summoned to do backing vocals. Their names were Martha, Rosalyn and Annette. They weren't paid much for their contribution – Martha reportedly got ten dollars per session if she sang, five if she clapped, and seven dollars fifty cents if she 'stomped'. But their efforts for Marvin Gaye gave them more than mere money. The artist thought they sang back-up so loudly they were stealing the show. They were 'vandals of music' – The Vandellas. Martha Reeves can be heard clearly on Marvin Gaye's first hit, 'Stubborn Kind Of Fellow'.

The tune entered the pop and rhythm and blues charts in October, 1962, beginning one of the richest runs in recorded music. Marvin Gaye was one of the ten most successful artists in the rock era, with literally dozens of hits. He found further fame with four female singing partners. He more quietly achieved as a writer for other artists, partly penning the classic 'Dancing In The Street' for Martha and The Vandellas and co-writing with wife Anna The Originals' long-running R&B No. 1, 'Baby I'm For Real'.

Gaye did all this while on one label, Tamla, until his first release on CBS twenty years to the month after 'Stubborn Kind Of Fellow'. In part, his succession of successes was a tribute to Berry Gordy's strategy of switching writers and producers to suit an artist's aims and abilities. After two more hits with William Stevenson, 'Hitch Hike' and 'Pride And Joy', the latter smash inspired by Marvin's love for his wife, Gaye was introduced to Brian Holland, Lamont Dozier, and Eddie Holland. They'd written a song Gordy thought great for Gaye, and Marvin agreed so ardently he cut it the very same day. This time the female backing group was The Supremes, though it wasn't quite as easy to hear Diana Ross as it had been to distinguish Martha Reeves. Marvin Gaye's autumn, 1963 classic, complete with one of the simplest but most exciting piano parts of all-time, was 'Can I Get A Witness'.

This track remains a monument of modern music, but Gaye didn't enjoy the actual recording as much as he thought he would. Brian Holland and Lamont Dozier made him sing at the very top of his register, several notes higher than he would have chosen himself. It physically hurt to do the song as they wanted. The singer who had lost love sounded pained and tense. Less than a year later, the Holland–Dozier–Holland team began working in earnest with the single's support singers, The Supremes, beginning their historic string of hits. They would also work with Marvin in 1964 on the marvellous 'Baby Don't You Do It'.

The way Gaye's voice worked so well with women gave somebody a bright idea. The motivation was also clearly commercial: Marvin was Motown's main man and Mary Wells the label's leading lady. It might be expected that teaming them might manufacture a hit single and album. The results exceeded expectations. Their first 45 produced two hits. Both sides, the up-tempo 'What's The Matter With You Baby' and the ballad 'Once Upon A Time', made the top twenty of *Billboard's* Hot 100, and 'Once Upon A Time' proved Marvin's first British entry. It was, alas, the end of the Marvin and Mary duo. Miss Wells had just turned twenty-one and was due to re-negotiate her Motown contract. As journalist Aaron Fuchs revealed, she was unhappy with Berry Gordy's royalty rate. Her new husband, a low-ranking Motown employee, advised her to accept an offer from Twentieth Century-Fox. The man who was then Twentieth's record boss, Morty Craft, told Charlie Gillett 'I told her how if she signed with us she'd get movie contracts and be a real star. That wasn't in the contract, of course, but why should I feel sorry I tricked her; if she's so crazy with overblown ambition she deserves what she gets.'

So goes the record business, and so went Mary Wells' career, out of the top ten for ever. Marvin Gaye wasn't so ambitious, and turned down all offers to appear in films, even rejecting the lead role in a proposed Sam Cooke bio-pic on the grounds that it would be 'morbid'. In retrospect it seems chilling that Marvin declined to play the role of a singer shot to death.

Gaye remained with Tamla Records, riding the charts solo at the same time as his two Mary Wells duets singing a Berry Gordy ballad, 'Try It Baby'. In early 1965, he scored with the personal favourite of his early hits, Holland–Dozier–Holland's 'How Sweet It Is To Be Loved By You', inspired by Jackie Gleason's television catch phrase, 'How Sweet It Is'. It was Marvin's favourite simply because it was his biggest pop hit to date, peaking at six. But another top tenner followed immediately, from a new source of material. Smokey Robinson lifted Gaye out of a temporary personal depression by long talks and hit songs, including 'I'll Be Doggone'. Another noteworthy number in Smokey's series was 'Ain't That Peculiar'.

During the mid-sixties Gaye continued to record regularly, but with less remarkable results. One of his greatest virtues was now providing a problem. Suitable for special handling by almost any fine writer or producer, he lacked a vital image of his own. His charm lay in drawing an audience towards him, rather than in projecting powerfully outward. Women found him sexy, but as a suave silent stud rather than a Tom Jones type. Unless it made for a great single, an ordinary pop song wouldn't draw sparks from Marvin. Berry Gordy's tactic of having him record LPs of Broadway songs and Nat King Cole classics didn't help the case, either.

A ladies' man needed ladies. This obvious truth had been over-looked since 1964, when, after Mary Wells departed Motown, a duet with Kim Weston called 'What Good Am I Without You' had been only a minor hit. In January, 1967 Tamla tried the long-overdue follow-up. A top twenty hit in both America and Britain, 'It Takes Two' served notice that the pairings with female partners made for good business and good music. Even the B-side, 'It's Got To Be A Miracle', was exquisite.

Then an unfortunate coincidence occurred. Like Wells, Weston walked. Gone from Gordy, she never regained her great glory, as in the case of Mary Wells. But Tamla wasn't going to waste time in pursuing the profitable pattern. The company suggested that Marvin vocalise with the young Tammi Terrell.

There was a bit of a risk. Unlike Mary Wells and Kim Weston, Tammi had not established herself as a solo artist, having only achieved two tiny hits. Furthermore, the proposed writers and pro-ducers, Nickolas Ashford and Valerie Simpson, were Motown new-comers.

Gaye gave it a go regardless. He thought recording with Tammi would be a challenge. Besides, he admitted, 'she was very pretty'.

So began the finest series of boy–girl duets in pop music. There was the dynamic debut, the original 'Ain't No Mountain High Enough', the slow and sensitive 'Your Precious Love', the tender testament of love from Marvin's own pen, 'If This World Were Mine'. The two-some scored four American top ten hits, including 'If I Could Build My Whole World Around You' and 'Ain't Nothing Like The Real Thing', while in Britain they nudged to No. 9 with 'The Onion Song'.

There was great meaning in the hit 'You're All I Need To Get By', more than the public realised. Tammi had collapsed in Marvin's arms while on stage in 1967. The single and album of the same name rep-resented her comeback. But eight operations failed to heal her. Tammi died of the complications from a brain tumour in 1970. Marvin would not perform in concert again for four years.

Ironically, while Miss Terrell was suffering her private hell, she was doing fine in the charts, and Marvin was enjoying his greatest gain as an individual. His historic hit was a fluke. 'I Heard It Through The Grapevine' had already been recorded by several Motown acts before his version was released. Jimmy Ruffin claimed that Barrett Strong, who wrote the number with Norman Whitfield, had intended it for him to issue shortly after 'What Becomes Of The Brokenhearted'. Whitfield cut 'Grapevine' on Gaye, but for internal political reasons the track was not issued. Gladys Knight and The Pips lived up to their name and pipped everyone. The family group's version, issued in the autumn of 1967, went to No. 1 on the R&B chart and No. 2 on the pop chart, becoming the Tamla stable's biggest seller to date.

Marvin's treatment was then placed on an album, and there it sat, until careful radio programmers pointed out Tamla was sitting on a smash. Marvin's version was brought out and it became No. 1 in America and Britain, overtaking Gladys' 'Grapevine' to become Motown's new all-time bestseller. 'I Heard It Through The Grapevine' is now universally recognised as a pop standard, so it seems shocking that Marvin Gaye discounted the disc. He thought the tune had run its course, and didn't even think his rendering would be released.

Gaye was finally launched on his delayed British chart career. 'Too Busy Thinking About My Baby', the follow-up to 'Grapevine', went top five in the UK as well as US. And then Britain got a hit the Americans missed. Dion had scored a comeback smash in the States with 'Abraham Martin and John', a song written by Dick Holler the day after the assassination of Robert Kennedy. But though Dion's version was a million-seller, it didn't even chart in Britain. Perhaps audiences here still expected vintage rock and roll from DiMucci; perhaps they weren't as profoundly penitent about the rash of assassinations as Americans were. Whatever the reason, the song 'Abraham Martin and John' had still not been a hit in Britain when producer Norman Whitfield took Marvin Gaye in the studio and turned out the lights. Singing in the dark, Gaye was literally as well as figuratively looking for light.

'Abraham Martin and John' reached the British top ten in 1970. It represented a turning point in Marvin Gaye's career. From now on he would be a topical artist, singing more about the problems and passions of real life than previously. He would also be his own man. There was something about the death of Tammi Terrell, something never publicly revealed, that made Marvin mad at Motown. He decided to write and produce his next album himself, despite scorn from the organisation. According to writer Peter Banjaminson, *What's Going On* was greeted with derision by Motown executives. Several reactions were vulgar. Berry Gordy told his brother-in-law he would not issue the disc. Gaye was quoted as replying 'Don't release it then . . . and I'm never going to do another album for you either.'

It wasn't a wild threat. Gaye already claimed to have stashed some of his best songs away for his children to publish after his death, just so Motown wouldn't get all his work. If this was exaggeration, it at least indicated his bad feelings about the company that had made him a star. The firm had no choice but to issue *What's Going On*.

The album was the greatest single achievement of Marvin Gaye's career. It spoke eloquently of various crises in contemporary life that together cried out for action. 'What's Going On' the artist asked in the first single from the album. 'The Ecology', he answered in the subtitle to the second 45, 'Mercy Mercy Me'. 'Inner City Blues', he replied in the third. All three were American top ten pop hits and soul chart No. 1s. In Britain a fourth track became a hit: 'Save The Children'.

The neglect of babies, the abuse of the environment, the horrors of the ghetto that 'make me wanna holler' – this had not been the stuff gold discs were made of. Tamla's initial antipathy was understandable from the business perspective. But anyone who could not hear the artistic achievement *What's Going On* represented should have been pensioned off with a tin handshake.

The US public heard Marvin's message immediately. The album went gold. The three singles all sold a million. The concerns of the people were the subjects of hit records. Black music had not just been influenced but altered. Major artists could now speak freely in their work of matters only the daring or the fringe could address before.

Gaye opened new ground, preparing an album devoted to the delights of sex. No one had dealt with that before and made it mainstream, but Marvin had no trouble getting it on. Millions of singles and albums raced out of the shops, almost as if under their own power, when *Let's Get It On* was issued in 1973. After *What's Going On* there had seemed nothing left to say, so Gaye had sensibly said nothing the next time, releasing the predominantly instrumental soundtrack to the film *Trouble Man*. The single, another American top ten effort, confirmed that Marvin was relying less on conventional pop structure and more on feel, oozing his way in and out of musical passages, altering the volume in his voice as one would as their moods changed in real life. Instrumentation loosened up to create a flexible groove. It was perfect for *Let's Get It On*. The music swayed, rather than rocked, and America was seduced.

Britain, obsessed with weenybop idols on the singles scene and progressive pop on the album side, underrated *Let's Get It On* but made up for the oversight by making the most of the 1974 duet project *Diana And Marvin*. Diana Ross firmly denied she was 'taking the place of' Tammi Terrell, and she was right to do so. Teaming her with Marvin was as natural in '74 as the pairing with Mary Wells had been in '64: Diana was now Motown's wonder woman. And, anyway, they'd been on the same record as long ago as 'Can I Get A Witness' in 1963. 'You Are Everything' was a top five single in Britain, where *Diana And*

Marvin proved a long-term bestseller. In the States, where the song had already been a major hit for The Stylistics, 'My Mistake' emerged as the top track.

Having come up with two classic concept albums and an acceptable double act, Marvin Gaye had done just about enough for the seventies, even though the decade had four more years left to run. The *I Want You* album carried his relaxed attitude to the point of vagueness, and the double album *Here My Dear* proved an unattractive purchase if only for its subject matter. Marvin's marriage to Anna Gordy had dissolved. Gaye, declared bankrupt in 1978 with debts of two million dollars, wasn't going to get away easily. Six hundred thousand dollars in royalties were assigned to Anna by order of the court. Since the *Here My Dear* story of their relationship was partly hers anyway, some of the money might as well have been, too.

The two most gripping moments in Gaye's late seventies product came on the LP *Live At The London Palladium*. The first took a mere minute. Awash with applause after a Marvin and Tammi medley, he stood on stage and said of the tribute, 'She would have liked that'. It was as if he felt that he was then, and always, in touch with her spirit.

The second highlight of the *Live* double album wasn't a concert recording at all. The fourth side was an extended dance piece called 'Got To Give It Up', and when Motown did give some of it up in favour of an edited version, the single was an international top ten hit. 'Got To Give It Up' was an American No. 1 and a British No. 7 in '77, but in the following years it appeared that Marvin Gaye was a write-off. No one, not even him, was going to have hits with titles like 'Funky Space Reincarnation'. And his personal habits became upsetting to his associates, who felt he was losing either control of himself or contact with everyone else. It was a particular triumph, therefore, when he returned gloriously in 1982 with the million-selling album *Midnight Love* and the worldwide winner, 'Sexual Healing'.

It was an adult song, but Marvin *was* forty-three, and he certainly wasn't going to wait until retirement to sing about sex. He had moved on yet another step from 'Let's Get It On', taking his diffident nature deeper inside his material, muttering and mumbling as if the microphone wasn't there. He had succeeded in making understatement not only a virtue but an art form. He had found a style for himself, writing and producing his own work with hand-picked associates away from Tamla.

On the morning of 2 April 1984, I was awakened by a breakfast television service asking if I could come in to the studio to talk about Marvin Gaye, who had been shot dead by his father the day before in Los Angeles. I never had such a terrible birthday.

Jerry Lee Lewis

I HAVE two intensely personal memories of Jerry Lee Lewis. The first is not nice. There have been interviews with artists I have been unable to use because the star was too shy or too inarticulate but Jerry Lee Lewis is the only performer whose interview I have been unable to use because of personal unpleasantness. He was rude and arrogant, dismissive of his late fifties fellows like Chuck Berry and Fats Domino. I considered his racist attitude an obscenity.

In contrast, my other memory is of a miracle. It was the Steve Allen show on live American network television. Lewis performed 'Whole Lot of Shakin' Goin' On' with a level of energy and commitment the Allen audience had never seen before. He moaned, he murmured, he screamed, he shouted, he chanted, he ad libbed, and he played the piano with his hands and his feet. Furniture flew across the stage and so did, for some reason, a rubber chicken. This was rock and roll as a spectacle. I and millions of kids like me were breathless.

Jerry Lee Lewis was born in Ferriday, Louisiana on 29 September 1935, the same year as Elvis Aaron Presley. His life was eventful from the start: the doctor who was to deliver him passed out drunk, and his father Elmo pulled him out of his mother Mamie. Mom named him Jerry after a silent film star whose last name she forgot. Pop gave him the Lee, but his parents couldn't agree whether that stood for grandfather Leroy or uncle Lee.

Elmo and Mamie were proud that their eldest son, Elmo Junior, had already distinguished himself in music. At the age of eight, he showed an aptitude for writing and singing. But one day, while mentally composing a song for church, he was run down and killed by a drunken driver.

The death of Elmo Junior left Jerry Lee as the only surviving Lewis son. He also showed early musical promise, and was almost but not quite as religious as his fundamentalist family. The first number he mastered at the piano was 'Silent Night' – boogie woogie style. He was dismissed from the Southwestern Bible Institute for playing a Pentacostal hymn in a boogie woogie version during chapel. Jerry Lee was only too aware of his natural sinfulness: his mother and cousin spoke in tongues, but he was never visited by the Spirit. His cousin Jimmy Lee Swaggart became one of America's top television preachers, and found occasions to plead to Jerry publicly for repentance. Throughout his life Lewis has suffered internal conflict between the call of the Lord and the siren sound of the Devil's music.

When he heard his son play 'Silent Night', Elmo Lewis was so thrilled he used his personal possessions as collateral to buy his boy an upright piano. Jerry Lee practised for hours every day, and inevitably started to play for money. In the autumn of 1954, he auditioned for the country music radio show *Louisiana Hayride*, but was turned down by star and scout Slim Whitman. In the summer of 1956, Lewis' cousin Mickey Gilley suggested he go to Memphis and audition for Sun Records, the company that had made a star of Elvis Presley. As biographer Nick Tosches tells the tale in his book *Hellfire*, Elmo Lewis sold nearly three dozen eggs from his hens to finance his son's trip to Tennessee. When Jerry Lee Lewis presented himself at Sun Records, owner and producer Sam Philips wasn't in, but assistant Jack Clement was. He was bemused by Jerry's claim that he 'could play the piano like Chet Atkins', since Atkins was a guitarist, not a pianist. Clement gave the twenty-one-year-old an audition, liked what he heard, and told him to return when he'd learned some rock and roll. The type of country numbers Lewis was playing were not commercial. On his second visit the Louisiana lad played an animated version of Ray Price's country and western hit 'Crazy Arms' at Clement's suggestion. Unaware that a recording was underway, guitarist Billy Lee Riley strolled into the studio and struck a strange chord at the very end of the song. The chord is still there today.

'Crazy Arms' wasn't a hit, but it did win Lewis some press attention. More importantly, it made him part of the Sun team. On 4 December, he played piano on the Carl Perkins session that produced 'Matchbox'. Elvis Presley visited his old friends that afternoon, and along with Carl and Jerry Lee performed an impromptu series of mostly religious songs. Johnny Cash sang with them until a photographer stopped taking pictures, then he went shopping. What had begun as a day's work for Lewis had turned into a place in the legendary Million Dollar Quartet – even though, at the time, he was a complete unknown.

Jerry Lee went on tour with Perkins and Cash, but his opening night performance was dull. His labelmates took him aside and offered him succinct but kindly advice. 'Get loose out there or you're gonna die', claimed Carl. 'Get Crazy!' Johnny joined in. The next night, Lewis stood up and kicked away his piano stool, and one of the great live acts in rock and roll was born.

He still wasn't a hitmaker, and played piano for other Sun stars. In January, 1957, he backed Warren Smith and Billy Lee Riley, appearing on Riley's classic rockabilly cuts 'Flyin' Saucers Rock and Roll' and 'Red Hot'. On the last number, Lewis not only invigorated the ivories but joined in the singing of the immortal line, 'Your gal ain't doodily-squat'.

'Red Hot' was the last record by another artist on which Jerry Lee Lewis appeared as session pianist. It wasn't so much that Jerry found reciting 'your gal ain't doodily-squat' undignified. He simply realised that Riley or any other credited act wasn't going to make Jerry Lee Lewis famous.

So the Ferriday fellow got down to making his own second single. On one side was a song written by Jack Clement called 'It'll Be Me', inspired by a visit to the bathroom. It's a long story, but a short record, and Clement and Sam Philips loved it and considered it A-side material. Cliff Richard loved it, too, taking it to No. 2 in Britain five years later.

But Jerry Lee preferred a number which had been written by country and western singer Roy Hall and rhythm and blues vocalist Dave 'Curly' Williams. While fishing together in Florida, the two had heard a big bang. When they asked what the noise was, they were told: 'We got 21 drums and a bass horn. Somebody's keeping time on a ding dong.' Hall and Williams were inspired by this incident to write 'Whole Lotta Shakin' Goin' On', recorded first by Big Maybelle in 1953.

Jerry Lee Lewis had not heard Big Maybelle's version when he decided to cut the tune in 1957. He was familiar, however, with the rendition by co-writer Roy Hall, who had given Jerry an engagement at his club. Hall's version had no piano in it, but Lewis automatically added the boogie woogie beat he favoured. He also changed the words because he couldn't remember them all. From such bizarre beginnings came a single that sold six million copies and made Jerry Lee Lewis an international idol.

'Whole Lotta Shakin' Goin' On' was a world wonder. In one week it was the No. 1 country and western hit, the No. 1 rhythm and blues seller, and the No. 3 record in the *Billboard* Top 100, though in another major trade chart it was also No. 1 pop. In Britain the side soared to No. 8.

Lewis had transformed an ordinary pop song into a heathen hymn. His pumping piano and leering lyric left little doubt what kind of 'shakin'' he was talking about. By altering the volume of his voice in the spoken section and going all out in the home stretch, pouring on the frantically repeated keyboard chords and glissando, Jerry Lee had surpassed the passion possible in unvarying rock tunes by pianists Little Richard and Fats Domino. Sam Philips may have considered the track a throwaway at first, but like everybody he loved a winner. For a follow-up in a similar vein he and his brother Jud chose 'Great Balls Of Fire' by Otis Blackwell, whose top tunes already included 'All Shook Up', 'Don't Be Cruel' and 'Good Golly Miss Molly'.

Jerry Lee didn't object to it because it was written by a black man, despite his personal prejudices. Music knew no colour bar. He resisted recording 'Great Balls Of Fire' for religious reasons. He saw it as sinful, and an argument raged in the Sun studios during the early morning hours of an October Sunday. Jack Clement turned on the tape and preserved the row for posterity. Philips persevered and prevailed. Jerry Lee Lewis laid down 'Great Balls Of Fire' and the first take was used as the single. It was a British No. 1 and an American No. 2, better pop placings than had been achieved by 'Whole Lotta Shakin' Goin' On', and it was a hit in, among other countries, Australia.

On a flight from Los Angeles to Hawaii, as the prelude of a package tour down under, Jerry was seated next to the fifteen-year-old headliner Paul Anka. He didn't like being second on the bill to anyone, and he didn't like Anka. The Canadian boy showed Jerry a song he'd been working on; the Louisiana lip dismissed it. Then Anka presented the words of his recent No. 1, 'Diana'. 'Don't make sense, write somethin' else', the Southern star sneered, and started writing his own words. So was born one of his best rock recordings, the 'Lewis Boogie'.

It was a rare beast: a Jerry Lee Lewis track written by the man himself. For the A-sides of his singles Sun stuck to works by other writers. 'Breathless', the follow-up to 'Great Balls Of Fire', was another Otis Blackwell tune, and another top ten smash on both sides of the Atlantic. But it took painfully long to climb the charts. Sam Philips had not sent out free promotional copies, figuring Jerry Lee was so hot radio stations would have to buy their own singles to please their listeners. Radio resistance to this tactic crumbled only gradually, so 'Breathless' needed another form of sales stimulus. It got help from television disc jockey Dick Clark, whose daily afternoon rock and roll show *American Bandstand* was so popular he was given his own Saturday evening prime time slot.

Jerry performed 'Breathless' live on the first programme. He came back again the following month to participate in a peculiar promotion. Listeners could get a copy of the single if they mailed in five wrappers from Beechnut gum, the show's sponsor, and fifty cents. Such an offer helped Clark as well as Lewis because Beechnut was unconvinced the show was selling enough gum to warrant continued sponsorship. Within a week, tens of thousands of gum wrappers had been sent in. The show was safe, and 'Breathless' was off and running into the top ten.

Even though this hit wasn't as big as the previous two, Jerry seemed secure because he'd been asked to perform the title tune of the youth-oriented film *High School Confidential*. His Jerry Lee Lewis trio played 'High School Confidential' at the very beginning of the movie, on the back of a flatbed truck. It was an electrifying sequence, just as exciting as the performance of 'Great Balls Of Fire' in *Jamboree*, retitled *Disc Jockey Jamboree* for British distribution. Jack Jackson was the UK deejay represented alongside such American greats as Dick Clark and the soul spaceman Jocko.

Lewis' career was in high gear. A tour was planned with Jerry Lee and Elvis Presley sharing the bill and fighting it out for the unofficial title of King of Rock and Roll. But before the itinerary could be confirmed, Elvis found a real-life role in the US Army. Jerry Lee seemed to have the field to himself.

Then things started going wrong – not just slightly wrong, but catastrophically. On an Alan Freed tour, Lewis was so upset at Chuck Berry topping the bill that in an effort to steal the show he not only performed with his usual energy but destroyed his piano, dancing on top of it, kicking it, and, one night, burning it. Word of mouth that this was a sensational show spread. Then one night in Boston, the overflow crowd outside the theatre rioted, provoked by police aggression. Subsequent dates were cancelled.

A worse fate awaited in Britain. In May 1958, Jerry Lee Lewis arrived with his new wife. From the start the tabloids took more interest in his partner than his playing. They didn't object too much to her being his cousin. But they were rather irate that this was his third spouse and that he had twice been a bigamist because of the sloppy timing of his divorces. And they positively drooled at the dispatch desk when they learned that the latest lady was only thirteen. What was not uncommon in the American South was outrageous to the self-appointed guardians of Britain's morals. They made Myra Lewis front page news and literally hounded her and Jerry Lee out of the country with the kind of gutter invective Fleet Street can summon so well.

This pitiful press crossed the Atlantic before the newlyweds did. Panic spread through the music business. Despite a full-page plea written by the Philips brothers and signed by Jerry Lee for *Billboard* and *Cashbox*, Lewis became too hot to handle. No promoter would touch him, and he had to return to playing clubs. Frightened of being stigmatised by association, Dick Clark refused to have his old friend on his TV shows, a form of censorship he felt guilty about for years afterwards. Worst of all, American radio support disappeared. Only in Britain was 'Lovin' Up A Storm' a top thirty hit in the spring of 1959. It reached No. 28, nothing much compared to Lewis's early hits, but a triumph considering the blacklisting he had suffered the previous year. Alas, it was an exception that proved the rule: Jerry Lee Lewis was through as a rock-and-roll chart star. Sun's attempts to bring him back to the bestsellers were usually unsuccessful, but at least they were interesting. First there was 'The Return of Jerry Lee', a novelty assembled by Jack Clement and deejay George Klein in which reporters asked questions answered by snippets from Lewis's hits. 'Lewis Boogie' was finally issued as the B-side of this oddity. Later Sam Philips had Jerry Lee record an instrumental, figuring that if he didn't sing no one would recognise it was him and the single might sell on its own merits. But 'The Hawk', the artist's alias, was equally as identifiable by his piano playing, and no one was fooled.

The only significant chart placings in the early sixties were attained with cover versions of late fifties rock hits. The revamped rockers were Chuck Berry's 'Sweet Little Sixteen', Little Richard's 'Good Golly Miss Molly', and, most important of all, Ray Charles's 'What'd I Say'. The latter cover crept into the British top ten in the summer of 1961. It was an inspired performance by the piano player, but the vision remained that of Ray Charles. Jerry Lee Lewis was no longer vital to the music business. He made his last records for Sun in 1963 and went to the Smash label. Sam Philips, a rich man from business investments that included a founding share of Holiday Inns, ultimately let Sun set. For five years, Jerry Lee walked the wilderness, encouraged by favourable receptions in Britain, discouraged by horrible developments in his personal life that included the drowning in the home swimming pool of his son Steve Allen Lewis, named after the TV host who had given him a big break in 1957. Jerry Lee's personal behaviour became so unpredictable and often so unlikeable that it has taken the biographies *Hellfire* and *Great Balls Of Fire* to tell the total tale.

Lewis had less than a year to run on his Smash contract, a pact which the company did not intend to renew, when the label's enthusiastic new Nashville executive Eddie Kilroy suggested cutting him country. He was over thirty now, so adult material was appropriate. The country audience had often supported him in his rocking days; perhaps it would accept him again.

The Smash hierarchy were unenthusiastic, and Jerry Lee was so unmoved by the experience he put down a dozen country songs and then left Nashville, forgetting about them. What he did not foresee was that one of those numbers, 'Another Place, Another Time', would change his life. The record was a dramatic departure for Jerry Lee

Lewis. It wasn't that he hadn't done country material before; he had, on B-sides and album tracks for Sun. But here was a song of real life, of hard knocks, of someone who had known what it was like to lose but wasn't going to give up until the final bell tolled. The single shot to No. 2 in the country charts. For a moment it seemed that the artist would not be able to capitalise on the surprise success, since he was doing extremely well as Iago in the stage production of *Catch My Soul*, Jack Good's rock version of *Othello*. Lewis won rave reviews, and told the *Los Angeles Times* 'This Shakespeare was really somethin'. I wonder what he would have thought of my records.'

If the Bard had liked country, he would have been delighted. When *Catch My Soul* failed to get a place on Broadway, Jerry Lee concentrated on records again. He scored another country No. 2, this one a song that transcended categories and years later became a top ten British hit for Rod Stewart. Playing on the advertising slogan 'The beer that made Milwaukee famous', Lewis sang 'What's Made Milwaukee Famous (Has Made a Loser Out of Me)'. The single made the Hot 100 as well as No. 2 on the country chart, but it was undoubtedly the country success that was most important. He was singing with a voice dripping with emotion and irony, immersing himself into the material in the whole-hearted way that drew Ray Charles to record some country music. It was a kind of white man's soul, and American southerners loved it. Jerry Lee made a deal with them: in concert he'd perform both country and rock, but on record he'd be strictly a country artist. So he was for six incredible years, a time in which he registered fifteen top ten hits.

Many of these had clever lengthy titles that gave a summary of the character's dilemma. 'There Must Be More To Love Than This', claimed a No. 1. 'She Still Comes Around (To See What's Left Of Me)', a No. 2. And then there was the best of them all, a masterpiece of misery by Mickey Newbury in which the pain is exposed not just by the circumstances but by the desperate lengths to which the vocalist will go to rationalise his lover's departure. Lewis used many of the tricks that made 'Whole Lotta Shakin'' great on the Newbury song, he just utilised them in a calmer fashion. The ad libs, the asides, the brief tinkling piano figures – they all added to the effect of the magnificent and moving 'She Even Woke Me Up To Say Goodbye'.

It was so delicious the listener could be forgiven for trying to eat it. The way Lewis recited 'It's not her heart, Lord, it's her mind' brilliantly captured the ambivalence of his attitude: she doesn't mean to be unkind, not in her heart, but she knows she has to be in her mind, and maybe her mind is deficient. Now he couldn't resist throwing a rock number into his country catalogue. His risk was rewarded with another No. 1. In Jerry Lee's version of the Big Bopper's 'Chantilly Lace', he moaned and mumbled as he hadn't since the late fifties. And he referred to himself by his nickname, 'The Killer'. As he once explained, the name dated from his school days. 'That's what all my friends called me', he related. 'I hated that damn name ever since I was a kid, but I been stuck with it. I don't think they meant it killer like, like I'd kill people. I think they meant it music'ly speakin'. But I am one mean sonofabitch.'

'Chantilly Lace' not only went to the top of the country chart, it reached the top half of the Hot 100. This gave Mercury Records, the parent company of Smash, the idea that Jerry should record with contemporary rock musicians. He came to London after invitations had been sent rather indiscriminately to Britain's top names, asking them to join him in supersession whether it made musical sense or not. As one invitation recipient, Elton John, put it, 'What am I supposed to do, play piano for Jerry Lee Lewis? And Rod Stewart, what's he gonna do on it, sing for him?'

The London sessions album was a moderate success, and the single 'Drinking Wine Spo-Dee O'Dee' nearly made the top forty, but it was all massively inconsequential. Jerry Lee's best discs remained the country pieces, for this form best expressed the reflective sadness that everyone knew was part of his own life. He lost his second son, Jerry Lee Junior, in a road accident. His fourth marriage floundered. He shot his bass player twice while firing at a Coca-Cola can for fun. He was detained in the driveway of Elvis Presley's home, Graceland, waving a gun and demanding to see the man who had eliminated all doubt and reigned as the true King of rock and roll.

These were only some of the incidents that let fans know Lewis was aging none too gracefully, which made his big early eighties hit '39 And Holding' supremely ironic. Actually, he was already over forty, and in none too good shape. He became seriously ill in 1982 and nearly died, his stomach savaged by heavy drinking. Public figures like Johnny Carson and Kris Kristofferson begged him to hold on, and he did recover, but though there was a great deal of love around him, Lewis found it hard to accept, damning his fans in one interview in the most obscene language. He was a larger than life figure because he embodied so many conflicts – between religion and depravity, love and lust, self-control and self-destruction. This awesome figure suits an awesome legend, one without whom Elton John might never have kicked away his piano stool and without whom the English language would be lacking one of its more colourful exclamatory phrases: 'Great Balls Of Fire'.

Paul McCartney

IT'S HARD to know what to say about him. That's because there's so much to say about him. He's rather like Walt Disney: where do you begin? And like Walt Disney it seems, at least to people who are younger than he, that he was always there, always a show business institution. It's almost impossible to believe he was an ordinary human being who worked to the position he occupies.

Surely he's always been around, quasi-divine, nearly omnipotent? A man behind the largest-selling single in British history, and the one it replaced . . . a man with nine American No. 1s *since* the break-up of The Beatles . . . a patriotic chap who would be proud to be told he is the world's most famous living Englishman. We don't need an envelope to reveal the identity of the amazing Paul McCartney.

Paul McCartney was born in Liverpool on 18 June 1942. He was born again in April 1970. It wasn't that he had a profound religious experience. That was when he released his first solo album, *McCartney*. British promotional copies included a self-interview that confirmed what insiders had suspected: The Beatles had broken up.

One of the former Fab Four expressed his admiration that Paul had been clever enough to use a fact with which they were all familiar to draw attention to his own record. *McCartney* was a musical event *and* a news event, and several album tracks were played like singles on radio stations around the world.

They weren't all new: 'Hot As Sun' had been written before The Beatles had become famous, and two tunes had been penned in India in 1968. They weren't all complete: to give the impression of a homemade LP, which this one was, Paul included several song fragments. But they did fit together to form an engaging whole, the pleasant kind of outing that reflected the circumstances of a group member suddenly out on his own trying new ideas and finding some of them worthy of lengthy consideration and some of little attention. Two superb songs gave the platter substance: 'Maybe I'm Amazed', a deep and deathless

discourse on the astonishment one feels when one experiences the full scope of true love, and 'Every Night', another romantic piece whose soulfulness was later emphasised in a hit version by Phoebe Snow. The *McCartney* album was a positive statement in the midst of negative news, and it zoomed to No. 1 in the American album chart and No. 2 in the British list.

The sleeve credits had read simply 'Instruments and voices by Paul, Photos and harmonies by Linda'. From that information, and the lilting 'The Lovely Linda' that opened that album, press and public should have got the impression that Paul's wife, whom he had married on the 12 March 1969, was not only his life partner, but his helpmate. Many people still thought of the ex-Beatles as individuals who could not possibly make music with lesser mortals, especially some unknown woman – a rather sexist attitude, on reflection – and these folk were stunned when the second so-called 'solo' album, *Ram*, was actually credited to Paul and Linda McCartney, with no apologies.

The standout track on the LP was 'Uncle Albert/Admiral Halsey', a marvellously complex production that went to No. 1 as a single in the United States. It was never issued as a 45 in the UK, which got 'Back Seat Of My Car'. McCartney put the omission down to his 'funky organisation', which wasn't 'that clued in to picking up tracks off albums', but the most important reason it wasn't a British single is that in 1971 it was considered unhip and unfair for major artists to release too many tracks from LPs. Nowadays, for commercial reasons alone, it is unthinkable that a proven hit song wouldn't be taken off an album.

Ram was a No. 1 on both sides of the Atlantic, but the press was apoplectic. One major review called it 'the nadir of rock'. Recently there has been considerable revisionism in the ranks, and the very publication that carried that notice now gives it four stars out of five. Other journals are also more generous in their estimation. What had happened was that *Ram* was the real confirmation from Paul McCartney that, to borrow John Lennon's words, 'the dream is over'. The Beatles revolutionised popular music and changed lifestyles. A man having fun down on the farm with his wife, his kids and a lot of animals wasn't going to alter society. The pop pundits, who longed for leadership, savaged McCartney to express their own sense of loss.

The man himself did not feel that emptiness. Far from it. As he put it, 'When you write millions of love songs, when you're finally in love, you'd like to write one for the person you're in love with.'

'My Love', written by Paul for Linda, had a four-week run on top of the American Hot 100 in June 1973. It also reached the British top ten. It was the first great worldwide success for Wings, the McCartney-led group whose first flights had been as turbulent as a plane trip with the seat belt sign on all the way. After the success of *McCartney* and *Ram*, and the international hit single 'Another Day', Paul had formed a new group and gone on the lowest of low-key tours. Wings even turned up unannounced at Nottingham University and asked if the students would fancy a gig. They most certainly did, and so was born a band. It was excruciating for McCartney having to fill a set without Beatle material, facing audiences who possibly expected and certainly wanted to hear the familiar standards.

It didn't help that the first few Wings' releases were ill-starred. *Wings Wild Life*, the late 1971 debut disc, was a take-off that resulted in a crash landing. Having heard that Bob Dylan had recorded an album in one take, Wings flew through one of their own in a fortnight. It sounded like it. A couple of songs, particularly 'Tomorrow', showed promise, but were unfinished. Paul admitted that sometimes the engineer didn't get the chance to achieve a proper sound balance. *Wild Life* remains the only Paul McCartney product to fall short of the British top ten album chart; it just got to No. 10 in America.

The band's singles start wasn't glamorous, either. 'Give Ireland Back To The Irish', an enraged reaction to the 'Bloody Sunday' killings in Londonderry, was banned by the BBC for being a political song and achieved McCartney's lowest chart placings to date in both the US and UK. 'I always used to think John's crackers doing all these political songs', Paul recalled. 'I understand he really feels deeply, so do I. But until the actual time when it is actually there on the doorstep, I always used to think it's still cool to not say anything about it, because it's not gonna sell anyway and no one's gonna be interested.' 'Give Ireland Back To The Irish' proved Paul's initial hunch was correct.

'Mary Had A Little Lamb' proved his first feeling incorrect. He thought there would be great public interest in hearing the full and authentic words to the famous nursery rhyme. There wasn't. When he made 'Hi Hi Hi' part of the double A-side of Wings' third single, he probably didn't realise it, too, would be banned by the BBC, for alleged references to drugs and sex. This only gave more airplay to the other side, 'C Moon', allowing a top ten placing at home as well as abroad.

With 'My Love' and the James Bond theme 'Live And Let Die', 1973 was a better year for Wings. But it took the album released that December to restore Paul McCartney's reputation. *Band On The Run* was a classic.

The first single from *Band On The Run* was 'Jet', though a preceding 45, 'Helen Wheels', named after the family Land Rover, was placed on the American LP to stimulate sales. 'Jet' was the offspring of a McCartney dog bought in a country petshop. The purchased pet, a brown

Labrador, would vault the wall around the family house in St John's Wood. Clearly, she had a consort, for one day she walked into the garage and had a litter of seven black puppies. 'Jet' was one of the pups.

After *Red Rose Speedway*, the album that included 'My Love' but was otherwise not special, *Band On The Run* was a revelation. It was rich with fully-developed rock numbers, well-produced pieces that showed in their changes of tempo and range of subject matter a confidence and accomplishment lacking in the two previous Wings albums.

This didn't say too much for the musicians who had been in Wings, because besides Denny Laine, they weren't on the album. Guitarist Henry McCullough had rowed with Paul, and drummer Denny Seiwell didn't want to go to Nigeria, where the set was to be recorded. They were the first of several Wings who flitted in and out, and to give them their credit it is not difficult to understand why. It had to be hard playing under the direction of a legendary musician who knew what he wanted and when he wanted it. Confined, contradicted, or unable to conform, the Wings went wayward. Only Denny Laine, who had immortalised himself with the lead vocal on The Moody Blues' 'Go Now', stayed in the unit for any length of time, lasting out the seventies, though the talented young guitarist Jimmy McCulloch might have stayed as long had he been able to adjust to his fame and control his consumption of drink. His unnecessary death was a true tragedy.

Band On The Run, made in Nigeria, featured only Paul, Linda, and Laine. Motivated by Stevie Wonder's drumming on his recent records, McCartney pounded the skins himself. The marvellous result restored him to the No. 1 position on both sides of the Atlantic. In addition to 'Jet', there was 'Drink To Me' a song written at the request of Dustin Hoffman, who was dining with the McCartneys and said he'd been moved by Pablo Picasso's last words, 'Drink to me, drink to my health, you know I can't drink any more'. Fans found 'Let Me Roll It' an affectionate tribute to John Lennon, even though Paul didn't intend it as such. And there was the imaginative title track, which when issued as a single went to No. 3 in Britain and No. 1 in America.

'Band On The Run' seemed a romantic notion that applied to Wings, recording abroad, having trouble maintaining a full quota of musicians, rebounding from pastings in the press and recovering from a drugs arrest. In fact it was based on a remark by George Harrison, who, frustrated at the one of many meetings designed to dissolve the Apple organisation, said 'If we ever get out of here'. McCartney picked up on his ex-partner's prison analogy and wrote 'Band On The Run'.

The circumstances that had seemed to make the title personally relevant would recur. Wings did record abroad again, beginning with

Nashville sessions in 1974, they did have a changing membership, and McCartney managed to get arrested for drugs again later in the decade, this time in Japan. But what distinguished the middle of the decade was that at least in commercial terms the band could do no wrong. Wings put together a string of eight consecutive top ten American hits, the longest string of its time. They followed *Band On The Run* with another international No. 1, *Venus And Mars*, featuring an exciting sax solo by Tom Scott on the chart-topping US single 'Listen To What The Man Said'. But even that success was dwarfed by a 1976 title that was the No. 1 hit of the year in *Billboard* magazine's year-end tabulation, 'Silly Love Songs'.

It is often said that if a person is criticised enough along certain lines, he or she will emphasise that part of his or her behaviour as a gesture of defiance, whether the accusation was accurate in the first place or not. Paul McCartney had been savaged in the seventies by some critics who relentlessly wrote that he produced 'silly love songs'. They may have seemed so to outsiders who didn't have a contented love life of their own, but that didn't make them silly. It's just that uncomplicated declarations of love and devotion, stated in an innocent and light-hearted form appropriate for the emotions themselves, have rarely been the stuff of classic pop. Rock audiences want the turmoil that reflects conflict and rebellion, the forces which gave birth to rock and roll and have motivated its best music ever since. McCartney was a heretic to this religion when he told the faithful he was happy.

He knew he was called on the critical carpet for writing twee twitterings. So he replied directly. In 'Silly Love Songs' he courageously confessed, and then said 'What's wrong with that?' This time there was no complaint, but instead a multi-million seller.

The song showed in a rather public way that McCartney was still sensitive to criticism, despite his historic accomplishments. He found great consolation in demonstrations of public affection, whether it came from an individual, such as the skier who while passing him on a slope yelled out 'Loved *Ram*, Paul' or the large audiences who sold out the 1976 Wings Over America tour, captured for posterity on a triple album that became No. 1 in the States. But the sales successes couldn't make him confident about the next release. That one was always untried, its reception always uncertain. He was not sure about the greeting a tribute to his Scottish homestead would receive, so he refrained from making it an A-side and made an up-tempo number called 'Girls' School' the other part of a double A-side, just in case. It was the most unnecessary precaution in British pop history. 'Mull Of Kintyre' was No. 1 for nine weeks over the Christmas of 1977, and became the first single to sell over two million copies in this country.

Denny Laine shared credit for the piece. It was typical of Paul's finest song-writing that on first hearing it sounded like a standard. Hadn't 'Mull Of Kintyre' been a traditional number? Melody was McCartney's greatest gift. When he was in fine form, his songs, no matter whether the lyric was brilliant or banal, were attractive to the widest range of listeners any pop writer has yet reached. Just as his best numbers have seemed timeless, they will prove to be so in the years to come.

'Mull Of Kintyre' replaced 'She Loves You' by The Beatles as Britain's all-time No. 1. Until 'Do They Know It's Christmas' sold over three million in 1984, 'Mull Of Kintyre' remained in front. But in America, it wasn't a hit at all. Paul's ploy of issuing a double A-side backfired. At the time of the record's release, the American charts carried an unusual number of ballads by female vocalists, led by Debbie Boone's long-running No. 1 'You Light Up My Life'. Programmers wanted a safe rocker, something to lift the listeners without losing them. An up-tempo tune by a star like McCartney was just what the radio stations wanted, and 'Girls' School' rather than 'Mull Of Kintyre' was played in the States. Because it wasn't very good, it didn't sell very well, and America missed McCartney's greatest hit, an unofficial national anthem for Scotland.

Record executives had further reason to tear out their hair when Paul refused to put 'Mull Of Kintyre' on his next album, *London Town*. Their position was that it would increase sales, possibly to a seven-figure sum. His stand, as eloquently phrased in 1979, was 'I just have to remember that this isn't a record retail store I'm running; this is supposed to be some kind of art. And if it doesn't fit in, it doesn't fit in.'

A track that did 'fit in' also stood out, a delightful ditty that proved another American No. 1, easing the pain of the miss of 'Mull'. Recorded aboard the motor yacht Fair Carol in the Record Plant Mobile Studio, anchored off the Virgin Islands, 'With A Little Luck' was vintage McCartney. It showed that he still had a great singing voice, one that could reach into the upper register without much obvious difficulty and one that could grow louder and louder without sign of strain. Paul cleverly kept from resorting to these strengths too often, so that when they were fielded they had great effect. He also never lost control of his voice, and in that self-control was contained a tension that might have been missing from the words.

One would have thought that with an artist of McCartney's stature that all his good material was widely well known. But this isn't the case. Sometimes there's been a good album track on an average album, that hasn't been heard since it wasn't a single. 'I'm Carrying' from *London Town* is an example. So is 'Arrow Through Me' out of *Back To*

The Egg, a top thirty entry in the US but never a 45 in the UK.

Then there's the unheard B-sides. In one case particularly, the second face was unjustly lost. 'Daytime Nightime Suffering' was originally going to be the A-side of 'Goodnight Tonight', a dance number recorded in 1978 that proved perfect for the disco boom of 1979. Just as he jittered over 'Mull Of Kintyre', McCartney wavered in his judgment, deciding to shelve the single. About a week later, he played both sides again and thought 'That's crazy, we've made it; it's stupid, why not put it out? Just because people are going to pan it.' The paranoia was unfounded. People didn't pan it. 'Goodnight Tonight' was hailed as a clever construction, an acceptable face of disco, and it became a worldwide winner. The American record company, Columbia, distributed review copies with the same song on both sides. It was terrified that if radio programmers heard 'Daytime Nightime Suffering', now the B-side, they would play that one, too, splitting airplay and perhaps damaging sales. So was lost one of McCartney's classiest cuts.

'Daytime Nightime Suffering' and 'Goodnight Tonight' were both left off *Back To The Egg*, Wings' 1979 release. This was extremely unfortunate, because they were both better than anything that *was* on the package. There were a few good tracks, such as 'Old Siam Sir', 'Arrow Through Me' and 'Getting Closer', but none were outstanding. *Back To The Egg* was the first Wings' album since 'Wild Life' not to produce a top ten single in either Britain or America. The difference was that no singles were released from *Wild Life*; for several months EMI and Columbia tried unsuccessfully to milk *Back To The Egg*.

Back To The Egg, indeed, back in 1980 to where he had been in 1970. Paul wished to issue another solo album, and *McCartney II* was the outcome of his labours. It resulted in one of the oddest chart coincidences of his career. 'Coming Up' shot to No. 2 in the British hit parade. But the American record company panicked upon hearing the gimmicky version, which had Paul's voice altered to sound like that of a mechanical Munchkin. Columbia were sure this disc would be greeted with derision in the United States, so they looked for another single. They didn't have far to search. There on the B-side of the single was the bonus track 'Coming Up (Live)', recorded by Wings in Glasgow in 1979. That rendition was pushed in the States, and became the band's last American No. 1.

It was ironic that Wings should be No. 1 in America at a time when they weren't a functioning unit. They were grounded for good in 1981. After the murder of John Lennon, Paul McCartney maintained a low public profile, for reasons that seemed as tasteful as they may have been cautious. Denny Laine, claiming that he wanted to be part of an active performing band, flew away.

The apparent lay-off didn't mean McCartney had been inactive. He'd been recording with George Martin, producer of The Beatle discs and Paul's 'Live And Let Die' theme. Martin proved to be the task-master the artist needed. Some of his lyrics had become uninteresting, clearly requiring more thought, and some of his songs, particularly on *McCartney II*, were either uninspired or unpolished. With a studio mentor he respected, McCartney could re-shape or discard material that didn't work. The eventual product, *Tug Of War*, proved that Paul didn't have to release an album every year to stay in the public eye and that hard work in the studio does pay dividends. *Tug Of War* was one of the outstanding albums of 1982, with several highlights. He faced up not just to the public expectation of a John Lennon tribute but the personal desire to do one with the beautiful 'Here Today', which achieved the difficult task of being moving without being mawkish. His funky workout with Stevie Wonder, 'What's That You're Doing', was full of fun, and their other collaboration, 'Ebony And Ivory', an international No. 1. It was a plea for interracial harmony that was loved by many and hated by some, who resented its simplistic presentation of a complex problem and the literal inaccuracy of the analogy with the piano keyboard: white and black keys side-by-side aren't in harmony at all. This critical carping didn't stop 'Ebony And Ivory' from being the most infectious single of the year. Even those who hated it couldn't stop humming it.

'Take It Away' proved a successful follow-up, an evocation of several aspects of the professional pop life. 'Tug Of War', the title track, may have been the best of the lot, a song full of wisdom and experience about the pushing and pulling that goes into almost every aspect of life. The press interpreted it as a song about Paul's relationships with his fellow former Beatles, especially John Lennon, and there's no doubt that some of that went into the song, because this piece seemed to encompass everything McCartney had lived through.

He keeps learning, keeps experimenting. After Stevie Wonder he collaborated with Michael Jackson, enjoying a six-week run at No. 1 in America with 'Say Say Say'. Paul recognised the importance of quality videos and won the first *Top of the Pops* award with what was voted the outstanding video of 1983, 'Pipes of Peace'. This clip helped the single of the same name become Paul's first solo No. 1.

It appears McCartney is anxious to move more into visual media, as evidenced by his film *Give My Regards to Broad Street*. Still, were he to call it quits tomorrow, his place in the pantheon of immortals would be secure. But it is exciting to realise that, if he retains his health as he has so far, his career is only half over.

Michael Jackson

I DON'T want to talk about the llama. You know, Louie the llama, who lives on the estate. I don't want to talk about the llama. I don't want to talk about the Perrier. You know, the mineral water he supposedly ordered to bathe in while staying in a London hotel during a water authority slowdown. I don't want to talk about the Perrier. And I certainly don't want to discuss the absurd rumours . . . that as a boy he was actually a midget, that as a man he's become a woman, that Diana Ross was his mother. I'm not going to discuss obviously false rumours. But that these stories exist, that people are interested in the bizarre and outrageous about him, are a reflection of the hysterically intense interest in him, interest generated by his charisma and his career. I do want to talk about him because he is the outstanding performer of the early eighties. As a singer and dancer, Michael Jackson *is* a thriller.

By the time their fifth son was born, Joe and Katherine Jackson had run out of exotic names. They'd used Sigmond, Toriano, Jermaine and Marlon on their first four boys. The child born on 29 August 1958 was more conventionally called Michael.

His mother insists that her oldest sons started making music at home when the television set broke down. Father Joe noticed something was going on when he realised one of them was using his guitar. He'd been in a group called The Falcons though now he was employed as a steelworker. Neighbourhood kids started noting the at-home rehearsals and threw stones through the windows. They would then shout criticisms through the smashed panes.

Michael joined his brothers when he was five. That year he sang 'Climb Every Mountain' from *The Sound Of Music* in his kindergarten class. The teacher cried, his fellow pupils gave him a standing ovation, and, as he remembered, he felt 'real good about the future'. *Ebony* magazine has reported that when his teacher asked him what three things he wished would happen, he wrote 'I would like to be a great entertainer . . . I want peace for the world and I'd like to own a mansion one day.'

111

When he was six Michael became the family lead singer. The group won several area talent contests, including one where they bested Deniece Williams, and recorded uneventfully for a local label, Steeltown. It is one of show business' many myths that Diana Ross introduced The Jackson Five to Motown. It was actually Gladys Knight who made the first recommendation and Joe Jackson himself who made contact. Once at Motown they let everybody know they were there with their very first single – 'I Want You Back'.

'I Want You Back' was the beginning of a historic string of hits. The first four Jackson Five singles all reached No. 1 on the *Billboard* Hot 100. No other act had debuted in such a fashion, and none has since. All four scaled the summit in 1970. In the thirty-year history of the charts, only Jimmy Dorsey, Bing Crosby, Elvis Presley and The Beatles had achieved as many as four No. 1s in a calendar year. Jermaine Jackson said the fabulous feat had been a goal of Motown head Berry Gordy. When the quintet first met Gordy, he told them he was going to launch them with three or four No. 1 records before anyone had a chance to see them perform. He assembled a songwriting team called The Corporation, consisting of Hal Davis, Fonce Mizell, Freddie Perren, Deke Richards and himself. Gordy went to the trouble of forming The Corporation because he realised that Motown needed a new young act. All his established stars were aging. Even Stevie Wonder was no longer 'Little'. To get the group additional attention he gave their first LP the title *Diana Ross Presents The Jackson Five*. The former lead singer of The Supremes was embarking on her own much-publicised solo career, and the connection could only help both parties. When the boys were featured on her TV special, the link between them became legend. By the end of 1970 The Jackson Five had been No. 1 in the United States for a total of ten weeks. 'I Want You Back' had been followed in rapid succession by 'ABC', 'The Love You Save' and 'I'll Be There'. The last song, the biggest hit of the lot, was the one on which they most sounded like a group, trading vocals to great effectiveness.

Listening to 'I'll Be There' is an unsettling experience when one considers the lead singer had just turned twelve. How could he sound so earnest about love and personal commitment when he could not possibly have experienced them? In retrospect Michael confessed he, too, was amazed at how his voice used to sound. But he had been singing for over six years already, and he'd grown up listening to the masters of rhythm and blues, not just to Tamla talents but to greats like Jackie Wilson and James Brown. When he won his record-breaking eight Grammy Awards in 1984, he brought the proceedings to a halt with an unexpected tribute to Jackie Wilson, the great artist of the fifties and sixties who had just passed away. Wilson, who made some of Berry Gordy's early song hits, had sung extremely emotionally and with great dexterity in the upper register. To this day Jackson, who can hit a low C, prefers to vocalise as a tenor because he knows it is a more popular and persuasive style.

Michael admired not just Jackie Wilson but several pioneering artists, including Chuck Berry, Ray Charles and Little Richard. He loved James Brown, and not just for the King of Soul's voice. Brown was the best dancer in popular music, an acknowledged influence on the stage movements of Mick Jagger. The young Jackson had watched him from the wings while on the same bill. 'I knew every turn, every move, every spin,' he told *Ebony*. 'Something is going on inside of him . . . natural talent . . . It's magic and when I'm up there, I feel the same way.'

Michael's multiple talents made him a natural choice to record as a solo artist. In 1971 The Jackson Five had two more major hits, 'Mama's Pearl' and 'Never Can Say Goodbye', and Michael had his first. 'Got To Be There', his premier performance, climbed to No. 4. The follow-up, a remake of Bobby Day's 1958 smash 'Rockin' Robin', matched the original's peak of No. 2. What was there left to achieve but a No. 1? Michael got it in 1972 with 'Ben', a beautiful ballad with a loving lyric by Don Black. How strange that it should be sung by a boy to a rat in a movie about rampaging rodents. One critic joked 'Trouble is, at his age, Michael Jackson won't be admitted to any cinema screening the movie!'

The teenager's first No. 1 seemed to herald chart success through the entire decade. But the hits dried up. From 1972 to 1975, their last years at Motown, The Jackson Five only made the top ten once in America, with 'Dancing Machine', while in Britain they hit it twice, first with 'Lookin' Through The Windows' and then with Jackson Browne's 'Doctor My Eyes'. Michael also ceased to be a chart force, though at least he had nabbed a bonus in Britain with Bill Withers' 'Ain't No Sunshine'. The launch of Jermaine as a teen idol had resulted in merely one hit, 'Daddy's Home', and that only in America. Motown had simply run out of ideas, energy or both when it came to dealing with the family. After the disintegration of The Corporation following the first few hits, no studio mentor could make the most of the young men's talents. And The Jacksons had other grievances, too. Whereas they'd once been thrilled to sing songs by top writers, they now felt frustrated they couldn't do their own material. Michael expressed his discomfort at having to sing other people's thoughts. The group reportedly were not allowed to play on their own records, though they did so on tour. And, according to writer Peter Benjaminson, they were on a low royalty rate of 2.7 per cent.

With the assistance of two co-managers, Joe Jackson and his sons took their act to Epic Records. Well, most of the act. Jermaine had married Berry Gordy's daughter Hazel and stayed with Motown. Little brother Randy took his place, but the fivesome couldn't call themselves The Jackson Five any more. Motown retained the rights to the name. Epic teamed The Jacksons with Kenny Gamble and Leon Huff, the writer-producers whose Philadelphia International label had dominated soul music in the early seventies. The collaboration did yield The Jacksons' first British No. 1, 'Show You The Way To Go', and an American top ten winner, 'Enjoy Yourself'. But from this point on Jacksons albums were merely collections of predominantly up-tempo tracks that contained a couple of hits, most notably the 1979 multi-million seller 'Shake Your Body'. The records that were important events were Michael Jackson's solos such as 'Don't Stop Till You Get Enough', which had one of the most curious beginnings in pop history. The singer's introductory whoop was actually the climax of a spoken prologue on the longer album track. Single buyers had no idea they were joining the song in progress. This quirky marketing had been used successfully by Motown nine years earlier when it began the single of the Supremes' 'Stoned Love' in the middle of a sentence of the full version. Still, who knew? Who cared? 'Don't Stop Till You Get Enough' was an American No. 1. It was a tremendous start to a stint on Epic and a marvellous introduction to the 1979 album *Off The Wall*.

The LP itself was the world's first glimpse at an adult Michael Jackson. Father Joe's co-managers decided to dispense with the cute kid image with which their client had been burdened. They dressed Michael in a tuxedo for the cover photograph to let the world know he'd arrived as a sophisticated grown-up. Jackson didn't want to appear completely conformist so had the sleeve artists give him glowing white socks.

That small but telling touch has been typical of Michael's moves in recent years. He surrounds himself with the finest supporting squad in the business and adds the simple element that has tremendous visual impact. The Adam Ant-cum-Sgt Pepper jacket, the single rhinestone-encrusted white glove, a brooch he wore when decorations were in fashion, all have had stunning impact. It doesn't take much energy to wear them, but it takes instinct and thought to know which of many possible accoutrements to put on.

The suddenly suave Michael Jackson hadn't finished his chart-topping with 'Don't Stop Till You Get Enough'. The next release in America, 'Rock With You', was an even bigger hit, standing astride the Hot 100 for a full four weeks in the winter of 1980.

When 'Rock With You' made it two No. 1s in a row from *Off The*

Wall, it was obvious something special was happening. What had happened was that Michael Jackson had formed a perfect partnership with producer Quincy Jones. It was one of those rare relationships in show business: when two great talents team together and become even greater than they are alone. Quincy Jones had been great for at least two decades. He had recorded such immortals as Count Basie, Ray Charles and Frank Sinatra. But in 1977, at the age of forty-four, he established a special affinity with the boy less than half his age.

Jones and Jackson met making *The Wiz*, a big-budget Hollywood musical that turned out to be a turkey. The signs had been good. The all-black version of *The Wizard Of Oz* had been a hit on Broadway, thanks in part to the electrifying performance of new star Stephanie Mills as Dorothy, portrayed in the original film by Judy Garland. Michael Jackson had seen the show seven times and was delighted to appear as the scarecrow in the new motion picture. Quincy Jones was the musical director. The veteran music-maker told *Billboard* that in rehearsals Michael consistently mispronounced the name Socrates 'Socrate-ease and nobody would correct him. When they took a break, I took him to the corner and said, "Michael, it's Sock-ra-tease." We kind of looked at each other and we felt a real strong bond . . . Our relationship began to grow from that point.'

The man who was unintimidated by the teen star's fame proved a perfect partner in the recording studio. On their most successful tracks, good pop songs are given life and animation that survive repeated hearings. They don't attempt ballads often, but the one they did on *Off The Wall* was a beauty. When Michael sang 'She's Out Of My Life', he cried. When he tried again, he cried again. Finally Quincy decided to leave the break-up on the record. The tears of his track made 'She's Out Of My Life' grimly gripping.

The song was the fourth and final top ten single from *Off The Wall* in both America and Britain. No other album by a solo artist had ever yielded so many top tenners. The group Fleetwood Mac had found four such singles in their set *Rumours*. Jackson's sequence of smashes was 'Don't Stop Till You Get Enough', 'Rock With You', 'Off The Wall' and 'She's Out Of My Life'. With so many hits in heavy radio rotation for nearly a year, it was inevitable the album from which they came would benefit. *Off The Wall* sold over eight million copies, and Michael Jackson was back on top of the music business as he had been ten years previous.

The lesson was not lost at Motown. The company had retained the rights to repackage its Jackson Five material, and did so on several occasions in generally tasteful fashion. In 1981, when no new solo releases were scheduled because the group was concentrating on its

Triumph album, Motown reissued 'One Day In Your Life', a single that had failed to chart on its initial issue six years before. Now it was Michael's first British No. 1, proving that there was gold in the Motown vaults. So there proved to be again in 1984, when the vintage 'Farewell My Summer Love' reached the top ten. Both second servings did poorly in the United States, where radio resists rehashes.

Michael could hardly have cared that 'One Day In Your Life' didn't succeed in the States, but he cared very much when *Off The Wall* received only one Grammy Award in the 1981 ceremonies. Even that was in a confining Rhythm and Blues category. 'It bothered me,' he admitted. 'I cried a lot. My family thought I was going crazy because I was weeping so much about it. Quincy said not to worry about it.'

Jones got Jackson out of his funk by pointing out that the enjoyment he had obviously brought millions of people was his real reward. Together, with the resource of a reported $750,000, they painstakingly assembled their next co-production, *Thriller*. The title tune was written by Rod Temperton, an Englishman who had first come to public attention penning hits for Heatwave. Temperton proved as terrific a teammate for Jones as a songwriter as Jackson was as an artist. He provided successes for several stars, but his style especially suited Michael. Temperton had three songs on both *Off The Wall* and *Thriller*, including the two title tracks and 'Rock With You'. He was an indispensable part of the history-making team.

The first the world heard of *Thriller* was 'The Girl Is Mine', a duet with Paul McCartney. It was neither man's best work, and indeed the dynamic duet they cut for McCartney's *Pipes Of Peace* album, 'Say, Say, Say', was far superior. But Epic Records had noted and wanted to exploit international interest in Jackson, and felt the relationship with the former Beatle was a way to do it. The single didn't hurt anybody's career, reaching the top ten on both sides of the Atlantic, but it gave many auditors a false impression of *Thriller*. Several CBS executives commented privately that the new album was not as good as the last. They were to happily eat their words when the next single from it, 'Billie Jean', was a worldwide No. 1 starting the popular hysteria over the *Thriller* album. Seven cuts became top ten singles in America, a new record. One could spend minutes reciting records set by *Thriller*, but the big one is that it had sold approximately thirty-six million copies by the end of the first half of 1984, surpassing the previous best-selling LP, *Saturday Night Fever*, by about ten million. Jackson wasn't just a gifted singer and songwriter. Those who marvelled at his ability to turn on the spot when a child star now saw a fully-fledged Terpsichorean who won the praises of even Fred Astaire. Michael's dance routine to 'Billie Jean' electrified studio and television audiences at

Motown's 25th Anniversary celebration, and helped the broadcast win an Emmy Award. He himself won eight Grammies in 1984, the highest for any artist in one year. 'Beat It' was Record of the Year, *Thriller* Album of the Year, but the award he said meant the most to him was the Best Children's Recording, his reading of *E.T.* made in conjunction with Quincy Jones.

Michael also won awards and set records in a new field, promotional videos. Since the arrival of MTV in the United States in 1981, the trade had been waiting for the first great video artist. Jackson's dancing and charisma helped make 'Billie Jean', 'Beat It', and 'Say, Say, Say' classic clips, and the videocassette *The Making of Michael Jackson's Thriller* became the bestseller in that configuration's short history.

Michael is a devout Jehovah's Witness. The world worshipped at *his* altar. *Time* magazine ran a cover story without an interview. He had wisely stopped giving them because he invariably came across as being either immature or foolish. Television networks ran details of his 1984 tour with The Jacksons on their news bulletins. And the crazies came out of the closet. Michael's new manager Frank Dileo related that one entrepreneur requested the rights to promote a Michael Jackson concert in outer space.

Fame is the reaction of other people. To look at what they are reacting to is to give insight to the Michael Jackson product. Visually, the artist has altered his appearance surgically, cosmetically and decoratively to seem racially and sexually neutral . . . a universal man. His disarming innocence and sincere religious beliefs make him lovable and safe. His multiple talents, in song, with dance and on the screen, make him an entertainment phenomenon. Unlike his predecessors as the biggest thing in the business, Elvis Presley and The Beatles, Jackson does not yet have social importance. He doesn't change lives by influencing behaviour or beliefs. He is, quite simply, a great performer; in Berry Gordy's opinion, the greatest alive.

When he takes his place in history, there will be outstanding records and visuals left to enjoy. And that thirty-six million plus sales figure of *Thriller*. Who will ever beat it?

Joe Jackson

IMAGINE A concert where the artist gives the audience its first glimpse of his current hit ... because he's refused to make a video. Where the artist performs his first hit in a completely different style than on the record. Where the artist brings them to their feet with an exciting version of his biggest hit ... then ends with a low-key piece. Where the artist thanks the crowd for its support during the last few years then tells them he won't be touring again in the foreseeable future. Imagine Joe Jackson.

Joe Jackson, the most independent pop star of the early eighties, had the rare good fortune of having a hit single and album with his first releases. The hard work that won him those successes began several years previously. While a teenager he studied for three years at the Royal Academy of Music and played in the National Youth Jazz Orchestra. He was the pianist in the short-lived groups Edward Bear and Arms and Legs. In his hometown of Portsmouth he worked as musical director of the Playboy Club, where he met a duo he briefly assisted, the *Opportunity Knocks* winners Coffee and Cream.

Jackson reflected on the value of this training when speaking to *Trouser Press* magazine. 'The Royal Academy of Music was probably one of the least useful things I've done in my career as a musician,' he said. 'I learned more having to back singers and read charts, thinking how to keep a pub full of drunken morons entertained for two hours and not be fired at the end of the evening.'

But Joe didn't leave it *all* behind when he signed with A&M Records in 1978. One member of his band, bassist Graham Maby, had been with him in Arms and Legs, and has stayed with him ever since through the many and sundry versions of the Joe Jackson band. The first incarnation, with guitarist Gary Sanford and drummer Dave Houghton, recorded an album's worth of demos that caught the fancy of A&M executive David Kershenbaum. He produced Joe Jackson's first album, the 1979 issue *Look Sharp!* One standout cut 'Sunday

Papers', chosen as a single, was a bitingly bitter satire on a British institution, trashy tabloids, and on the people who read them. 'Is She Really Going Out With Him' and 'One More Time' were also exciting singles, providing a no-nonsense perspective on love. In 'Fools In Love', a tender tune prettified an insightful lyric. But at first none of the songs were hits. It took success abroad to get Britain interested in its own son.

American radio had shown little interest in punk, terrified that its shrill sounds would drive away listeners and hence alienate advertisers. Any new late seventies act who performed tunefully and professionally had a far better chance of exposure. And Joe Jackson had a strange coincidence working in his favour. Baseball's most famous scandal had been the case of the 'Black Sox', members of the Chicago White Sox who accepted bribes to throw a championship series. One of the stars of the team was 'Shoeless' Joe Jackson. After hearing of the charges against his idol, a young fan approached Jackson and uttered the now famous line 'Say it ain't so, Joe'. Joe remained silent. He couldn't say it wasn't so.

Now, sixty years later, here was a modern-day Joe Jackson, whose first album cover bore a photo of the artist from the knees down. He wasn't shoeless. He was wearing gleaming shoes – white shoes. It was a great talking point, and it seemed a clever visual pun. The only thing that ruined the story was that Joe Jackson had never heard of his baseball namesake. But 'Shoeless' Joe had helped get some valuable attention for *Look Sharp!* and its first single, 'Is She Really Going Out With Him?' The latter entered the America Hot 100 in June 1979, and rose to No. 21. As has often happened with records ranging from 'Fool' by Chris Rea to 'Roxanne' by Jackson's A&M labelmates Police, success across the Atlantic rebounded back to Britain, and Joe had a home hit in August.

Critics in the UK compared him to another recently emerged soloist, Elvis Costello. Both were supposedly angry young men and both didn't visually fit the pop mould. The latter point was undeniably true. Jackson was well over six feet tall, exceedingly slim and prematurely balding. But the 'angry young man' label annoyed him. As he later recalled, 'It never made sense to me. I get angry sometimes, like anyone else. How can I be angry all the time?' The Costello critique got under his skin, and he was at first quoted calling the latter-day Elvis 'totally obnoxious' and asserting that the only way he would want to meet him was at gunpoint. But later he mellowed, shrugged off the comparison, and expressed admiration for his fellow artist. He added tellingly, 'People really must have more respect for my intelligence than to think that I would deliberately rip people off.' Such fraud was obviously a subject to which Joe had devoted thought. The title track of his second LP, *I'm The Man*, was explicitly about a con artist who anticipated and created public appetites for worthless fads. Jackson had been in a shop that sold both John Travolta and punk key rings, and he wondered if both markets were being exploited by the same manufacturer.

'I'm The Man' was both delightful and disastrous. As a comment on artificially inflated mass demand for nearly valueless objects, it was a caustic comment on capitalism. As a commercial choice for another hit single, it was a failure. It was quite simply too loud and too close to punk to win widespread radio play in either the US or UK. This was not a subject that caused the artist himself much lost sleep. As he once explained it, no act can be certain of having a hit with a given record. Therefore he must make the work that satisfied himself and at least guarantee that success. To have to live for the rest of his life with a compromise that failed would be a terrible burden.

Here is where Joe Jackson has been uncommonly heroic in his career, always moving in the direction his artistic temperament takes him regardless of the possible commercial consequences. It's an admirable trait in an industry that always wants more of what it has just had if what it has just had has paid the bills.

Jackson has been fortunate in his stance in not only having a sympathetic manager but a co-operative record company. As he has publicly admitted, it may not be fashionable to acknowledge that one's label has been consistently supportive, but A&M Records backed Jackson on even what may have seemed his strangest decisions. And, like a fairy tale, there was always a happy ending. 'I'm The Man' may have stiffed as a single, but a subsequent release from the same album gave Joe Jackson his first top ten hit.

'It's Different For Girls' reached the top five in the winter of 1980. No one was more surprised than the artist himself. Joe Jackson had considered it too slow and subtle to chart, but A&M had insisted it could be a hit. When they were proved correct, he threw up his hands and allowed the company to choose future singles from albums. He was too close to the project to know which piece would be most commercial.

At this time the Joe Jackson band was one of the leading live attractions in pop music. By now firmly familiar with the material, they always delivered energetic and exciting renditions of the songs, and Joe's live persona was unique. He quite willingly replied to comments from the audience, sometimes calling a concert-goer's remark 'stupid', despairing at the inevitable clamour for his hits, and at one show at the Palladium in New York pouring beer over a troublesome patron.

Instead of taking offence and picking a fight, the wet watcher lifted his arms in triumph, as if he'd been singled out for special treatment from his hero. Jackson seemed to walk a tightrope on stage, risking a riot that never came. As long as he made the music they wanted to hear, audiences didn't mind being barracked by the star. Perhaps they sensed Joe's unexpected affection. If he really hated them, he asked, why would he do long sets?

Some numbers on the group's repertoire wouldn't fit on the third album, so they were released on one 45 to 'get them out of the way', as Joe phrased it. The A-side he wanted to 'get out of the way' unfortunately 'got away', but it remains a fine version of a great song, Jimmy Cliff's reggae classic 'The Harder They Come'.

In 1980 Joe tried many different approaches to his work. He produced his third album, *Beat Crazy*, himself, without the aid of David Kershenbaum. In the video for 'Mad At You', a single from the album, he portrayed not only the lead character but his wife. A rejection of sexual stereotypes was also the topic of the track 'Fit', partly inspired by a transsexual friend rejected by the gay community as a transvestite. Jackson tried to take a stand against racism in the same song, a subject on his mind because his girlfriend of the time was black. On the song 'Pretty Boys' he roasted record companies and television producers who give exposure to brainless but attractive youths rather than talented but unsexy musicians. Another number, 'Battleground', was dedicated to the black poet Linton Kwesi Johnson. A very ambitious project, *Beat Crazy* turned out to be too much to take on. As the liner notes confessed, 'This album represents a desperate attempt to make some sense of Rock and Roll. Deep in our hearts, we knew it was doomed to failure. The question remains: Why did we try?'

Beat Crazy drove Joe Jackson crazy. Running in and out of the control room and lacking someone to exchange ideas with proved exhausting and unsatisfying. Joe learned that in future he should work with a producer. Even more unhappy was the disintegration of the band that followed. His career on a downturn and suffering from glandular fever, Jackson was cheered by listening to tapes of forties artists like Louis Jordan and Cab Calloway. It was while sick that he got a healthy idea: 'Jumping Jive'.

'Jumping Jive' was originally popularised by one of its co-writers, Cab Calloway. It was Calloway and other jump blues artists of the forties who lifted Joe Jackson out of his personal low and inspired him to assemble his own group to perform their material four decades later. Jackson was particularly fond of Louis Jordan, nicknamed 'King of the Jukeboxes' at a time when the jukebox was the major exposure recorded music had. Jordan's humorous stories of troubles and traditions were played by a jump band in a style that clearly preceded rock and roll. The single greatest influence on Chuck Berry's story-telling lyric style was Louis Jordan. Many of the tunes performed by Joe Jackson's jazz band had been in Jordan's repertoire. They formed the basis of an exhilarating set that gave showgoers in the UK and US some of the best fun they'd ever had at a pop concert.

The album of the material was called simply *Joe Jackson's Jumping Jive*, because the leader wanted his fans to know he was involved but that it wasn't a new album of new numbers. The only thing 'new' about these old tunes was that Jackson lengthened some of the instrumental sections. The original recordings had to fit on 78 rpm discs, and the solos were brief. *Jumping Jive* was, as Jackson confirmed, a 'total sidestep' in his career. Some commentators thought it might be suicidal, but it enhanced rather than detracted from Jackson's reputation as an eclectic artist. Some purists sneered it was an outrage he should draw large crowds when Louis Jordan played to pitifully small audiences just before his death. Jackson countered that he was happy to introduce thousands of young people to Jordan's music, and that neither he nor they could be blamed that they had not attended performances that took place before their birth. An inevitable question at each Jumping Jive gig was: what will Joe do next? He wasn't saying, but he knew. He had already started writing some of the songs for his next album.

In 1982 Joe Jackson released the best work of his career to date, the album *Night And Day*. The LP was inspired by its maker's residence in New York City where, he said, he felt more at home than any place else on the globe. Considering himself a night person, he was particularly drawn to the city's night life. Authentic jazz and salsa artists seen regularly in New York hardly ever appeared in Britain, and Joe feasted on this musical fare. *Night And Day* incorporated funk, jazz and salsa elements in an album that captured the feel of living in the Big Apple. It was cleverly divided into a 'Night' side and a 'Day' face. Unlike what one might have expected, with slow material for night and up-tempo for the day, patterns were reversed. The faster numbers were linked together on the 'Night' side, and as one might have a continuous array of sounds in the city that never sleeps. The 'Day' material comprised ballads to relax and recover by, songs like 'Breaking Us In Two', an American top twenty hit, and 'Real Men', an Australian top ten winner.

'Real Men' was a particular gem. Jackson observed the state of play in the sexual games men play with women and each other. Are the real men the ones who treat their women roughly or with tenderness? What about the reversal of male stereotypes, where large segments of the gay community dressed as tough guys à la Village People, and straight men wore make-up and dyed their hair? It was one of the most perceptive songs Jackson had ever written. As he pointed out, it took him twice his normal count of words to tell the tale. He reached another lyrical peak with 'Steppin' Out', which won a Grammy Award nomination for Record of the Year, and earned top ten placings on both sides of the Atlantic. *Night And Day* was the bestselling album of Joe Jackson's career.

Interest in his next work was higher than ever before. How ironic, then, that hardly anybody heard it. Like many successful pop writers, Joe Jackson was asked to score a motion picture. His film was *Mike's Murder*, written, produced and directed by James Bridges. With box-office favourite Debra Winger as star the movie seemed guaranteed large paid attendance figures. But things went terribly wrong. The film tested badly and was drastically recut. Much of Joe Jackson's music went the way of the deleted footage. What remained had to compete with new music composed by John Barry, who hardly shared Jackson's style.

Mike's Murder was seen by only a small number of filmgoers in the United States. Debra Winger was so upset she vowed to form her own production company. For Joe Jackson the consequence was an album very few of his own fans know about. 'Memphis', the single from the album, was lucky to stagger into the bottom part of the *Billboard* Hot 100. Fortunately, another success was not far away. Jackson has calculated that he is only capable of writing between ten and twelve decent songs per year. The 1983 ration appeared on the 1984 release *Body And Soul*, recorded in a stone and wood hall in New York City. The reason for using the former Masonic Lodge, often used for classical recordings, was that both Jackson and co-producer David Kershenbaum wanted to capture a live sound generally missing in modern music. They managed to complete the entire LP in five weeks, the equivalent of running a four minute mile by current recording standards. Kershenbaum had rejoined Joe for *Night And Day*. Now, with *Body And Soul*, it became apparent that he was the perfect partner for Jackson. Somehow he best brought the potential of the songs on to tape. Kershenbaum had co-produced all of Jackson's hits: 'Is She Really Going Out With Him?', 'It's Different For Girls', 'Real Men', 'Steppin' Out', 'Breaking Us In Two', and now the American top twenty success 'You Can't Get What You Want (Till You Know What You Want)'.

The last title seemed a sentiment applicable to Joe Jackson's own career. He always conceived his goal and then achieved it, rather than stumbling directionless through a career and missing opportunities for self-fulfillment. He conducted his career as he felt correct, not how it should be done for financial reasons. If he had to change the musical styling of 'Is She Really Going Out With Him?' to retain interest in the song, he would make it an a cappella number or play it with piccolo, accordion, violin and tambourine. Better to be excited about a concert selection than to walk through a lifeless version of a single. When he felt that the music industry's obsession with videos had gotten out of hand, he wrote an open letter to major publications. In the spring of 1984 both *Billboard* and *Variety* published his criticisms at length. It couldn't have been lost on readers of the article that 'You Can't Get What You Want' had reached No. 15 without benefit of a video on MTV. Although a tour is, like a video, considered necessary to pro-mote album sales, Jackson stunned his followers by announcing both on stage and in print that he is tired of the international circuit and will not go on long roadtrips for some time to come. These are all parts of a picture of pop's most unpredictable star. When once asked what he was going to do next, he replied 'It's not too soon to know, but it's too soon to tell.' That's a good attitude. It asserts the freedom of the artist in the face of business pressures and show business convention. It helps make Joe Jackson a real artist and a real man.

Bobby Darin with his wife Sandra Dee

Bobby Darin

BOB DYLAN first won widespread public acclaim in 1963. A friend was appalled when the singer complained he couldn't walk down the street without being recognised. He asked Dylan, 'Do you think you're Bobby Darin?' It wasn't a ridiculous remark. Bobby Darin had scored nine top ten hits in five years and was one of the highest paid live entertainers in show business. But he was best known for having the largest ego in popular music. He'd announced his intention to be the biggest thing in show biz by the time he was twenty-five, a legend at thirty. If Bob Dylan was really looking for a model of stardom, he needn't look far from the spelling of his own name. Change a few letters and there he was, starring at the Copacabana and releasing five feature films in one year. There was Bobby Darin.

Walden Robert Cassotto was born on 14 May 1936. His father had died several months before. Young Cassotto's mother was so poor that during the first year of his life the boy had to sleep in a drawer in a dresser. Walden spent a great deal of time on his own, learning to play piano, guitar and drums. After doing well at the Bronx High School of Science and spending a year at Hunter College he terminated his education. Cassotto wanted to be an actor, and no university was going to get him a part. The young Italian-American anglicised his name by looking in the local phone book. He liked the look of Darin and became Bobby Darin, although a more colourful story has him spotting a partially unlit sign at a Mandarin Chinese restaurant – the 'm', 'a' and 'n' had burned out, leaving 'Darin'. He joined a troupe of travelling players and landed his first role as an Indian chief.

When his acting attempts led nowhere, Bobby started writing jingles and songs. One tune he wrote with his friend Don Kirshner so impressed Connie Francis' manager George Scheck that Scheck landed Darin a disc deal with Decca. Four singles were released and all were flops, even though Darin had significant television exposure in 1956, including appearances on the Tommy Dorsey and Jackie Gleason pro-

127

grammes. Fortunately for Darin, Don Kirschner was able to convince Atlantic Records executives Herb Abramson and Ahmet Ertegun that he deserved another chance. They signed him to their Atco label, but three more stiff singles followed. Abramson and Ertegun began to lose interest in the Bronx boy. Their partner Jerry Wexler was never that crazy about him anyway. Sensing that his contract might be terminated, Darin paid a personal visit to Ertegun and Wexler, giving a performance of a new song right in the office. Ertegun thought the tune had a chance, and allowed the brash youngster an hour and a half studio time in which he cut four sides, including a song that had one of the most unlikely origins in pop history – 'Splish Splash'. Bobby Darin had been at the home of rising New York disc jockey Murray 'the K' Kaufman. When Darin claimed he could write a song about any subject, Kaufman replied 'OK, wise guy. Write me a song that has "splish splash I was takin' a bath" as one of the lines.' Bobby went to the piano and did it. At least, that was Darin's version of the story. Other accounts had him collaborating with Kaufman's mother or wife, and it was the mother, Jan Murray, who actually shared composer credit.

Darin and Kaufman didn't only collaborate on 'Splish Splash'. When the singer had feared Atco would drop him he had made a record for Brunswick under the name The Ding Dongs. Murray Kaufman supervised the session. When Ertegun and company heard the disc – 'Early In The Morning' – they were disturbed. The similarity between Darin and The Ding Dongs was too great to be a coincidence. It might not have mattered if they were going to drop the artist, but 'Splish Splash' was breaking out across America. When Darin admitted he was The Ding Dongs, Atlantic threatened to sue Brunswick. The latter company surrendered the recording, but sensing the song was a hit had one of their star acts cut it immediately. So it came to be that Buddy Holly recorded a song by the unknown writer Bobby Darin.

The composer wasn't unknown for long. 'Splish Splash' was released on Atlantic Atco's label, entered the Hot 100 in June 1958, and quickly climbed to No. 3. Brunswick rush-released Buddy Holly's version of 'Early In The Morning', forcing Atco to go into battle. Since Darin was already in the charts they had to release his original under a different name: The Rinky Dinks. The unprecedented sight of a chart battle between Buddy Holly and The Rinky Dinks ended with the final tally Holly 32, The Dinks 24. In this kind of competition, the lower number wins. In the course of one summer Bobby Darin had both made his top ten debut and bested one of rock and roll's biggest stars. Of course Holly wasn't overly worried. He was in the charts at the same time with The Crickets' number, 'Think It Over'. Bobby Darin collectors today value most highly the pressings of 'Early In The

Morning' with the silly names. A near-mint pressing by The Ding Dongs will now fetch over $40. The Rinky Dinks go for $10, and Bobby Darin with The Rinky Dinks for a mere $4.

Both 'Splish Splash' and 'Early In The Morning' owed obvious debts to Negro rock and roll pioneers, and Darin confirmed he'd been influenced by Ray Charles, Fats Domino and Little Richard. When listening to Bobby's early hits it's not difficult to identify the inspiration. Fats Domino was the obvious source for the style on Darin's second top tenner. 'Queen Of The Hop' scored in the autumn of 1958, after both 'Splish Splash' and 'Early In The Morning' had run their course. But though the gap in release dates was about four months, 'Queen Of The Hop' had been recorded at the same session as 'Splish Splash'. Two million sellers each written in less than an hour were recorded together in less than ninety minutes.

Record hops were a phenomenon with which Bobby Darin was well acquainted. Even before 'Splish Splash' he'd become a good friend not only of Murray 'the K' Kaufman but America's most influential disc jockey, Dick Clark. The Philadelphia-based Clark had found national fame with his television show *American Bandstand*, and Bobby was always willing to work with Clark at less glamorous record hops as well as on TV. At record hops star DJs would spin hit discs and artists would drop by to mime to their latest release. Clark credited Darin with a dynamic stage performance even when he was only lip-synching. The men became firm friends, so much so that when Clark received a prime time Saturday evening slot very similar to today's *Top of the Pops* Darin sent him an opening night gift – a box of gold spray painted horse manure. It was just one example of his curious cockiness. Before the release of 'Splish Splash' he told Clark's bouncer, Ed McAdam, 'After it hits, you come to work for me; you can be in charge of keeping the thousands of screaming girls at bay. The surplus'll all be yours and I can assure you it'll be more exciting than fighting off the occasional grandmother this one attracts.'

When he had won his first two top ten hits Darin realised he wanted fame beyond the confines of rock and roll. He was a great admirer of Frank Sinatra and, like that long-lasting star, wanted to win the widest possible audience. He used strings instead of saxophones on his next release, and demanded thirty-two takes before the elements of the record fused properly. One of those parts was piano. 'Dream Lover' was based on a chord progression Darin had discovered at the keyboard. The pianist on the session was Neil Sedaka.

'Dream Lover' was a spectacular success, reaching No. 2 in America and No. 1 in Britain. Darin decided to go for broke and record an album of pop standards in a big band style, aiming right at the adult market. The first track on side one of *That's All* was 'Mack The Knife'. The standout song from *The Threepenny Opera* had been a hit for six different artists in 1956. Darin based his reading on Louis Armstrong's version.

When he informed *American Bandstand* he was going to release 'Mack The Knife', Dick Clark told him he was crazy and producer Deke Hayward advised that if he wanted to turn his career into chopped liver, so be it. But Darin knew what he was doing. He was taking the kids with him and adding their parents to his fan following. 'Mack The Knife' was one of the biggest hits of all-time, reaching No. 1 in America for nine weeks and Britain for two. Even today it remains one of the most powerful performances in pop.

'Mack The Knife' was America's No. 1 record for most of the autumn of 1959. Coming on top of 'Dream Lover', it made Bobby Darin the star of the year. He won Grammy Awards for Best New Artist and Record of the Year ('Mack The Knife'). The sixties seemed his. He had managed to do something almost impossible, to both rouse rockers and please parents. The generation gap had been an abyss in pop music since the advent of rock and roll, and Bobby Darin seemed the ideal artist to appeal to both sides. He was also the first to share the credit for 'Mack The Knife', a public act of generosity that Dick Clark considered typical of the humanity that lay beneath the humbug. Darin singled out band leader and arranger Richard Wess as the leading contributor to the single's success. Wess' style can be heard throughout the album *That's All*, which led off with 'Mack The Knife' and continued with 'Beyond The Sea'. This second song was an English adaptation of a 1945 French hit, 'La Mer' by Charles Trenet. One can easily hear stylistic similarities in the arrangements of 'Mack The Knife' and 'Beyond The Sea', the crisp swinging brass and the heavy drum emphases. More than ever, Darin pays homage to Sinatra. One can imagine Fabulous Frank singing the song almost identically.

'Beyond The Sea' was another top ten winner for Bobby Darin on both sides of the Atlantic. He was the brightest new star in show business, and he lived the life of a star, romancing leading female singer Connie Francis and glamour girl Joanne Campbell, who found record fame of her own with her novelty hit '(I'm the Girl on) Wolverton Mountain'. (Joanne's most bizarre outing was a title based on a TV commercial 'Mother Please I'd Rather Do It Myself'.)

The ultimate dream for the gossip pages was Darin's marriage in 1960 to the film star Sandra Dee. The ultimate venue for a pop singer of that time was New York's legendary nightclub the Copacabana. At the age of twenty-three, Bobby was the youngest act ever to headline there, at least until the nineteen-year-old Paul Anka achieved the feat later in the year. By that time Darin had become the youngest artist to ever have his own television special. Besides, a live album of his Copa performance became his third consecutive top ten LP. In the pre-Beatle era, only a handful of rock and roll stars sold albums as well as singles.

Was Darin still a rock and roller? If not, what was he? He continued releasing jazzed up versions of pop standards, but without band leader Richard Wess the arrangements lacked zest. Even more alarming, Darin no longer seemed to be singing the song but rather imposing his own personality on it. 'Clementine' and 'Won't You Come Home Bill Bailey' both charted, but in lower positions than the recent hits. Some American DJs turned over 'Bill Bailey' and started playing 'I'll Be There'. This minor hit was covered by Gerry and The Pacemakers and became a top twenty hit for them in both the US and UK in 1965, the greatest success for a Darin song performed by someone other than Bobby.

Bobby Darin the songwriter was at work in 1960 and '61 on music for films more than his own albums. Indeed, he met Sandra Dee in Italy on the set of a film for which he'd written the music. His score for the motion picture *Come September* resulted in not only a fine hit vocal, 'Multiplication', but an instrumental title theme that managed to crawl into the British top fifty. The artist credit read 'The Bobby Darin Orchestra', though there was no such permanent group.

Darin worked extremely hard now that he finally had his Hollywood chance. In 1961 he acted so consistently that the following year he had important roles in five feature films, a record at the time. The 1962 release *Captain Newman, M.D.* won him a Best Supporting Actor Oscar nomination.

With this concentration on films, his records inevitably suffered. An anthology album with a few moments of spoken commentary titled *The Bobby Darin Story* was followed by *Love Swings*, a set of standards like 'The More I See You' and 'It Had To Be You' that alarmingly peaked at No. 92. *Twist With Bobby Darin*, a set of previously released tracks Atco thought suitable for twisting, failed to cash in on the dance craze as hoped. *Bobby Darin Sings Ray Charles*, a well-meant but unmemorable tribute to one of Darin's heroes, fared worst of the lot. Bobby's presence on the airwaves was maintained in 1961 by more standards, most successfully by 'You Must Have Been A Beautiful Baby' and the British No. 2, 'Lazy River'.

He had tried to do too much. He could not be a teen idol, a big band singer, a nightclub draw and a film star all at once. This wouldn't bother most artists, who would be happy to be one of those things. But Darin wanted to be everything. Even for a form known for hype,

Darin's LP liner notes were breathtaking in the claims they made. 'With this LP, Bobby permanently takes his place among the greats of American popular song', the *That's All* sleeve had read. 'He could sing any song in any style with equal facility, taste and skill', another claimed. A third jacket informed readers that 'Bobby had his sights set from the beginning on being an artist, on making a contribution to show business and to the cultural life of this nation.' Promotion is one thing, vanity another. There comes a time when words are worthless unless there are things to back them up.

In the summer of 1962, Bobby found just such 'Things'. This composition brought him back in to the top three of the US and UK charts in 1962. It was one of those rare records that can be called charming without either insulting it or being pretentious.

Atco didn't, however, get the chance to follow through on the success of 'Things'. Darin was lured to Capitol Records in the middle of 1962. Insiders always look for the real reason behind a label jump, and this time they came up with a tantalizing theory. Capitol had recently lost Frank Sinatra, who had started his own company, Reprise. Label heads believed Darin could be the next Sinatra and hence replace him on the roster. Unfortunately it wasn't that easy. *Oh! Look At Me Now*, Darin's first album for Capitol, yet again featured swinging standards with big band accompaniment, this time Billy May's group. It was the lowest charting album of his career to date. His first single, the film theme 'If A Man Answers', was only a small hit. It was time for Darin, who had made the transformation from rock and roller to adult entertainer, to make another switch. He took full note of the folk music boom sweeping America and the increased number of country and western cross-over records, many by his hero Ray Charles. Darin went, to use the title of one of his 1963 LPs, *Earthy!* and scored two consecutive top ten hits, 'You're The Reason I'm Living' and 'Eighteen Yellow Roses'. At this time his guitar player on live appearances was Jim McGuinn, who two years later found fame as Roger McGuinn of The Byrds.

All human beings are to some extent victims of history. It's just that for some circumstances are kind. Bobby Darin was one of many American solo artists dealt a body blow by The Beatles, who swept America in 1964. The British invasion of the Hot 100 followed the Fab Four. Folk music was suddenly uncommercial. Pretty boy solo singers from the early sixties were passé. Without warning, Bobby Darin found himself part of the past. For two years he unsuccessfully tried to find a new niche. He reunited with 'Mack The Knife' band leader Richard Wess for an album of easy listening hits clumsily titled *From Hello, Dolly to Goodbye, Charlie*. The second half of the title proved prophetic. In 1965 he recorded another set of middle-of-the-road favourites and missed the LP chart completely. Bobby Darin the Copacabana character was dead as a dodo in the music business of the mid-sixties. Finally he found something current that he loved and could do. He was drawn to the songs of Tim Hardin and scored with a beautifully understated version of 'If I Were A Carpenter'.

This tender tune returned Darin to the top ten. It was delivered so delicately Bobby seemed a totally different artist from the belter of big band ballads. His album *If I Were A Carpenter* featured five Tim Hardin tunes and two by John Sebastian, leader of The Lovin' Spoonful. The following LP had two more songs by both writers, and each composer provided Darin with small single successes.

But the late sixties were not happy times for Bobby Darin. In 1967 he and Sandra Dee were divorced. Bobby was shattered by the assassination of Robert Kennedy, whom he had met and admired. According to friend Dick Clark's memoir *Rock, Roll and Remember* Darin became 'a latter day hippy', growing his hair, wearing jeans, and living in a caravan in northern California, throwing his money away on a movie that was never released. He formed his own label, Direction Records, and recorded an album of socially aware material. 'Long Line Rider' was about the discovery of human remains on an Arkansas farm. 'In Memoriam' was a lengthy lyric for Robert Kennedy. To show how honest an artist he had become he named the LP *Bobby Darin Born Walden Robert Cassotto*. He went further. He announced he would play only colleges, not clubs. He legally changed his name to Bob Darin. A cynic might well have asked who he thought he was . . . Bob Dylan?

It was ironic that in 1969 Darin's greatest success came not as an artist but as a writer, and that the performer who charted with his song was Tim Hardin. Roles were reversed on the last Darin composition to reach the American top fifty. Hardin sang 'Simple Song Of Freedom', a piece that sounded like a very personal creed. In the following year America began moving away from simple statements and humble homilies of peace and love, and Darin moved with it. In the early seventies he returned to nightclub work, found new television fame through the help of a comedian he had once helped, Flip Wilson, and signed to Motown Records. Berry Gordy's company put him on a Jackson Five TV special and gave him his last chart entry, the love theme from *Lady Sings The Blues*.

But Bobby Darin wasn't allowed to enjoy his comeback. In 1971 he had two heart valves replaced. In 1973 he died after six hours of heart surgery. He was only thirty-seven years old. It was then that Americans learned that Darin had always known he had a bad heart. Dick

Clark believed he always knew he would die young. This was why he was desperate to achieve everything he could at an early age.

This theory explains so many aspects of Bobby Darin's career that might otherwise seem odd – why he was anxious to befriend and impress important contacts as soon as he could, why he told anyone who would listen how talented he was so he could get a chance to prove it, why he changed styles like a chameleon not just to stay in vogue but to get them all in while he could. This knowledge of his own frailty humanises a figure who might otherwise seem obnoxious, and makes him mythic. That a human being can aspire to the heights knowing he is doomed to crash to earth – that is the stuff of dreams.

The Kinks

'"Sunny Afternoon", "Waterloo Sunset" or "Sitting By The River-side" suggest the world of T'ang Chinese poets conversing and drinking wine by moonlight or, closer to home, the streams and meadows of Izaak Walton's angler.'

No, I didn't say that. I *couldn't* have said that. Until I looked them up in a reference book I didn't know who T'ang poets and Izaak Walton were. Jonathan Cott said it. He's America's most literary rock critic, and for him to respond so blissfully to The Kinks' music suggests there is something of literary value in the songs. When one listens to the group's best work from the past twenty years, one realises that for the past two decades Ray Davies has been Britain's poet laureate of rock. No one has better captured the people and places of this country, its strengths, its scandals, its sunsets.

Like many British pop stars of his era, Ray Davies owes a debt of gratitude to Alexis Korner for his start in show business. Unlike the others, however, Davies never actually performed with the bluesman. Korner was playing at Hornsey Art College, where Davies was taking a theatrical design course. The student approached the star and said 'Look, I'd like to be a musician. Can you get me a job?' Instead of saying 'Get lost, kid,' the typically generous Korner gave the boy his phone number and told him to call the following Sunday. Davies did, and was put in touch with Giorgio Gomelsky, who placed him with the Dave Hunt Blues Band. For a year the teenager played jazz and blues on the London club circuit.

In 1964 Ray joined a unit that was literally closer to home – his brother's group. Dave Davies, three years younger than Ray, was one of The Ravens, no pun on his sibling's name intended. A young businessman named Robert Wace thought he himself might make a good lead singer for the group, but realised that the older Davies was perfect for the part and wisely withdrew, instead agreeing to manage the band in partnership with stockbroker Grenville Collins. Music business

living legend Larry Page also got involved. He named the Davies' group The Kinks and gave one of their demos to producer Shel Talmy. He in turn recorded one of Ray's songs, 'I've Got That Feeling', with a Liverpool schoolgirl trio named The Orioles. More importantly, he referred The Kinks to Pye Records, who paid for two studio sessions. The first of these brought forth flops – a version of Little Richard's 'Long Tall Sally' sung à la Beatles and 'You Do Something To Me'. During the second session The Kinks got the goods. 'You Really Got Me' started their chart career.

It had almost ended it before it began. According to Ray Davies, Shel Talmy produced the original version. Davies hated it and threatened 'If you put this record out I'm leaving the business, I'm not going to promote it or anything.' The Kinks re-recorded the number, though Talmy was still credited as producer. As released the single was pure primal power. Ironically for a group that would ultimately be praised for its subtlety and sensitivity, 'You Really Got Me' was the hardest rock record ever to have topped the British charts when it scaled the summit in September 1964. Much of the credit for its impact must go to Dave Davies, who perhaps unknowingly took a guitar figure from The Kingsmen's 'Louie Louie' and refined it to the rawest riff. Indeed, there are some who say that with 'You Really Got Me' and its follow-up, 'All Day And All of The Night', The Kinks were doing nothing less than laying the foundations of heavy metal.

'All Day And All Of The Night' proved 'You Really Got Me' had not been a fluke by soaring to No. 2. The Kinks were off on a historic string of singles. Of twelve consecutive releases, eleven would make the top ten. Three would go to No. 1. The team responsible for this achievement was Ray Davies on vocals and guitar, Dave Davies on guitar and vocals, Mick Avory at the drum kit, and Peter Quaife playing bass. They'd been together since they were The Ravens, and would remain so until Quaife left in 1969. Shel Talmy produced The Kinks through 1967, the last year of their hit streak, so the evidence suggests that despite his differences with Davies he was a crucial element in their success. Ray acknowledged the debt when he recalled 'he was good for us 'cause I'm the sort of person who will do things time and time again, past the point where I think it's good, and Shel would always say "that's it, that's the first take, that's what this band is all about," so I learned a lot from him.' Jim Rodford, who joined The Kinks many years later, was in a group that played on a package tour with them in late 1964. 'There was Dave down on his knees playing his guitar to the ceiling,' he remembered. 'The kids had never seen anything like it before . . . they didn't know how to react. So they rioted. Every night. That power . . . it was animal.'

It wasn't solely on the singles charts that The Kinks scored. Their debut album, bluntly titled *Kinks*, reached No. 3 at a time when The Beatles had a hammerlock hold on the top spot. With fourteen tracks, it gave good value for money. But with those fourteen numbers committed to vinyl and 'All Day And All Of The Night' also used up, Davies faced a sudden song shortage when it came time to record the band's first single of 1965. He wrote a melody on the train and lyrics during a coffee break, but the result sounded like he'd worked on it for weeks. Released in January 1965, 'Tired Of Waiting For You' became Britain's bestseller in February. Had not The Beatles and Rolling Stones dominated the time, more attention would have been paid to The Kinks. Two No. 1s and a No. 2 single, a top three album, and two top three EPs, *Kinksize Session* and *Kinksize Hits*, began the Kinks' blitzkrieg. Across the Atlantic all three hit singles reached the American top ten.

But if The Kinks were on top of the world, Ray Davies didn't feel it. 'I never really felt I belonged in the sixties,' he told journalist Giovanni Dadamo years later. 'That was the worst time for me.' The Beatle-bonkers world wanted another Fab Four, and The Kinks were too iconoclastic to oblige. Davies suffered from the pressure to conform. He agonised over bad business deals and reportedly once ran the eight miles from his Muswell Hill home to Denmark Street, London's 'Tin Pan Alley', carrying all his money in a sock. Trivially but embarrassingly, Davies was unhappy about a space between two front teeth. Publicity photos show he always kept his mouth closed lest he reveal the unglamorous gap.

The Kinks responded to stardom by not doing what was expected of them. 'Tired Of Waiting For You' was a mid-tempo piece radically removed from power pop. 'See My Friends', a top ten triumph later that same year, was influenced by Indian chanting, Davies having the ocean near Bombay in mind when he wrote the song. Late in the year, The Kinks released on the EP *Kwyet Kinks* a track that was a new direction both for them and for British rock. 'A Well-Respected Man' was brilliantly observed social commentary, picturing in words and music a type of Englishman only too familiar to record buyers. The *New Musical Express Encyclopedia of Rock* called the track 'one of the most famous rock songs never to have been a British hit'. By that the author meant the recording never became a hit single. But in the mid-sixties separate EP charts were published, and *Kwyet Kinks*, which contained 'A Well-Respected Man', was the act's second No. 1. The cut *was* a hit single in America. Even though the title character was quintessentially British, he had his American suburban counterpart, though the line 'He likes his fags the best' had a drastically different meaning in the States.

Success with pop portraiture excited Ray Davies. He set out to achieve it again, this time with 'Dedicated Follower Of Fashion', a words-and-music picture of a clothes-mad Mod striving to stay in style. Swinging London was leading the land into buying colourful clobber. Although Mods made up a major part of The Kinks' core constituency, Davies was upset. Someone told him that when you're angry the best way to express yourself is with humour. He sat down at the typewriter, at which he was not nimble, and painstakingly pounded out 'Dedicated Follower of Fashion'.

With this release, at No. 4 the highest placed of the last five Kinks singles, the quartet moved into another peak period. Ray Davies attributed the slight drop in singles sales and album quality in late 1965 to the band's disillusionment with the money men of music. Lawsuits had sapped energy and cut creativity. But with 'A Well-Respected Man' and 'Dedicated Follower Of Fashion', Davies had discovered a different kind of song at which he excelled. No one could capture the character and customs of Britain better than he. A cluster of classics came from The Kinks in 1966 and '67, and one, 'Dandy', in an American hit by Herman's Hermits. 'Sunny Afternoon' told the tale of a successful young man who'd lost his loot to the taxman, but was still determined to enjoy a pleasant *post meridiem*. If the sound of the song was a bit more middle-aged than one might expect of someone of tender years, it was probably because at the time of writing it Ray was listening almost exclusively to Frank Sinatra's *Greatest Hits*. Ironically, the men nearly had back-to-back No.1s. 'Strangers In The Night' and 'Sunny Afternoon' were separated at the top only by The Beatles' 'Paperback Writer'.

Few groups would follow a No.1 with a song inspired by a mining disaster. But it's a symptom of the true artist that he is a prisoner of his own inspiration. When struck by an idea, he has to bring it to fruition as a sort of emotional exorcism. So it was that the Aberfan tragedy, in which a landslide of coal slack killed scores of school children, inspired 'Dead End Street'. In this song Ray Davies demonstrated his ability to write a song from both within and without his subject. He could comment on a social phenomenon with the objectivity of the onlooker while conveying the subjective stance of an individual affected by it. This combination made his successful songs doubly effective. 'Waterloo Sunset', the follow-up to 'Dead End Street', remains equally evocative of the pandemonium at Waterloo Station during rush hour and the beauty a person perceives if he takes notice of the sun setting over the Thames.

Only two months after 'Waterloo Sunset' peaked at No. 2 Dave Davies had a top three hit with a single released under his own name. It actually was co-written by brother Ray and had both he and his wife singing backing vocals. The Kinks were the musicians on the record. Why 'Death Of A Clown' should have been issued as a solo single seems inexplicable unless Pye wanted to establish Dave as a spin-off artist to give the company two hit acts rather than one. Radio might be more responsive to playing two records with different lead singers than two with the same vocalist. Whatever the strategy, it was botched. No solo album was ready to cash in on the popularity of 'Death Of A Clown', and when two successive singles didn't duplicate its success Dave's solo career was abandoned. Additional tracks ultimately turned up on American albums, and years later Dave did release a solo LP, but the time his name was most in the public eye remained the summer of 1967.

When 'Death Of A Clown' reached No. 3 and the next Kinks single, 'Autumn Almanac', did the same, it appeared that all was well. But a major change was about to occur. *Something Else By The Kinks*, the autumn release that included 'Waterloo Sunset', 'Death Of A Clown' and 'David Watts', was the last of the band's albums to be produced by Shel Talmy. Davies had pronounced the version of 'Waterloo Sunset' supervised by Shel as 'awful, just awful,' and had managed one himself. The three-year association which had been so immensely profitable for both sides was terminated. Ray wanted to refine The Kinks' musical style and produce coherent works on album. His first attempt bore the long-winded title *The Kinks Are The Village Green Preservation Society*. This wasn't pretentious posturing. Davies was casting The Kinks as guardians of the best of British. Among the items he sought to save were strawberry jam, vaudeville, draught beer, tudor houses and billiards. Ray realised the things that make you different make you special. Without them, you're just like everybody else.

The record-buyers of 1968, however, were not interested in maintaining the status quo. If they bought pop political philosophy at all it was that which called for change, perhaps even revolution. The singles-oriented Pye Records wasn't comfortable either when Davies delivered the tapes of the LP. When asked which tracks were the singles, he announced none were. It would be nearly three years before The Kinks had another top ten record.

'Lola', a No. 2 in the summer of 1970, followed a series of setbacks for The Kinks. The *Village Green Preservation Society* album hadn't charted in either Britain or the United States. Its homespun nostalgic values and picturesque characters were not the stuff of sales success. In America, the basic Englishness of the project baffled would-be buyers. After four top ten LPs and several minor entries, The Kinks were shut out. When another concept album, *Arthur or the Decline and Fall of the*

British Empire, also failed, they could well have felt ignored. By all, that is, except for a small band of devotees who were convinced that these works were more important than anything they'd ever done. These loyal followers believed that *Arthur*, originally written for a television play that was never performed, had been unjustly overlooked in the commotion over another rock opera of the time, *Tommy*. The new Kinks fans were fascinated by the vision with which Ray Davies saw his world, and supported his LP projects through commercial thick and thin. It may have been lost on the broader public that 'Lola' itself was part of a larger piece, *Lola Versus Powerman and The Moneygoround . . . Kinks Part One*. The long player was the story of The Kinks' unhappy experiences in the music business. In one track the band's three original mentors were all mentioned by their Christian names. Another cut on the album, 'Apeman', became another smash single, but 'Lola' was the stand-out, with its ambience and its ambiguity. What did Davies mean when he wrote he was glad he was a man and so was Lola? Was the Soho transvestite glad that Davies was a man or that he himself was a man? Was Davies merely stating that he and Lola were both men? It was marvellous musical mischief, and a hit around the world.

The same could not be said for the group's first effort for RCA Records, the 1971 set *Muswell Hillbillies*, nor the 1972 double *Everybody's in Showbiz*. It may have been because of its length that a masterpiece in the latter LP, *Celluloid Heroes*, was not given more exposure. There could be no other excuse. 'Celluloid Heroes' was one of the most perfectly realised pieces of pop to come out in 1972. It poignantly placed the private person behind the Hollywood star alongside the fantasy figure created by the myth-making machine, and conrasted both with the inadequate narrator who felt the need in himself to yearn for the cinematic immortality even he knew was illusory.

Everybody's in Showbiz was only a minor success, and most of the business it did do was in the United States. Ray Davies' marriage disintegrated. Personally and professionally overwrought, the leader of The Kinks caught his colleagues by surprise when he announced his retirement from the stage of a festival at White City. Even the exit was anxiety-producing. Announced half-on and half-off microphone, it had fans and press alike wondering what he had really said and if he had really meant it. As it turned out, Davies and The Kinks returned to issue further thematic albums on RCA, a two-part project in the *Village Green Preservation Society* vein called *Preservation* and an adolescent romp titled *Schoolboys In Disgrace*. These unified sets, and a live show that was part rock show, part vaudeville, endeared the band to ever more Americans. When The Kinks moved to Arista Records in

1977, they were back to the threshold of the American top thirty. 'A Rock 'n' Roll Fantasy' put them inside.

Just as Ray Davies had bit the hand that fed him when he parodied the 'Dedicated Follower Of Fashion', now he admonished the young man who sits in his room for hours on end listening to LPs. 'Maybe I am telling him to take off his headphones now,' Davies explained, 'because it just doesn't pay to be enclosed in your own world any more.' The accurate yet affectionate admonition won its top thirty berth in 1978, the year The Kinks' fortunes were truly revived. A new generation of musicians revived vintage Davies material. Van Halen scored their first American top forty hit with an update of 'You Really Got Me'. In Britain The Jam covered a song about a real person Ray had envied in school, 'David Watts'. The Pretenders made their successful disc debut with a number from the very first Kinks album, 'Stop Your Sobbing'. A second stab at the songbook, 'I Go To Sleep', provided The Pretenders with a 1981 top tenner. More importantly for lead singer Chrissie Hynde and Ray Davies, the affinity was not just musical. Their friendship resulted in the birth of a daughter, Natalie, although in 1984 Chrissie married Simple Mind Jim Kerr.

The Kinks' improved American fortunes not only gave them their most successful studio album ever, *Low Budget*, but their first top five single, a success that ricocheted across the Atlantic to bring the band their best British showing in thirteen years. 'Come Dancing' was another example of Ray Davies' ability to set a scene and place people within it. In this case, he told the story of Britain's declining dance halls as it related to the fortunes of a family. Davies wasn't just talking about preserving the nation's endearing eccentricities. He was looking back nostalgically, admitting his middle age, wondering where his past fitted into his present. The tremendously touching follow-up, 'Don't Forget To Dance', let a lady who was no longer young partner males half her age and do it well. In The Kinks' 1984 release 'Good Day' Ray revealed that he once fancied another of the nation's institutions, Diana Dors.

By not pretending to be the young man he once was, by writing from the vantage point of the man he is, Davies has laid claim to ground never before developed in rock. With a still strong band behind him, there is no reason he cannot continue to make music of not just quality but interest. Davies likes to downplay his role in rock. Observing the mild success of past albums and several stage and television projects, he described himself in 1980 as 'not very rich, not very successful, and certainly not very famous'. He admits to frequent frustration, pointing out that nothing achieved in the past helps to write the next song. If he could take the long view for a moment and observe the lives of his listeners as candidly as he has the subjects of his songs, he might see how many days he has brightened and he might allow himself the pleasure of a sunny afternoon.

James Brown

I HAVE seen David Bowie in his finest form, where every gesture and every movement complemented his music, where only one false move would have broken the spell. I have seen Elton John in Madison Square Garden fomenting hysteria with his hits and then introducing John Lennon to an audience so enthusiastic one felt the roof would physically be raised by the rumpus. I was present at the Lyceum for Bob Marley's famous celebration of love and unity, and at the Spectrum in Philadelphia where Bob Dylan and The Band played together and got twelve thousand young adults to unselfconsciously stand as one in the darkness and sing 'Like A Rolling Stone'.

But none of these thrills matches the excitement of watching James Brown at the peak of his powers. Performing in an obscure theatre in the round in Connecticut in the mid-sixties, Brown displayed more energy and a better sense of timing than I had ever seen or ever hoped to see. It was as if someone had opened the stage door and in rushed a singing and dancing whirlwind. Whatever anyone had been exposed to before, this was a new bag.

James Brown has achieved sixteen No. 1s in the American rhythm and blues chart, but his importance transcends ethnic groupings. James Brown has also been the second most successful artist on the *Billboard* Hot 100, according to statistics compiled by chartologist Joel Whitburn. Brown is the runner-up only to Elvis Presley and, no disrespect to the King of Rock-'n'-Roll, the King of Soul was a better dancer.

James Brown was born on 3 May 1933 in Barnwell, South Carolina, and was raised across the Savannah River in Augusta, Georgia. His father was a failed blues singer and guitarist who worked pumping petrol. James' boyhood years were spent in a kind of poverty Americans like to think no longer exists. As he recalled, he 'picked cotton, worked on a farm, worked in a coal yard. I had to walk home along the railroad tracks and pick up pieces of coke that fell off the trains. I'd take that home and we'd use it to keep warm. I was so poor my underwear was made out of flour sacks.'

To pick up extra money Brown shined shoes outside radio station WDRW. Years later he bought the station. He danced for friends and for soldiers at the local army base, who gave him coins for his efforts. When his parents separated, he moved in with his aunt in nearby Macon.

He got two important breaks through sports. He was trained by the former boxer Beau Jack, winning sixteen of seventeen professional bantamweight bouts. It was in his footwork drills that the young pugilist mastered moves that would be the basis of his stage act. James was also a fine baseball pitcher, and it was while hurling for Alto Reform School, where he spent three years for theft, that he had an on-field collision with gospel singer Bobby Byrd. After the game the troubled teen talked to Byrd and asked him to support his parole plea. The local celebrity and his family agreed to sponsor the boy and found him a job, winning his release. In changing James Brown's life, Bobby Byrd changed his own, more than he could have dreamed.

Byrd had been lead singer of The Gospel Starlighters. He invited his protégé Brown to join just as the group changed styles in favour of rhythm and blues. They changed their name to The Famous Flames, requiring the adjective because another outfit were already known as The Flames. The new act worked for over two years before making a demo of 'Please Please Please' in a studio of radio station WIBB. The number had become a showcase for James Brown, who repeated the word 'please' in a frenzied chant inspired by a Georgia group's 'Baby Please Don't Go'. The taped performance didn't even have any instrumentation on it, but that didn't stop WIBB from giving it airplay. Listeners loved it, and so did King Records talent scout Ralph Bass. Bass claimed he went to a club and saw Brown 'crawling on his stomach and saying "please please please" – he must have said "please" for about ten minutes.' He decided to record The Famous Flames. When he did his superior told him that 'this man sounds like he's stoned on the record, all he's saying is one word.'

This story is told at length in Cliff White's mammoth liner notes on the compilation *Roots of a Revolution*. Only White, Britain's foremost James Brown scholar, would be capable of writing over a thousand words just to cover the two-year period between 'Please Please Please' and the star's second hit, 'Try Me'. These two years were a testing time for James Brown. The 1956 debut disc did reach the top ten of the rhythm and blues chart, but its million sales were accumulated over time rather than in a few months. Consequently, there was no great incentive for The Famous Flames to go on. Knowing that James had come to dominate the act anyway they disbanded in the spring of 1957.

Brown got unexpected live work when Little Richard found religion and needed an artist to take over a tour. James found new Famous Flames and continued to bill himself on record as James Brown and The Famous Flames until 1968 whether a group actually appeared on the disc or not. Bobby Byrd rejoined James after the recording of 'Try Me', a tune The Flames claimed Brown found in Florida while working a club called The Palms. 'Try Me' managed to make it to No. 1 for a week in February, 1958, between Jackie Wilson's 'Lonely Teardrops' and Lloyd Price's 'Stagger Lee'. The national success of the single won James Brown and The Famous Flames an appearance at the Apollo, Harlem's headquarters for Negro entertainment. The group were stunned when they were outclassed by The Vibrations, whose major hits 'The Watusi' and 'My Girl Sloopy' were still years away. As Bobby Byrd put it, 'they ate us alive'. During the next four years, as James Brown gradually became an established chart artist, he and The Famous Flames developed the best live show in rhythm and blues. Eventually it was the finest in popular music. When they played the same Apollo Theatre on 24 October 1962, James had the show recorded at his own expense. The historic result showed how involved his audiences had become. The crowd answered him and screamed for him, sometimes at a louder level than that of his own voice. The concert remains almost unbearably exciting to hear. Heaven knows what it was like to be there.

James Brown Live at the Apollo was an absolute breakthrough. It was understandable that King Records head Syd Nathan had found the prospect of recording a live performance unattractive, since there had never been a hit rhythm and blues concert album. As a matter of fact, there had never been a gold R&B LP, period. Negro record buyers had always selected singles. That the Apollo package could climb to No. 2 on the *Billboard* album chart was a prospect no one had even considered, let alone taken seriously. But James Brown knew how loyal his following was. In the years between 1956 and 1961, when he was struggling to achieve some sort of chart consistency, he was touring first the southeast and then the entire United States at a pace that would have forced less dedicated artists into retirement. In so doing he built a broad base of support and tightened up his backing band.

It was no surprise, then, when Negro audiences demanded to hear a James Brown live recording. They first wanted it on radio, deluging R&B stations with requests to hear the Apollo show on the air. Some outlets played it like a single, some at the same time every day. Then the sales started and, in early 1963, white people joined in to purchase the perfect party platter. With one stroke James Brown enticed both racial groups to purchase rhythm and blues long players for the first time.

The first half of 1963 saw Brown's breakthrough on the pop singles chart as well. On 17 December 1962, less than two months after the Apollo recording, he used a chorus and strings for the first time. 'Prisoner of Love' had been a No. 1 for Perry Como in 1946, when The Ink Spots also had a top ten version. Seventeen years later James Brown's urgent gospel-flavoured interpretation brought the song back to No. 18. The familiar JB delivery – the 'you, you, you' at the end is directly descended from 'Please, Please, Please' – was couched in a lush backing that made it palatable for pop people.

The orchestra was a tool used to get Brown into the top twenty. It couldn't become a permanent part of his act because it wasn't his style. The *Prisoner of Love* album, compiled of newly-recorded ballads and old tracks overdubbed with strings, failed. It's just as well. It's impossible to contemplate James Brown going cabaret. His next hit was nearer the roots of The Famous Flames. Not only did 'Oh Baby Don't You Weep' boast a call-and-response interplay between lead and backing vocalists typical of gospel, it was actually inspired by a religious recording, The Swan Silvertones' 'Oh Mary Don't You Weep'. James Brown sang and played piano on the studio recording, which was overdubbed with audience reaction because another live album, *Pure Dynamite*, needed some songs that hadn't been on the Apollo package. The tampered track reached the American top thirty in early 1964.

James Brown had been voted America's number one rhythm and blues male vocalist in a 1962 deejay poll. Now he was a pop personality as well, and he worked at a superhuman rate to consolidate his career. He had become known as 'The Hardest Working Man in Show Business' because of his interminable itinerary. He released records at a more prolific rate than any other major artist before or since, not just on himself but on various associates. One reason why even his greatest admirers write off some of his work is that he was not overly selective about what he put out.

In 1964 he went into overdrive on the overdoing it, issuing discs on two labels. While still under contract to King, with whom he had had several squabbles, James cut for Smash, and managed three chart singles and two albums before the courts stopped him. One of the 45s, 'Out of Sight', reached the pop top thirty.

As early as 1960 James had popularised the Mashed Potato, but it wasn't until the middle of the decade that he became America's master of the dance, replacing Chubby Checker. The go-go boom knew no boundaries, and Brown's ability to dance better than anyone in the business and his talent for making great dance records made him a massive pop star. In 1965 'Papa's Got a Brand New Bag', which mentioned many stylish dance steps, broke him into the American top ten and the British top thirty for the first time. The follow-up, 'I Got You' kept him there. It was at this point that I caught the concert that is still the best show I've ever seen. James Brown was a tornado struggling to get out of the human body into which it had been unfairly confined. He would dash around the stage and suddenly fall to his knees, pleading, begging to his woman to have mercy. He would bolt upright and slide across the stage on one foot, one of the most often, and most badly, imitated moves in all show business. He would grunt, growl, sweat and shake until the viewer could not stand the suffering. The *coup de théâtre* was the cape act, in which the disconsolate Brown, sobbing his way through 'Please Please Please', would be comforted by an attendant, raised from his knees, and helped off stage, his shoulders covered with a cloak. Still screaming 'Please . . . please' from the sidelines, Brown would throw off the cloak and dash back to the microphone, pleading anew and again falling to the ground. Once more an attendant would offer a cape and usher the star away. Once more James would return, visibly possessed. Brown would get through blue, red, silver, gold and leopard-spot capes before he finally finished. It was the most brilliant combination of soul singing and ham acting anyone has ever offered.

'I Got You' was the biggest pop hit James Brown ever enjoyed, reaching No. 3 in early 1966. As typified dance records of the time, it was featured in a forgettable film, in this case a winter sports epic called *Ski Party*. 'I Got You' was a reworking of 'I Found You', a number Brown wrote for Yvonne Fair in 1962. The only substantial change was the substitution of 'got' for 'found' in the title, yet the new version sounded far superior. James and his band leader Nat Jones were refining a dance groove that was tight and taut, omitting any sound that wasn't essential.

But Brown wasn't confining himself to dance music. The releases were still flying thick and fast. A new recording of 'Try Me' from the Smash sessions was issued. Though the timing may have been inopportune, the practice of re-cutting his own classics was common. Brown revisited several of his vintage hits, some of them more than once. That he had a sense of his own importance was further evidenced by his spectacularly grandiose production of his own 'It's a Man's Man's Man's World'. The title was a take-off of the 1963 film *It's A Mad, Mad, Mad, Mad World*. As a commentary on the battle of the sexes it sounded like it must be a joke, and the over-the-top introduction reinforced that feeling. But Brown put so much feeling into the record audiences took him seriously, and took him again to the American top ten and the British top thirty.

So much of James Brown's life at this time sounded like it had to be

false. He would send interior decorators to cities in which he was due
to play so they could redesign the rooms in which he would stay. He
would open bank accounts in each of these cities, so he never would be
marooned without money. 'I always intended to be my own man
wherever I went,' he explained, 'and if I had my own money anyplace
then I was my own man. Nobody was going to own me.'

James Brown had six Hot 100 entries in 1967. The outstanding
effort, another R&B No.1, was 'Cold Sweat', a track that was more
than just another million-seller. Brown collaborated with new bandlea-
der Alfred Ellis to create a modern musical sound. He moved away
from melody and standard song structure into a free-flowing form
where nervous guitars repeated riffs, brass blared musical punctuation
and the drummer drove the track. Indeed, on part two of 'Cold Sweat',
the B-side of the single, Brown barked the famous command, 'Give the
drummer some', and Clyde Stubblefield duly obliged.

To put it succinctly, James Brown was inventing funk. In almost all
his singles of the late sixties and early seventies the musicians establish
a framework within which Brown declaims and they respond, but
there are no chord sequences or melodic development as rhythm and
blues had previously known.

In 1968 James accumulated eight hits. One, the live recording
'There Was a Time', was based on a chart single he had made only a
year previously, 'Let Yourself Go', but the concert performance was so
riveting it had to be released on its own. Though it was highly unusual
for a pop star to give himself a mention in his own record and to talk
about his own prowess as a dancer, it was in character for this star. In
the course of his career Brown or his associates have named him 'The
Hardest Working Man in Show Business', 'Mr Dynamite', 'Mr Please,
Please, Please', 'The King of Soul', 'Soul Brother Number One', 'The
Little Groove Maker Me', 'The Godfather of Soul', 'Minister of
New Super Heavy Funk', and 'The Original Disco Man'. His ego is
part of his image, but this penchant for self-promotion is another
reason why some earnest music critics haven't taken James Brown as
seriously as they should have. It seems unbecoming a great artist. But
although it is ludicrous to a sophisticate, his constant re-titling of himself has kept him current and vital to his public, as if he were a comic-
book super-hero. Indeed, one year he wore a silver suit with a
lightning bolt on the chest that looked as if it might have been the
costume of a caped crusader. Another tour he wore a top with the
words 'sex machine'.

'Get Up I Feel Like Being a Sex Machine' was an international hit
for James Brown in 1970. It was recorded in Nashville one night after a
live show. Brown had been chatting to then-President of King Records

Hal Neely when he got the idea for the song. He borrowed Neely's pen, wrote the words on the back of a poster, and had his engineer drive three hundred miles from his home in Cincinnati for the session. Brown supervised the laying down of the rhythm tracks and did his own vocal in one take. The result was yet another gold record. And yet another multi-part song. Brown's forays into funk were so lengthy they couldn't fit on to one side of a single. Both the A- and B-sides were used to accommodate the cuts, the result being that his sequence of hits read like this list from 1970: 'It's a New Day (Part 1 and Part 2)', 'Funky Drummer (Part 1)', 'Brother Rapp (Part 1 and Part 2)', 'Get Up I Feel Like Being a Sex Machine (Part 1)', and 'Super Bad (Part 1 and Part 2)'. *The Book of Rock Lists* thought this habit so hilarious it printed a category '35 Multipart Hits by James Brown', the most ridiculous-sounding of which was 'Let a Man Come In and Do the Popcorn (Part 2)'. Brown had invented the dance The Popcorn, had reached the top thirty of the pop charts in 1969 with an instrumental written to go with it, then vocalised for an even bigger hit, 'Mother Popcorn (You Got to Have a Mother For Me) (Part 1)'. This was followed by 'Lowdown Popcorn' and 'Let a Man Come In and Do the Popcorn (Part 1)', which in its turn was succeeded by Part 2. With titles like these Brown started losing his white audience. He was becoming a parody of himself, travelling in ever-diminishing lyrical circles. And, painfully, he lost his leadership of the dance music market, which followed a different and more synthesized drummer in the mid- and late seventies. Only occasionally was the voice of James Brown heard urging dancers to 'Get Up Offa That Thing'.

No artist could have lasted long with silly songs that were mostly furious funk were it not for a solid standing won for other reasons, and James Brown had earned respect for the best reasons imaginable. He had incarnated the American rags to riches legend. His triumph over racial discrimination and economic deprivation was no less admirable because it became the stuff of myth. When he earned the respect of his people and the love of his country, he repaid them. After touring a San Francisco ghetto in 1966 he wrote and recorded 'Don't Be a Drop-Out', and he printed this slogan on his record labels for some time thereafter to further encourage students to stay in school. When Martin Luther King was assassinated in 1968, he performed live on television in first Boston and then Washington to cool tempers and discourage riots. He promoted patriotism, as in 'America is My Home', but constructive, critical patriotism, as in his album *Revolution of the Mind*. He made one of the first significant anti-drug records, 'King Heroin'. And, most important of all, in 1968 he issued 'Say It Loud – I'm Black and I'm Proud'. It may have been natural that America's foremost black artist should have articulated the change in his people's self-awareness from Negro to Black, but it was still a courageous step considering his broad audience. James Brown, who revolutionised R&B and fathered funk, was not an Uncle Tom. And, unlike Elvis Presley, he did not have a Colonel Tom to exploit him. He ran his own business and remained proud. He stayed in touch with the times, too, recording with Afrika Bambaataa in 1984. If non-Americans, if non-blacks, do not fully appreciate the contributions of James Brown nor realise the magnitude of his success, that is, in the end, their problem, for Brown knows what he is. He is black, and he is proud.

Elvis Costello

DURING THE mid-seventies I was the American correspondent in London for *Rolling Stone* magazine. The editors in San Francisco loved receiving up-to-the-minute reports on Paul McCartney, Elton John and other British artists who were world leaders in popular music. But as the second half of the decade began it became more difficult to interest my editors in stories on new UK talent. Glam rock had hardly crossed the ocean – even Roxy Music were only minor stars in the States – and punk didn't export at all. I encountered increasing resistance to suggestions for articles on British acts that weren't in the American charts.

The last straw came in the summer of 1977. A new artist had with his very first album shown himself to be a perceptive songwriter, a distinctive vocalist, and a highly individual personality. When the *Rolling Stone* editors didn't want to hear about him I directed my enthusiasms elsewhere. But I suppose I shouldn't have been surprised when they laughed at my suggestion. Who, without ever having heard him, could take seriously an artist named Elvis Costello?

Declan Patrick McManus was born in London in 1955. A computer operator for Elizabeth Arden cosmetics, he was a husband at nineteen and a father at twenty-one. This is hardly the stuff of legend, so it should be quickly pointed out that two connections with the music industry make his early life story at least sound interesting. His father Ross McManus was a singer with the Joe Loss orchestra, quite useful for a would-be pop star. Not only was there father's singing to hear but the records he brought home. The orchestra always did cover versions of current pop hits, so the originals were always in the McManus home, not only on the radio but on the hi-fi.

The second useful association was one formed when young Declan lived in Liverpool. A Beatle buff whose first record had been 'Please Please Me', he went to the Cavern Club in 1974 and met Nick Lowe, member of Brinsley Schwarz. In 1976 Lowe signed to the new Stiff

Records as a solo artist and producer. He met Declan on the London underground and encouraged the frustrated young singer to submit his first demonstration tape to the founders of his label, Jake Riviera and Dave Robinson. They signed him.

If was Jake Riviera's idea to give Stiff's new signing a noticeable name. His invention subsequently seemed a stroke of brilliance, but it should be remembered that in its early days Stiff also promoted Wreckless Eric and Magic Michael, men with marvellous monickers who none the less never charted. Declan McManus had ability as well as a billing.

Elvis Costello was a name nobody even remotely familiar with popular music could ignore. 'I thought he was completely mad', the artist later said of Jake. At first it seemed an obnoxious move. How could anybody dare name themselves after the King of Rock and Roll, who was still living and occasionally still having hits? And, even more sacrilegiously, how could anyone do so irreverently? 'We here at Stiff say Elvis is King', a 1977 liner note read, without even stopping to worship at the temple of the original Elvis.

For a short time in 1977 the move appeared like it might backfire. Elvis Presley died, without consulting either Jake Riviera or his namesake. Harmless jokes can seem to be in bad taste when millions are mourning, but the perpetrators of this merry prank got away with it. They achieved what they wanted – to be noticed. Everyone's first reaction would be to ask why the young artist called himself Elvis, though few if any enquired whether it was the comedian Lou or the gangster Frank who inspired the Costello. Once they noticed an Elvis Costello record, they listened. Once they listened, they could not help but be impressed.

A phrase from 'Alison' gave Elvis Costello's debut album its title, *My Aim Is True*. The ballad was the artist's third single from the set, following 'Less Than Zero' and 'Red Shoes'. The album was produced for Stiff by Nick Lowe and recorded with the American group Clover, many of whom went on to become members of Huey Lewis and The News. Elvis Costello was the first artist on the label to earn a significant chart placing when *My Aim Is True* climbed to No. 14 in the British album chart. He promoted his songs through the summer on the fondly-remembered 'Stiff Live Stiffs' package tour which sent Elvis around the country with Stiff stablemates Ian Dury, Wreckless Eric, Larry Wallis and, of course, Nick Lowe. Costello was backed by the recruited trio of keyboard player Steve Naive, bassist Bruce Thomas and drummer Pete Thomas. Despite their surnames, nobody in the group was related, but they complemented each other so well musically that Elvis Costello and The Attractions became a permanent unit.

In the autumn of 1977 the band achieved its first hit single. It is an often-told true tale that Elvis wrote the song after listening to the first Clash album for thirty-six consecutive hours. He told the *Sunday Times* 'There's quite a bit of humour in the songs, and that gave The Clash a genuinely human feel – as opposed to the earnestness everyone was peddling then.' He gave wit and energy to his own song, spinning a sinister story about a girl who, like so many television viewers of the time, was 'Watching the Detectives'.

The track was added to the American version of *My Aim Is True*. The set captivated critics. And why not? They made their living writing, and here was a composer who could use words intelligently. His music affected the brain as well as the body, and rock reviewers could write reams of copy about his lyrics whereas they'd be stuck to generate more than a paragraph on punk platters.

Because he was the acceptable face of New Wave in the United States, winning radio and press attention when everyone other than The Sex Pistols was getting none, Elvis was invested with the anger and energy of the New Wave movement. He couldn't have just been an ordinary wimp who happened to make it because he could write a clever lyric and carry a tune. 'Declan was a lonely, frustrated teenager', one American author claimed. 'Short, awkward, bowlegged and bespectacled, Declan became obsessed with his own sexuality.' If he had plenty to be angry about, a second scribe thought he sounded like it. 'He wields a seductively soft vibrato like Dionne Warwick with fangs', he wrote.

Elvis encouraged his instant incarnation as the bad boy of rock. He insulted his concert audiences, refused to give interviews, and seemed to snarl while singing some songs. When he said '(I Don't Want to Go to) Chelsea', it came over as '(Try to Make Me Go to Chelsea and I'll) Punch you in the Face'.

The hits '(I Don't Want to Go to) Chelsea' and 'Pump It Up' were included on *This Year's Model*, Costello's 1978 issue. It appeared on Radar Records, Jake Riviera's new company. In America the set came out on Columbia Records, which had released *My Aim Is True*. Any claim that Costello's aim was anything less than world stardom was refuted by that simple fact. The American arm of CBS was as large a label as they come, and while it may have been tactically clever to be with a credible independent firm at home, it was necessary to go with a major to sell records in the States. Elvis had courted Columbia in a memorable move when he busked in Park Lane outside the hotel where the outfit was having its annual international convention.

Costello enthusiasts knew early on they were in for considerable expenditure if they were going to get all his collectables. The single of

'Less Than Zero' had been different from the album track. *My Aim Is True* had come with a choice of four different colours on the back cover, and the American edition had carried an extra track. The US single of 'Alison' had added a string synthesizer and was then reissued with a different B-side. With *This Year's Model* Costello and Riviera's packaging ploys reached a new plateau, with a bonus single appearing in only the first five thousand British copies, an off-centre cover in the UK contrasting with a correctly centred US sleeve of a slightly different photo, and a slightly different track listing. Instead of 'Chelsea' and 'Night Rally' Americans got 'Radio Radio'. Home audiences were given 'Radio Radio' as a single. 'The 7-inch picture sleeve of this release is now quite rare', *Record Collector* announced in 1983, 'but rarer still is the 12-inch promo, only a few hundred of which are rumoured to have been pressed. A publicity statement that only a handful escaped, however, appears to have been slightly exaggerated, and you shouldn't have to pay much more than £20 for a copy.'

If Elvis Costello was sending his staunchest supporters to the poorhouse, he was sending shivers up the spines of pop programmers. 'Radio Radio' didn't just seem like, it *was* an indictment of airplay policy at leading stations. 'I want to bite the hand that feeds me', Costello clearly claimed.

It is difficult to convey rage without ruining a record, without being inarticulate in choice of words or sacrificing the melody of what is, in the final analysis, still a pop *tune*. In 'Radio Radio', as in some of his other best early work, Costello mixed the elements marvellously. Words and music fed his fury.

He had a cause for complaint, too. Playlisters had ignored New Wave discs selectively in Britain and completely in America. The only way they could play 'Radio Radio' without swallowing extremely hard was to think that Elvis was talking about the situation across the Atlantic. Frightened that Radio 1 might ban this brilliant record, I quickly made it Record of the Week while deputising on a daily programme. I needn't have feared. The national network was magnanimous and supported the single. Maybe it was about America. Columbia never released it as a 45.

For 'Radio Radio' to remain an album track in the States wasn't an insult. Costello's three first albums were all outstanding, containing too many top tracks to be spotlighted. 'Lipstick Vogue' won particular acclaim among the *This Year's Model* collection, and the next set, *Armed Forces*, had many more winners. In addition to its singles, it carried 'Green Shirt', a piece of tension and tightness, and, in its American incarnation, 'Peace, Love and Understanding', an affectionate cover of an old Brinsley Schwarz song. Perhaps because it was written by Nick Lowe and in this version produced by him, Costello had it released in Britain as the B-side of his mentor's 'American Squirm' under the billing 'Nick Lowe and His Sound'.

In an act of considerable wit, Columbia Records issued a special promotional single for radio station airplay around the time of Valentine's Day, 1979, coupling Costello cuts suitable for smooching, 'Peace, Love and Understanding' and Elvis's version of the evergreen 'My Funny Valentine'. The single was pressed on red vinyl with tiny hearts all over the label.

Columbia couldn't put out the Radar single, 'Oliver's Army', because of the phrase 'white nigger'. Although the expression has a valid use to British ears, adding impact to the lyric, the word 'nigger' is a racial taboo to most Americans, regardless of its purpose. Costello was undoubtedly deprived of his first Hot 100 entry. In the UK, 'Oliver's Army' got to No. 2. In the US, the replacement single, 'Accidents Will Happen', didn't happen.

Armed Forces was released in January 1979, perfectly timed to be acclaimed as The First Important Album of the year. It remains Elvis's best chart performer, reaching No. 2 in Britain and remaining in the list for twenty-eight weeks. Both are his best figures. In America it was his first top ten LP.

Costello could have stopped then and his place in pop history would have been secured. He had delivered three superb albums in three attempts and had established a lasting reputation as the leading solo artist of the New Wave and the man who put the droll in rock and roll. He may have wished he had stopped when he drank too much one night after a concert in Columbus, Ohio, got into a disagreement with members of the Stephen Stills Band, and referred to Ray Charles in racially abusive terms. Publicity-seekers made sure the comments got in the press, and his career in America was set back for years.

Here was incredible irony. Even the most cynical observer in the galaxy would have been stunned into silence by Costello's quandary. The great rebel had offended public sensibilities without trying to and without meaning to. In Britain everyone knew the real man as a lover of black music, including the work of Ray Charles. He had played at Rock Against Racism rallies and that very same year produced the integrated group The Specials. But Americans knew only what happened in their country, and what he had said about Ray Charles was far more of an insult than impudently naming himself after Elvis Presley. It was Topic A until finally, in 1982, *Rolling Stone* ran a cover interview on him and headlined it 'Elvis Costello Repents'.

If only they'd heard his disparaging comments on *Roundtable* about Linda Ronstadt's cover versions of his songs! The mere prospect of generous royalty checks wasn't enough to bribe him into praising product he hated. More welcome publishing payments came, however, when Dave Edmunds reached No. 4 in the British charts in the summer of 1979 with his reading of Elvis's 'Girl's Talk'. It was a perfect pop single, well worth rehearing years afterwards.

Costello's love of black music manifested itself again on his 1980 album *Get Happy*, a twenty-track tunefest that included a cover of Sam and Dave's 'I Can't Stand Up for Falling Down'. A B-side for the original artists, it became an A for Costello, but only after a sequence of curious events. Elvis so enjoyed working with The Specials, a collaboration that resulted in a top five album, that he gave them a single for their label Two-Tone. He could do this, so he thought, because Radar had just been purchased by WEA and his own recording future was in doubt. WEA saw to it that the thousands of Two-Tone pressings could not be sold. Given out free at several Christmas concerts, but not received by all patrons because several Scrooges scored several copies, the disc became an instant collector's item, which could quickly enrich any owner choosing to sell by about £15.

'I Can't Stand Up For Falling Down' was the second top five single for Elvis Costello and The Attractions, but it none the less began a decline in the quality of their work. *Get Happy* was a disappointment. The act of putting twenty tracks on to one album proved overly ambitious rather than generous. A subsequent album, *Trust*, also suffered from overloading. Costello diluted the impact of his best work by insisting on also releasing material that wasn't of the same standard.

The temptation to keep the arm of the composing churn turning must have been irresistible. Costello was famous for keeping notebooks in which he would write down any potentially useful phrase that came to him, regardless of where he was at the time. Even someone who didn't enjoy his early eighties work had to admire him for both his love of composition and his affection for the work of other artists.

That affection extended to quality country music, and in May 1981 he travelled to Tennessee to record a set of country favourites. Working in Nashville with the rightfully legendary Columbia producer Billy Sherrill, Elvis recorded the album *Almost Blue*, highlighted by a remarkable rendering of personal hero George Jones's 'Good Year for the Roses'. The two discs revived Costello's slumping chart career in Britain. The project also served a personal purpose. 'It was an exorcism of the unhappiness I felt at the time', he told London's *Time Out* magazine. 'I really meant *Almost Blue* ... a very sad and depressed record.'

Perhaps he was cheered by the album's British success or that of his Squeeze production *East Side Story*, which boasted two of their very finest cuts, 'Tempted' and 'Labelled with Love'. Maybe he was elated by the experience of playing with the 92-piece Royal Philharmonic Orchestra at the Albert Hall on 7 January 1982. Whatever the reason, he began a return to form with that year's *Imperial Bedroom*, and was in classic condition for his 1983 effort *Punch the Clock*.

He told *Time Out* that he had learned the hard way that he had to write for the general public, not just the coterie who regularly bought his records anyway. He addressed an audience no smaller than the entire nation when under the pseudonym The Imposter he put out 'Pills and Soap'. The title came to Costello when he saw the activist documentary *The Animals Film*. As he remembered, pills and soap are 'by-products of the misuse of animals. And then I started to expand the idea to the misuse of the human animal, in all its many ways ... particularly with reference to misplaced sentiment, including patriotism.'

Because he felt his song pertinent to the forthcoming General Election and his next album wouldn't be ready until after the date, he issued the single on its own. He used the pseudonym 'The Imposter', the title of a track on *Get Happy*. This was because only Steve Naive and Elvis were on the record, so it wasn't really an Attractions record, and because the group's next single, 'Everyday I Write the Book', was due shortly anyway. When it came out it stunned reviewers who long ago stopped wondering what Elvis's first American hit single would be by reaching the top forty of the Hot 100.

This was more a triumph of timing than any indication of value. In the second half of 1983 a long list of British acts were getting their first exposure on American 'Hot Hits' radio. There was a far more impressive piece of work on the new album, *Punch the Clock*.

In 1982 Elvis had supplied the words to Clive Langer's tune 'Shipbuilding', an ironic comment on the Falklands War that was given an emotionally moving reading by Robert Wyatt. Costello added a trumpet solo by Chet Baker and managed to make his version even more chilling. 'I found it very sad that people could be manipulated into crying and weeping in the streets about a country that doesn't belong to them', he explained. 'It was a very cheap emotion.' His lyrics went behind the flag-waving to examine the effect of the war on construction men who would get employment knowing their product killed.

'Shipbuilding' was a high point in Elvis Costello's career. As he had in 'Radio Radio', he had singled out a target and done a demolition job on it. But his manner of expressing rage had matured. 'You can only shout for so long at somebody', the former angry young man related, 'and you either lose your voice or they stop listening ... I have learned better ways of putting the point over – and you don't always have to shout!' Indeed, while 'Shipbuilding' and 'Radio Radio' both moved minds, it was 'Shipbuilding' that also moved listeners to tears.

The successor to *Punch the Clock*, *Goodbye Cruel World*, was a set that at least occasionally satisfied and offered three noteworthy singles, The Imposter outing 'Peace in Our Time', the soul cover 'I Wanna Be Loved', and an original with harmonies by Daryl Hall, 'The Only Flame in Town'. One of Costello's better if not best efforts, it indicated that the revival of fortunes brought about by *Punch the Clock* was continuing.

The future must be bright for an artist who combines talent with a personal dedication to music. Only an artist who cares tremendously about his field would go on to a radio show like *Roundtable* and plug not his own new release but the debut of a group on an independent label – 'Gangsters' by The Specials. Or produce first tracks by an unproven group for which there was no demonstrated demand – The Bluebells. Or search the shops of the world for records he doesn't yet have in his collection from every field of popular music. To see him expand his range with a supporting acting role on television's *Scully* was a pleasure. To see him back near the top of the singles chart would bring even more satisfaction. It's bound to happen sooner or later because this New Wave survivor has proved he's in for the long run. Like Oliver's Army, Elvis Costello is here to stay.

Frankie Valli and The Four Seasons

RARE INDEED is the voice so unique it can be recognised after only a few notes. Ray Charles has such a voice. When you hear his soulful, mournful cry you know it has to be the Genius. If you hear a rock tune by a singer who appears to be gargling with gravel, you can bet money it's by Rod Stewart. And when you hear a close-harmony number with a lead line so high it could intercept Concorde in mid-flight, you can be certain it's the sound of Frankie Valli.

Francis Castelluccio was born in Newark, New Jersey on 3 May 1937. He made his first public performance as a schoolboy, singing 'White Christmas' in a holiday recital. The young Castelluccio was heard by a country and western artist named Texas Jean Valley, who thought him good enough to get a New York audition. She pretended the lad was her kid brother, Frankie Valley. The name stayed with the Italian-American his entire career, but the spelling changed. Texas Jean had spelled her name ending with 'e-y'. Frankie tried 'e-y', 'i-e', and just 'e' before settling on the 'i' that appeared on all his hit records.

Those hits were a long time in coming. Valley's first release, 'My Mother's Eyes', was made in 1953. His second try, 'Somebody Else Took Her Home', failed in '54. The following year Valley teamed with The Variatones to become The Four Lovers. Their 1956 effort 'You're The Apple Of My Eye' took them to No. 62 in the *Billboard* chart and to Ed Sullivan's television show, but they couldn't follow it up. Subsequent singles failed, and the friends had to resort to background singing and demo discs to make ends meet.

In 1961 half the quartet departed. One of the two replacements was Bob Gaudio, who had made the novelty hit 'Short Shorts' with The Royal Teens. The new group needed a new name. One night they were playing the cocktail lounge of a New Jersey bowling alley. The lounge was called The Four Seasons. It may have been the first occasion on which an act assumed the name of its venue.

The first single by The Four Seasons, 'Bermuda', flopped, leaving

163

the group without a record deal. Bob Gaudio wrote the second, 'Sherry', in fifteen minutes, and the group recorded it after several days' rehearsal.

Songwriter and producer Bob Crewe had become a friend of Frankie Valli's when they collaborated on a 1958 single, 'I Go Ape', released under the name Frankie Tyler. Crewe subsequently had used The Four Lovers as background singers on sessions by artists like Freddy Cannon and Danny and The Juniors on the Swan label he co-owned with Frank Slay. In 1962 Crewe took the finished version of 'Sherry' to a record convention. A company named Vee-Jay offered the best deal, and 'Sherry' was issued in the summer of 1962. But it didn't become an instant smash. It bubbled for a month and a half until Dick Clark played it on *American Bandstand*.

Today music industry analysts are well aware of the important roles played by MTV in America and *Top of the Pops* in Britain in breaking hit records. But they mustn't forget that television exposure has long been a way of getting new acts off the ground. In the late fifties and early sixties, *American Bandstand* was *the* pop music show. 'Sherry' sold over a hundred thousand records the day after Clark's broadcast, and it went to No. 1 for five weeks.

Only two records, 'Monster Mash' and 'He's A Rebel', had turns at the top before The Four Seasons were back. Bob Crewe had been watching a Clark Cable film in which the star had admonished a weeping woman with the words 'Big Girls Don't Cry'. Crewe thought he heard a hit song title there, and with Bob Gaudio proceeded to write The Four Seasons' second No. 1. Once again they were on top for five weeks.

The group consisted of Valli, Gaudio, Nick Massi and Tommy DeVito. DeVito had been one of The Variatones who had joined forces with Valli in 1955. Now, like Frankie, he was being rewarded for his perseverance. When 'Walk Like A Man' became one of 1963's early No. 1s, The Seasons had scored three chart-toppers in succession, not counting a Christmas ditty, 'Santa Claus Is Coming To Town'. No vocal group had ever performed that feat. It was precisely the long years of hard work and repeated disappointment that kept the foursome from losing their perspective when they suddenly became America's hottest act.

It was just as well they kept their feet on the ground or they would have been rudely reawakened when their next attempt, a remake of Fats Domino's 'Ain't That A Shame!', peaked just outside the top twenty. But they bounced back in fine form with the top three tune 'Candy Girl'.

The Four Seasons' early hits depended on Frankie Valli's unearthly falsetto and the close harmony work of the group. It was a form of male singing clearly derived from the doo-wop style of urban Negroes in the American Northeast. In an interview with *Goldmine*, an outstanding Wisconsin publication devoted to record collecting, Valli recalled he started doo-wop singing in high school. 'We used to do it in the locker rooms and in the boys' bathrooms,' he related. 'Under bridges, in hallways, anywhere where you could get that natural echo going.' The Four Seasons sang doo-wop, and when they looked for a distinctive sound decided it had to be a variation of the method they loved so much. Having grown up in the New York area, they could do it convincingly. Whites brought up outside the Northeast rarely managed to sound authentic. The other outstanding white doo-wop inspired act, Dion and The Belmonts, had come from the Bronx, closer even than The Seasons to the original source.

Hearing one's first Four Seasons record with Frankie Valli's banshee-like howl, one might have thought one was listening to a novelty record. But it wasn't a novelty that was tiresome. Philips Records realised that the group's best days were not yet behind them, and lured The Seasons away from Vee-Jay with a lucrative offer. Philips' reading of the market proved correct, and The Four Seasons hit the top three with their first outing on the label, 'Dawn'. It would have gone higher had it not been for The Beatles, who dominated the American chart for months after their first entry in January 1964. Indeed, The Four Seasons had two in the top twenty the first week of April, the famous seven days when The Beatles had Nos. 5, 4, 3, 2, and 1 in the *Billboard* Hot 100.

The other Seasons success was 'Stay', a remake of Maurice Williams and The Zodiacs' 1960 No. 1 put out by Vee-Jay to get more mileage out of the departed group's catalogue. The original arrangement of 'Stay' seemed perfect for The Four Seasons treatment. Indeed, Charlie Gillett has downgraded the contribution of the quartet to popular music, writing that their style had already been heard on hits by The Diamonds and The Zodiacs.

The release of the 45 wasn't Vee-Jay's most outrageous repackaging of the men's material. In 1964 the company promoted *The International Battle Of The Century: The Beatles vs The Four Seasons* with, as the cover copy put it, 'each delivering their greatest vocal punches'. 'You be the judge and jury!' the sleeve shouted.

It was a preposterous double album, but an understandable one. Just as Vee-Jay had signed and lost The Four Seasons, it had leased the earliest Beatles material, including 'Please Please Me' and 'Twist And Shout', and failed to follow through. Both acts were red-hot, the Fab Four historically so, and Vee-Jay had no new material on which to capitalise. *The Battle Of The Century* set was less bizarre than a similar coupling with the hits of Frank Ifield. The winner of the fictitious fight was, in the end, the clever collector. The album is The Four Seasons' most valuable disc, currently selling at over $100.

Even in the year of The Beatles the New Jerseyites were not to be eclipsed. They made it to No. 1 that summer with what may be their best record, 'Rag Doll'. This title went to the top in New York City in one week. It sounded an instant anthem from the very first drum beats, perhaps borrowed from The Ronettes' 'Be My Baby'. It also sounded richer and fuller than the earlier No. 1s, a musical enrichment brought about by arranger and conductor Charles Calello. He arranged many of The Four Seasons' biggest hits over the next few years and was an important shaper of their sound, though Bob Crewe and Gaudio continued to write the singles.

During the mid-sixties The Seasons benefited from the added input of Denny Randell and Sandy Linzer. Along with Crewe they co-wrote the international hit 'Let's Hang On'. Randell also arranged a single of particular importance to Frankie Valli. When asked by *Goldmine* to nominate his favourite Four Seasons hit, the lead singer surprisingly named one, 'Big Man In Town', that only scratched the top twenty in the US and did not even chart in Britain. Indeed, The Four Seasons, considered a quintessential sixties group, had more top ten hits in the UK in the seventies than they did in the sixties. One reason was that during the group's peak period Britain was wrapped up in its own beat boom. Many fine American records were slighted. There were no radio programmes of the US charts to inform listeners of outstanding releases across the Atlantic.

Another explanation is that many Four Seasons sixties songs did make it in Britain by other artists. Singles, B-sides, album tracks and Frankie Valli solos all were covered to good effect. The Walker Brothers went to No. 1 in 1966 with a reworking of 'The Sun Ain't Gonna Shine Any More'. A year later The Tremeloes scaled the summit with their version of 'Silence Is Golden'. The Bay City Rollers got a chart-topper out of 'Bye Bye Baby' in 1975 and in 1980 The Detroit Spinners led the list with 'Working My Way Back To You'. That's four No. 1s with four songs whose most successful original got to No. 5. There have been other smash covers, too. The Osmonds took Frankie Valli's 'The Proud One' to No. 5, exactly where Andy Williams topped out with his interpretation of the soloist's million-seller 'Can't Take My Eyes Off You'. That so many top tunes could be resisted in their original performances yet loved when sung by others suggested that The Four Seasons really did sound best on their home turf. The young men from New Jersey singing in the street corner style of New York did mean most in those places. They even sang the theme song of New York's top mid-sixties evening deejay, WABC's 'Cousin Brucie', Bruce Morrow.

It was gratifying, then, when they did hit in Britain, as when they reached No.12 in 1966 with 'I've Got You Under My Skin'. Performing a standard was risky business in 1966, when groups playing their own material were dominating the chart. But The Four Seasons had found that staying ahead of their audience's expectations was the way to survive in a business which had left rock and roll on the rubbish heap of pop history. Nothing is deader in popular music than a star or a style that is recently dead, before the passage of years can give the subject nostalgic appeal. In the mid-sixties late fifties forms and fancies were passé. The Seasons were forced by commercial considerations to leave the doo-wop behind and modify their sound, through the epic pop aria 'Rag Doll' to the hard-rocking 'Let's Hang On' to the lushly arranged Cole Porter classic, 'I've Got You Under My Skin'.

They had even begun 1966 in the charts as The Wonder Who, performing Bob Dylan's 'Don't Think Twice' with an ultra-high Frankie Valli vocal. The novelty was the result of Valli having fun with the previously recorded instrumental track and the producers liking what they heard. Anything to be different, and that included a Valli solo. 'Can't Take My Eyes Off You', which reached No. 2 in America in the summer of 1967, took Frankie Valli to a new level of popularity. He had scored across the board with a ballad without The Four Seasons. He seemed set to take his place as one of America's leading adult attractions.

But at this point The Four Seasons' ability to take the correct turn at each intersecton deserted them. Valli's personal follow-up, 'I Make A Fool Of Myself', was all too obviously son of 'Can't Take My Eyes Off You', and appeared foolish. His overblown 1968 drama 'To Give (The Reason I Live)' was an embarrassment.

The most disastrous step, however, was left for the group as a whole. In 1969 they attempted a progressive LP with some serious sociology. Lillian Roxon wrote cruelly but accurately when she said 'The resulting album, *Genuine Imitation Life Gazette*, truly grossed out their die-hard fans. It stiffed and, in effect, the foursome had slit their professional throats.' With tracks like the opening cut, 'American Crucifixion Resurrection', they weren't about to have many hit singles from the set.

Despite Valli's insistence that the album was better than its reception, it did lead to the break-up of the band. Nick Massi had quit in 1965 because he didn't like touring. Now, in 1970, Tommy DeVito called it quits, too, and Bob Gaudio followed in '71.

But Valli did not give in. With new Seasons he signed with Motown, promised personal guidance by Berry Gordy. But the company founder was too busy with Diana Ross films to pay attention to yesterday's yodellers. After a fruitless few years Frankie and The Seasons requested and received ownership of many of their masters. They then had cause to be thankful to Father Time. Valli had been kept alive as a soloist in the UK charts with a 1970 re-release, 'You're Ready Now'. In 1975 The Seasons scored on Motown's Mowest label with the long-forgotten 'The Night' and Frankie registered an American No. 1 with a track he'd bought back from Motown, 'My Eyes Adored You'.

The Seasons never had been album artists. Their most successful LP in the British charts had been a greatest hits set named *Edizione d'Oro (Gold Edition)*. In 1976, two anthologies made the top twenty LP lists but so did a new package. Bob Gaudio made a massive commitment to his old friend Frankie. He wrote the music, co-wrote the lyrics and produced an entire LP of new material, *Who Loves You.*

The title track was an international top ten single in late 1975. It was just the beginning of a Seasons surge. The album was a success during '76, spurred on by the group's first British No. 1 track, 'December 1963 (Oh What A Night)', also their first American No. 1 in twelve years.

What was most startling about the reception given the single is that Frankie Valli didn't start singing lead until the middle of the song. Drummer Gerry Polci was out in front. Indeed, he led all the way on the follow-up, 'Silver Star', which reached No. 3 in the UK. Valli felt relieved rather than aggrieved. He reminded interviewers that The Seasons show was over two hours long, and if he could have a brief rest from vocalising he was delighted. He was also content having three hits on his own, 'Swearin' To God' and 'Our Day Will Come' in America and 'Fallen Angel' in Britain.

Polci was a new face as well as a new voice. Indeed, with the exception of Frankie Valli and the returned Bob Gaudio, there had been a complete change in the line-up. A 1981 *Record Collectors Price Guide* calculated that there had been twelve different Seasons, but most pop fans were unaware of the changing membership. Because the group never had a visual image and the vocal trademark was always Frankie Valli's voice, only the record buyer paying the closest attention noticed when there was a replacement. Vallie owned the name The Four Seasons, so theoretically could enlist whomever he wanted.

In 1978 he didn't need anyone's assistance to achieve yet another American No. 1. Barry Gibb was asked by Robert Stigwood to write and produce a title theme for the movie musical *Grease*. The Bee Gee was only too happy to oblige, and felt that there was no one better able to evoke the feeling of the rock and roll era than the man who had been there himself, Frankie Valli. Their collaboration and the clever credit sequence that accompanied it constituted a high point in the film.

It may be appropriate that the last great hit from Frankie Valli was a fond appreciation of the early days of rock and roll, for that is where he and The Four Seasons had their roots. It may be an accurate criticism that what they did was based on the work of people who never found the fame and fortune they did. It may be true that others took a similar sound into the charts earlier. But no act accumulates fifty-nine chart records without having something special, and Frankie Valli's voice was, and is, indefinably special. As enthusiastic critic Nik Cohn wrote, 'There's not much to say on them, they're not analysable. They're perfect, that's all.'

As long as he lives Frankie Valli has a chance of having more hits. His age and appearance have nothing to do with his appeal. Given the right song and production, he could be back up there again, with or without The Four Seasons. There ain't no good in our goodbyin'.

Queen

THE FIRST time I saw them I walked out. It wasn't that they were bad, they were just loud – menacingly aggressively, painfully loud. I'd had an accident in gym class when I was twelve that gave me a slightly perforated left eardrum and ever since a highly amplified bass makes my head buzz as if there is a squadron of kamikaze pilots dive-bombing my brain.

I'd come to see Mott the Hoople at the Hammersmith Odeon, and their support group had driven me away. Sadly, I never did see Mott the Hoople, but I've seen their support group a couple of times since. They're playing the biggest halls available now, so the sound is no longer a problem. Yet, if I may be excused a very bad pun, I still get a buzz from Queen.

Queen had its royal roots in London's appropriately named Imperial College. Guitarist Brian May recruited drummer Roger Meddows-Taylor and vocalist Tim Staffell to form Smile. May had been in other bands before, and The Others had even cut a single titled 'Oh Yeah' in 1964, but this was his most serious musical project to date. Meddows-Taylor had been in several groups in Cornwall, first as a guitarist. As he remembered it, 'Drumming was an incidental thing. I had an old drum and I picked up a few more drums and it turned out that I was better at drumming than anything else.'

Smile occasionally played on the same bill with Wreckage, whose lead singer preferred Freddie Mercury to his real name Fred Bulsara. Born in Zanzibar and educated at Ealing College of Art, Freddie thought there could be a place for a group who did to hard rock what he had done to the name Fred Bulsara – present it in modified form with show business values. He persuaded his Kensington market stall partner Taylor, and Brian May to try the project, which he called Queen. Having finished college and lost singer Staffell to a band named Humpy Bomp, the duo agreed, though not without initial reservations. After sampling several bassists they asked John Deacon to join them.

171

Queen got a break in 1972 when De Lane Lea studio in Wembley needed demonstration material to prove to would-be users that their facility was capable of recording hard rock. The quartet got to record demos for free and used them to seek a contract.

When they took the tapes to record companies they were turned down everywhere, even though one of the labels, EMI, eventually signed them, and one of the demos, 'The Night Comes Down', was to be issued on their first album. As Roger Taylor bitterly recalled, 'Some guy from EMI came up, didn't have a stereo tape machine, found some old Grundig from about 1918, and eventually played it. In mono.'

Salvation came in the forms of John Anthony and Roy Thomas Baker, staff engineers at Trident Studios. Anthony had produced a single by Smile, released only in the United States, and Baker had just set up his own production company and was looking for someone to record. Trident itself wanted to expand its musical interests beyond mere studio ownership. Queen, who had no manager, liked the multiple opportunities on offer, and signed with Trident. They were to be managed for Trident by Jack Nelson and produced by Baker, though early on the group's relationship with Roy became one of co-production.

Trident 'shopped' the tapes. Roy Featherstone of EMI heard the recordings at MIDEM, the music industry's annual business bash at Cannes in the south of France. The EMI label was just starting, and Queen seemed a good prospect as the 'heavy' group the company was seeking. So it was that a firm which had turned them down signed them on the basis of tapes made in London being heard in France.

Yet still there was frustration. The release of the first album, *Queen*, was delayed, and when it was put out it petered out quickly. The debut single, 'Keep Yourself Alive', also failed to chart. But at least the quartet landed a top tour, supporting the then-hot Mott the Hoople.

In early 1974 they were given reason to thank Mott's one-time mentor, David Bowie. *Top of the Pops* were going to include 'Rebel Rebel', but the artist couldn't make the show. Queen were booked to promote 'Seven Seas of Rhye' instead, and the result was the first of two top ten hits they enjoyed that year. The second was 'Killer Queen'.

Mere months separated the two tunes, but they were among the most memorable of the band's career. Everyone retains the memory of their first successes, and for Queen March 1974 is particularly worth recollecting. 'Seven Seas of Rhye' entered the singles chart the week of the 9th of March. A fortnight later *Queen II* came into the album list, eventually reaching No. 5. The last week of the month their first LP finally joined the bestsellers.

The double dose of Queen in the album charts was intriguing

because the two discs were clearly made at different stages in the act's development. As Brian May put it in 1976, the first platter 'had the youth and freshness which was never regained, because you're only young once. It had a lot of rough edges, a lot of bad playing, a lot of bad production, but obviously we didn't have that time to spend on it which we did subsequently.'

The success of both albums was the good news. The bad news was that May suffered a severe attack of hepatitis just after the start of the group's first American tour. When he returned to Britain to recuperate, it was discovered he also had an ulcer. He was out of action for months.

The reactions he and his fellow musicians had to this setback demonstrated their priorities. May at first despaired of continuing. Surrounded by negative press cuttings from the British pop press and utterly sapped physically and creatively, he thought he might have to abandon his craft. Only when he faced that terrible possibility did he realise how much he loved music. When he did pick up his guitar, he realised anew his commitment, and vowed to continue.

During May's recuperation, Deacon, Mercury and Taylor refused to replace him. They started recording their third album around him, doing those bits that didn't require a guitarist. Once again a Queen LP had a different feel to it, this time because of the unusual way it was recorded. Yet no one was disappointed. *Sheer Heart Attack*, its title conceived by Roger, was their biggest success yet, reaching No. 2 on the album charts. 'Killer Queen', the single from the set, climbed to the runner-up singles slot.

Queen were poised for a No. 1. In November 1975 they got it. 'Bohemian Rhapsody' was the first single in eighteen years to spend nine weeks at No. 1. It led the list from 29 November 1975 to 24 January 1976. At just under six minutes it was the longest No. 1 since 'Hey Jude' in 1968.

As is sometimes the case with lengthy hits, 'Bohemian Rhapsody' wasn't conceived as a single. While it was still No. 1 writer Freddie Mercury claimed 'It was just one of those pieces I wrote for the album; just writing my batch of songs. In its early stages I almost rejected it, but then it grew.'

It grew indeed, becoming pop music's most famous mini-opera. It changed tempo and style several times, running the range from Mercury's aria to May's scorching guitar solo. One choral fragment required 180 vocal overdubs.

'Bohemian Rhapsody' set Queen apart from every other heavy group that ever existed. Freddie was delighted. 'I really wanted to be outrageous with vocals because we're always getting compared with other people, which is very stupid,' he said at the time. 'If you really listen to the operatic bit there are no comparisons, which is what we want.'

To promote 'Bohemian Rhapsody' Queen did something else that set them apart from the crowd. They took off four hours from rehearsing and made a film of the song with director Bruce Gowers, spending £4,500. Shown every week on *Top of the Pops*, this clip helped keep the single at No. 1. There had been promotional films before, but this was the first time a visual treatment of a record was seen to have a direct impact on sales. Just as film historians point to *The Jazz Singer* as the first talkie, pop people point to 'Bohemian Rhapsody' as the first vital video.

In the autumn of 1975, without the benefit of hindsight, the single merely seemed the best of Queen's finest album yet. *A Night at the Opera* also demonstrated what would be Queen's greatest strength. All four members contributed songs. Mercury's efforts including the scathing 'Death on Two Legs', dedicated to the early management the group had now left behind. Brian May offered the epic 'The Prophet's Song', a rock arrangement of 'God Save The Queen', and two numbers on which he sang lead. Roger Taylor vocalised on his own 'I'm In Love With My Car', and John Deacon penned 'You're My Best Friend'. The latter cut was the cherry on top of the cake. 'Bohemian Rhapsody' had spent its historic time at the top and gone on to be Queen's first million-seller in the States. *A Night at the Opera* had been the quartet's first No. 1 album. Now came the bonus: 'You're My Best Friend', a track the group at first resisted releasing because the LP had already been so successful, but which became an international hit none the less.

The four members of Queen were very different personalities, and this was reflected in their individual songwriting. They rarely collaborated, they contributed. This variety was their greatest strength. The tendency to repeat something that had been successful was their greatest weakness. *A Day at the Races*, the follow-up to *A Night at the Opera*, was in this respect a disappointment. There was the obvious use of a second Marx Brothers film title to name the album. More damaging, 'Somebody To Love', the first single from the set, seemed to be derived from 'Bohemian Rhapsody'. The follow-up 45, a Brian May blisterer called 'Tie Your Mother Down', ran into radio resistance in both Britain and America for the mere suggestion of mayhem against mum. It took *Queen's First EP*, led by 'Good Old Fashioned Lover Boy', to bring the band back to the top twenty.

A Day at the Races was briefly a No. 1 album, and it was the first set the foursome had produced on their own. But it did give the impres-

sion that they had peaked. They had offered the best, and were now re-
cycling it. This would be a feeling one would occasionally get from
Queen's work. Fortunately, the men who had forty-two 'A' and 'O'
levels between them were always bright enough to rescue themselves
with the exciting and the unexpected.

I was driving through the highest mountain pass in Vermont in the
autumn of 1977 with my old college friend John Marshall. John had
asked over dinner if I still got The Feeling like I used to at the Dart-
mouth radio station. The Feeling was the thrilling combination of awe
and anticipation that a record I was hearing for the first time was a
future smash. As we travelled through the pass we heard unfamiliar
music on the radio. It was a distant transmission from Boston, fading
in and out on the night air. We strained to hear the new piece, praying
it wouldn't disappear before it ended. When it was over, I turned to
my friend and said, 'John, things haven't changed. I just got The Feeling. I don't know who that is, it sounds like Queen, but whoever it is,
that is a smash. We are going to be hearing that for months.' I was so
carried away it was a good thing John was driving.

What I'd heard was one of the finest double-sided singles of all-time,
'We Will Rock You' and 'We Are The Champions', best heard back-
to-back, as they were on the album *News of the World* and as they were
on many American radio stations, which treated them as a single work.
Though Brian May had penned the first song and Freddie Mercury the
second, they complemented each other perfectly. After the earthy excitement and statement of purpose of 'We Will Rock You' came the
reflective and proud 'We Are The Champions'. The double anthem
was Queen's biggest success yet in America, selling over two million
singles in the United States. In Britain 'We Are The Champions' got to
No. 2.

News of the World boasted a cover painting by Frank Kelly Freas
based on a 1953 *Astounding Science Fiction* magazine cover. Freas was
latterly famous for his work with *Mad*, but had earlier been a noted sci-
fi artist. His picture showed a giant robot with two unconscious band
members in his hand and two falling to earth, the expression on the
metal man's face asking 'Did I do all this?' Of the four members of
Queen, one, Freddie Mercury, is bleeding profusely and apparently
deceased. Trust the most flamboyant member of the outfit to upstage
the others, even off stage. Mercury had emerged as the most outrageous singer in rock, a supremely confident leader who strutted
across the stage like a demented peacock, thrusting his chin forward,
holding his head high, and wearing a shocking range of costumes.
Through the years he has worn a kimono, a motor-cyclist's leather
gear, shorts, a clinging glitter suit, and the drag of 'I Want To Break

Free'. His critics consider him The Ponce of Pop, and in 1977 the *New Musical Express* even headlined an interview 'Is this man a prat?' But millions of worshipping fans, who accept Freddie's stage orders like true faithful, understand that it is all part of a show, a well-conceived and carefully-executed entertainment. Brian May had recognised Mercury's charisma when he suggested the sleeve of the very first Queen album picture the singer on stage in a spotlight. 'He looks right for it and he acts right for it,' Brian said. Mercury proved May right.

Freddie once explained that his apparent arrogance was a survival mechanism. Early business associates, it was claimed, exploited the group. 'I felt that anybody who approached me, you just kept your defences up,' the vocalist explained. 'Some people think he's arrogant,' Brian May elaborated, 'but in fact he's only arrogant when he knows he can afford to be.'

Part of Freddie Mercury's public posture is theatrical. He has a keen interest in show business and glamour. Some of his stage gestures reveal the influence of Liza Minnelli and his choice of 'Big Spender' for an encore showed affection for Shirley Bassey. He revered the dancer Nijinsky, and duplicated one of his costumes. Freddie's love of dance also inspired him to attempt one of his most courageous stunts. In the summer of 1979 Mercury appeared in a ballet gala at the Coliseum in London. The troupe of star dancers, some from the Royal Ballet, performed an interpretation of 'Bohemian Rhapsody' for which he provided a live vocal. At one point he had to leap horizontally on to the outstretched arms of two rows of dancers, still singing into a microphone mere centimetres from his mouth. He never came closer to losing his prominent teeth.

For a well-deserved encore Freddie urged the audience to sing along on 'Crazy Little Thing Called Love'. He seemed to forget that while Queen had recorded it weeks before, it had not yet been released, and there was no way anyone in the hall other than he knew the words.

'Crazy Little Thing Called Love' was the latest of several daring singles released just when it seemed Queen were passé. The semi-operatic style had gone sour on the 1978 double A-side, 'Fat Bottomed Girls/Bicycle Race', which was received as a poor sexist joke rather than a coupling of two worthy tunes. Despite Brian May's lovely 'Leaving Home Ain't Easy', the LP *Jazz* was not the band's best. They once again needed to offer something new. 'Crazy Little Thing Called Love', a modern rockabilly number, was just what the disc doctor ordered. It topped out at No. 2 in the British charts and went four weeks at No. 1 in America. The single was the perfect introduction to the forthcoming album *The Game*, a staggering set that may be the firm's finest. Contained within its grooves are Roger Taylor's superb 'Rock It (prime jive)', Brian May's attractive aria 'Save Me', and some dynamic disco from John Deacon.

Queen's bassist was the player with the lowest public profile, perhaps because he was the youngest in the band, perhaps because he was at peace in his personal life, but his contribution to the group was too easily underestimated. He was the member most capable in business and legal affairs, and, as befits a man with an electronics degree, he was the most familiar with the tons of equipment required for the Queen stage show. Deacon could write a strong song, too, as he showed with 'You're My Best Friend', but he never tried to make more than the occasional contribution. 'Both Brian and Freddie are really good at songwriting,' he once said, 'and I always had the feeling I could never come up with anything good enough.' One of the two tracks he supplied for *The Game* was more than good enough. 'Another One Bites The Dust' was another US No. 1 for Queen, selling over three million copies there and giving them two of 1980's five bestselling singles. Borrowing a bass line from Chic, John Deacon crafted a cut that appealed to dancers as well as rockers, and the group were thrilled when blacks constituted a substantial part of a Madison Square Garden concert.

The prolonged popularity of 'Another One Bites The Dust', which remained in the Hot 100 for thirty-one weeks, worsened an unusual dilemma that faced the band. Both their soundtrack to the film *Flash* and a greatest hits collection were ready for release at the end of 1980, but *The Game*, a No. 1 on both sides of the Atlantic, was still strong in the States, where it ultimately went multi-platinum. The anthology was delayed a year, but the movie music couldn't be held back. It had to be released in conjunction with the film, and so came out only five months after *The Game*.

Flash consequently seemed an anti-climax to the public, but it was a valuable experience for Brian May in particular. It was he who co-produced the album with Mack and wrote the bulk of the predominantly instrumental material. May had always been serious about his music, an attitude that seemed to the cynic to be at odds with Queen's pomposity but actually vindicated it. He had with his father built his own guitar while a schoolboy, and though it only cost £8 it was made with such care and precision that the so-called Red Special remained his favourite model even when he could afford any other. The *Flash* soundtrack required Brian to submit himself to the new discipline of timing music to action on the screen. Later he recorded a recreational album with his friend and fellow guitar ace Eddie Van Halen.

Queen's chart chances were again revived with a change of pace. They were recording in their studio in Montreux, Switzerland, a city famed for its music festival and one where David Bowie had a home.

Bowie and John Deacon had become friends so it was perhaps inevitable that the Thin White Duke should visit the Mountain studio. It was not inevitable that the resulting jam would evolve into a single, and when he left David apparently was unaware that what he had done informally could be refined for release. It could be, and was.

'Under Pressure' by Queen and David Bowie was a No. 1 in the autumn of 1981. It was perfect publicity for the finally released *Greatest Hits*, which was No. 1 on the album chart for a month. Strangely, 'Under Pressure' wasn't on the UK collection, which with seventeen tracks gave great value for money. It was included on the American anthology, which had fewer selections, but neither single nor album were as well-received in the States as they had been at home.

The band was in fact beginning a downturn in their American fortunes, one which worsened with the release of the 1982 package *Hot Space*. As had happened with Rod Stewart after 'Da Ya Think I'm Sexy?' so happened with Queen after 'Another One Bites The Dust': a massive No. 1 led a top act down a musical cul-de-sac. Queen's detour into dance was not appreciated, being either late or lousy, depending on one's point of view. A re-evaluation of direction was needed.

In 1983 Queen celebrated the tenth anniversary of their debut record by releasing nothing, nothing at all. It was the first year in which they had remained silent. There was no reason they had to resume. Financially they were finally secure, having structured their own business organisation and in consequence become the most highly paid company directors in the United Kingdom. They did not need to make another Queen album to express themselves musically. Not only had Brian made his album with Eddie Van Halen, Roger had recorded two on his own and Freddie had partnered Giorgio Moroder on 'Love Kills', a song from the soundtrack of Moroder's reconstituted version of Fritz Lang's silent film classic *Metropolis*.

Queen continued because they felt they still had more to offer, and in 1984 they came up with the goods. *The Works* generated four hit singles 'Radio Ga Ga', 'I Want to Break Free', 'It's a Hard Life' and 'Hammer to Fall', each written by a different member of the group. The band were four strong individuals. It was well-known that they often argued, and they admitted it publicly. But they subjugated their egos to the interests of the group, and in so doing ironically gave themselves better lives.

Critics have always been dismissive of Queen's work. *The New Musical Express Encyclopedia of Rock* called them proof of the 'vacuum effect' – that when a top act, in this case Led Zeppelin, disappears, a less talented attraction takes its place. In his summary of 'heavy metal' Lester Bangs, who coined the expression, referred to them simply as

'the aptly named Queen'. Dick Clark's *The First 25 Years of Rock &
Roll*, which ended in 1980, didn't mention them at all. In 1984, the
Times, comparing the band's volume to its content, cleverly wrote that
Queen use 'a sledgehammer to crack a walnut'. Rock historians tend to
favour inventors of styles, socially critical lyricists, and the indigent
artist overlooked by the general public. Loud mass-audience pastiche-
offering pleasure-seekers leave them cold. Maybe critics shouldn't
always be so serious. We need a few loud mass-audience pastiche-
offering pleasure-seekers, especially when they occasionally come up
with a single that sends chills down your spine and makes your radio go
ga-ga.